Sarah,

It was
wonderful
seeing you again.
Best of luck in ?

Sincerely,

W
C

PEACEWOOD, THE MOST POWERFUL MAN IN THE WORLD

Wezley Calvin

Cover design by Eric Lugo.

Paperback ISBN: 978-09990089-0-4

www.wezleycalvin.com

A novel for the dreamers.

PART I: The Scattered Pages of Peacewood

Chapter 1

Thirty-one Tylenol, a glass of zinfandel, and a partridge in a pear tree. Famed novelist Johnathan Peacewood had concocted a magical death elixir. He wanted something poetic and powerful. He had to go out with a bang, of course!

Jonathan lay in bed, imagining the headlines. Tabloid writers never wrote good headlines anymore. They weren't romantic enough. Too sterile. Too stiff. Not enough passion. Not enough prose. But of course, they could never measure up to Johnathan anyhow.

If Picasso was a master with paint, if Balanchine one with movement, then Johnathan Peacewood was a master with words. His last novel, *Somerset Eternal: The Disco Era*, had sold nearly seventy million copies. And the Somerset series, which so far included six novels, was ranked (along with the Bible, the Kama Sutra, and those Harry Potter books) amongst the world's most widely read. Johnathan's novels had gotten him appearances on *The Tonight Show*, a star on the Hollywood Walk of Fame, and lunches with a slew of Pulitzer Prize winners. Yet, while Johnny experienced the glamour and excitement of a Mick Jagger (parties and privilege and press conferences), he suffered the emptiness and angst of a Marilyn Monroe (pills and pain and prostration). It was a travesty, really. All that success yet still no joy.

Johnathan had made millions writing about Somerset, an immortal African princess who would die upon discovering her first true love. But the trick was that Somerset never did. She never could find love. She was born in western Africa in the 1500s and swept off to America a hundred years later on the Middle Passage. Once there, she was mistress to Thomas Jefferson, Billy the Kid, and even Roy Holston. She took a shot at Langston Hughes during the Harlem Renaissance, too, but she wasn't really his type.

In all that time—in the five centuries and in the multitudes of men she had known—she had never felt true love. So she could never die. And so Johnathan kept writing. He wrote of her heartbreaks and her tears, of her restless spirit and its constant discontent. Somerset had captivated readers with her perpetual pursuit of true love. But with six novels down, Johnathan was sick to his stomach of that undying bitch.

Here he was, mid-thirties—older than Kurt Cobain, Amy Winehouse and Janis Joplin, older than Hendrix and Morrison, too (hell, older than Christ at crucifixion)—and he was just like his Somerset, never finding love. There were short affairs in the dark, and occasional, ephemeral trysts. And of course, there was sex— lots and lots of sex. Sex with models and actors. Sex with doctors and generals and laureates and comedians and restauranteurs and moguls and athletes and prostitutes and even a few priests. But love? No, there was no love for Johnathan Peacewood.

Charlotte Swanson, his obnoxious (though business savvy) publishing agent, had admonished him against coming out publicly. Johnathan's homosexuality would have inhibited book sales. He had to consider his target demographic, after all. Housewives in rural Texas weren't going to read novels written by a fudge packer—that's for sure. They'd feature his work at their annual town book burnings if they found out Johnny liked boys instead of girls. To add, not only would his fans find his lifestyle morally objectionable, they would never connect to his stories because of it. No one would buy Somerset if they knew she was a gay man's anecdotal summary of his own, perverse sex life. Isn't that right? So he kept it quiet. Johnathan hid all his affairs in shadowed corners and secret gardens so that his fanbase never suspected a thing. And this couldn't have helped his love life. It just couldn't have.

So Mr. Peacewood luxuriated in his labyrinths of money, buying himself the world to forget about love. Unfortunately, love was his career. One success and the world wants a thousand more. That's the way of it. First, book signings, then lectures, then talk shows and movie rights and screenplays and lawyers and contracts. This all led to penthouses with chandeliers and vacations with his rock star and singer and rapper friends, one who had recently had a big hit on the Billboard Hot 100, rapping about the size of his penis (but didn't they all rap about that?). There was caviar and Versace. And don't forget about those tea dates with all the young, celebrity heiresses and the golfing with his buddy the U.S. senator, who'd snort coke and share hookers with Johnny before going home to his lovely wife and kissing her conservative Republican cheek. There was drag racing with the prince of You Name It and hang gliding with the CEO of You Guessed It. But there was no love.

And alas, the luxuriation never led to fulfillment. The drugs and alcohol never led to sustenance, and the glamour never led to love. But again, love was his job. So now Somerset made him his maddest.

He was so mad that he decided the seventh novel would have to be the last. He would finally kill the dame off without having her find love at all. In the seventh novel, which he had already started, Somerset had met a new lover named Clifton. He was a handsome veteran. Fought in Iraq. Wanted to sic the bastards responsible for 9/11. But Clifton had a sick side, unbeknownst to everyone. He had a penchant for blood—fresh blood. He loved to feel it in his fingers and on his face and in his mouth. He loved to see it trickle from the body all red and rich. He had first communed with the Devil over in the Middle East, where he'd kill detainees when no one was looking, cut their throats just to watch them bleed. And when he got back to the states, boredom drove him to kill again and again and again. Clifton had become a serial killer as demented as Bundy and Gacy and Dahmer. And Somerset was just his type: graceful, black and timeless. And as soon as he got the chance, he was going to rip her to shreds, just like all his other victims.

But Johnathan couldn't do it. He couldn't bring himself to finish that novel. His soul was parched—dry as the Gobi and completely without motivation. So with thirty-one Tylenol, a glass of zinfandel and a partridge in a pear tree, Johnathan Peacewood would to kill himself while the "Twelve Days of Christmas" played on the stereo in the background (even though it was July).

Ba boom!

Ba boom!

Ba boom!

The elixir was setting in. His heart raced. His muscles tensed. His pupils dilated. Johnathan lay there alone in the penthouse, gazing out the window as the moon illuminated the waves on the lake. What a beautiful, quiet evening to die. What a poetic and profound way to pass.

He watched the sailboats float toward the horizon, disappearing under the ghostly silver moonlight as Willis Tower beamed bright, its antennae glowing a festive red, white and blue for the Fourth of July. And he knew all the drunken heathens in this city were down on the streets, pretending they were still frat boys without mortgages and wives and children. They were screaming and whistling and drinking as though tomorrow didn't exist. Pretending that they were more than just boring accountants and lawyers and stock brokers. Johnny knew that the fireworks would start soon, competing with the moon for the space in the summer sky.

Ba boom!

Ba boom!

Ba boom!

And no one would suspect a thing. No one would miss him for days.

Eventually, though, maybe in a week or so, his obsessively maternal agent (that old bag) would call about the new book, filling his voice mailbox with messages of deadlines and contracts and angry publishers. She would call and call and call. And when he didn't answer, she would come to his apartment. She had a key, of course. She would let herself in and come clacking along the hardwood in her Louboutins and find herself some caviar in the kitchen. She'd call for him but hear nothing at all. And eventually, she'd come through the bedroom, walking past his pathetic, decomposing corpse, as though nothing were unusual. She'd smell his rotting human ass, but would assume that he had had another male hooker orgy the night before—homo sex left a certain smell, you know? Then, she'd go into his bathroom and snoop around in the medicine cabinet for some painkillers or cocaine or bath salt. She wouldn't find any, though. Johnathan would have already popped, snorted, smoked, ingested and injected everything in the place, including the paint thinner from the broom closet.

Then, she would look to the mirror and reapply her lipstick, tossing her hair a few narcissistic times, telling herself that she was as radiant as she had been in her thirties. Still, it'd be time for a touchup: a little lift for those circles under the eyes, a little Botox for the ever-deepening trench in her forehead.

Then, she would turn out the light in disgust and walk back into the bedroom. She'd start talking to him about how delightful it must be to be him—to sleep his life away while the rest of the world was off grinding its gears. How wonderful it must be to be Mr. Johnathan Peacewood, never answering to anyone about anything. "What a spoiled brat you are, Johnny," she would say. "You are the most ungrateful piece of garbage that I have ever had the dishonor of representing. But you're brilliant. You're fun. And most important, you're worth a fortune to me," she would say. "Now, get up and write me my novel, you licentious little reptile!"

But Johnathan wouldn't get up. He would just lay there cold and dead, wouldn't he? She would go into the kitchen to retrieve a chilled bottle of Evian from the refrigerator (she would never drink tap). Returning to the bedroom, she would gently unscrew its cap and pour the water onto Johnny's face. "Wake up, Betty Davis," she would say. But Johnny wouldn't wake up. He would just keep on being dead. So she would slap his pretty face. Still dead though. So she would check his pulse. Yes, he would absolutely be dead. Dead as a doornail.

"Well, damn," she would say. "You've really done it this time, Betty Davis." That's what she'd say. Then, she would get in bed with him, her back resting against the headboard, her hand stroking his lifeless, decaying face. She would light a cigarette and take a puff. "Well, Johnny," she would say, "now you're worth even more."

But that's not quite how things unfolded. Johnny felt death touch him, all right—in fact, he stopped breathing. And for a brief moment, his soul lay there in his dead body, gazing out that window as the roman candles opened up the heavens.

Ba boom!

Ba boom!

Ba boom!

The pills had stopped his heart and his soul was just waiting to be recycled by the universe, and this was his escape. He only hoped now that he looked handsome when the paparazzi snapped photos (he really should have worn his Oscar de la Renta tux for this).

Ba boom!

Salvation! He sensed a warm, white light. The Christians were right, or maybe this was the Jewish light. Or maybe this was Nirvana. Did Hindus see light at death? The broken particles of Johnathan's soul stopped sinking away to the darkness, and they reassembled as though some magnet at his center was pulling them back. Broken shards of memory came back together, and he felt as though he were reliving several simultaneously. That time he fell off his bike when he was seven and cried until everyone on the block came out to find him bleeding and screaming in the street. That time he wet himself at school in the sixth grade—the doctor said it was a staring seizure, but really, he just wanted to get out of that math test. The night he stayed at home writing a short story instead of going to his senior prom. His nineteenth birthday, when he lost his virginity to a very friendly prostitute named Dylan who dreamed of being on television. The memories were sewing themselves together into one long ribbon. Johnathan's spirit had disconnected from his body so that he could feel nothing. His soul itself had the consistency of water, fluid and pellucid, as he lay there, still and deceased.

For a moment, the room got very quiet, but then he heard a voice singing.

"Time for love. No time for death. Peacewood, take another breath!"

A playful spirit stood near the window, translucent and beautiful, wagging his finger with admonition as he sang. "All the spirits want to play. Peacewood lives another day!" Then, the spirit leapt up onto the mattress and began jumping up and down and flapping his tongue over his teeth. "Time for love. No time for death. Get up, Peacewood! Take a breath!"

"No!" Johnathan groaned. "Love isn't real."

Then, Johnathan felt the softest hand caressing his head. It was another spirit, this one female. She smiled graciously, holding him in her arms as the light in her watery eyes sparkled like starlight. Slowly, tears dripped from her cheek, falling upon Johnathan's chin. "You're hurting, Johnathan," she whispered. "I am sorry for that. This is not the way things should be for you, my dear."

The playful spirit flounced about on the bed, and he sang, "Johnny, you're a silly man. But I am your biggest fan!"

"Please stop," he groaned.

"Ain't no lover in your bed. So you want to lay there dead!"

"Enough! Enough!" the female spirit shouted, scowling at the playful one. She frowned a bit, her angelic face rumpling into a knot. But then, looking back to Johnathan, her peaceful countenance was restored, her voice calm again. "Johnathan, it isn't your time, sweet love. We're sending you back."

"No," Johnny groaned.

"There are better days ahead for you," she said. "I promise."

Doing a backflip off the bed, the playful one ran over to the window to see the view. As the roman candles burst out in the sky, he danced around smiling and singing. "Johnny Peacewood, dry your tears. You will live a million years!"

"I said enough!" the female spirit shouted again, pointing her finger at him with scorn.

But of course, he could not be deterred. He sang, "I am Wesse! Who are you? You can't tell me what to do!"

Looking over into the doorway, Johnathan saw that a third beautiful spirit had arrived. This one had a striking musculature, with the wings of an ostrich. Though his face remained veiled within the shadows, his eyes glowed through the darkness with a bright red, like lava.

"What's happening to me?" Johnny asked. "Who is he?"

"That is my brother Curte," the female spirit replied, holding Johnny by the hand. "He is the guardian of the passageway between life and death. He will not let you pass."

"But I—I died," Johnathan stuttered. "I—I'm dead. I know I'm dead. I can't feel my body—my breath—my heart."

"Yes," she said. "But we will start it back. This is not your time."

"Peacewood cannot have his way! He will live another day!"

Then, Curte came into the room, his wings dragging the floor like the train of a wedding dress. As he approached, Johnathan could hear a steady thumping sound. It was healthy and loud, and the closer Curte came to the bed, the louder the thumps grew.

"What is that noise?" Johnny cried.

"There's nothing to fear," the female one said, gently running her hand along his cheek.

Slowly, Curte extended his arm with a closed fist. The thumping was now more intense. And when Curte opened his hand, there was Johnathan's heart beating away, all pink and veinous.

"Your heart still beats, Johnathan," the female spirit said. "It has not given up, and neither should you."

"Life is joyous. Love is gay. Live to see another day!" the playful one sang.

Curte threw the heart at Johnathan, and it was swallowed up by his chest. It was as if a rock had been thrown into a pond and had disappeared underneath the black ripples in the water. Suddenly, Johnathan could feel his heart beating again. He inhaled. He exhaled. And suddenly, life was surging through his body again.

Unfortunately, he could feel his stomach too, and it had begun to do the tango inside of him. His throat opened up and emptied the contents of his belly out onto the sheets—all thirty-one Tylenol (and every other poison he had swallowed). The spirits all vanished one by one, their translucent selves fading into the shadows in the room. And then...

...there was nothing.

Darkness.

And from the darkness sprang unconsciousness. Johnathan's mind went blank for fourteen hours, specifically.

He woke up late on the fifth of July, dizzy (hungover, actually). He lay there in a pool of his own vomit, atop his 1000-threadcount Martha Stewart sheets. The suicide attempt had failed, and here he was still alive, still breathing, and still aware of his existence. But he was too weak to move, so he went back to sleep.

Darkness.

Once more.

Johnathan's mind re-emerged again early on July sixth. This time, the hangover had subsided, at least. So how long does it take your liver to repair itself after thirty-one Tylenol, a glass of zinfandel, and a partridge in a pear-shaped rocks glass filled with gin? About forty-eight hours. But he was still weak and still entirely deflated.

"Dear God!" he cried.

Then, he remembered that there was no God. The last priest he had made out with, in the bathroom at that hotel bar in Monaco, had told him so. And he remembered that time when he was nine and tried to sell his soul to the Devil to pass his algebra exam. He'd failed that exam anyway, and his mom beat his little ass for not having studied, proving the Devil wasn't real either.

The phone rang.

Who the hell was it?

Charlotte, his obnoxiously maternal agent. He didn't have to answer. He knew what she wanted. How's the book coming along? That's what she would ask. It's not. It's not coming along in the slightest. He let the call go to voicemail. It was the seventeenth one Charlotte had left this week. What a nag!

Then she called again. And again and again. There were also text messages. There were ninety-seven text messages. And don't forget about all the emails. But what did any of that matter now? He would just lay in bed until the spirits rethought their position on his life.

△ △ △

A week passed before Johnathan left the penthouse. He had not eaten because in all that time, he had slept eighteen to twenty hours each day. Even in his waking hours, he had remained in bed. Each morning, he would wake with the awareness that his millions of dollars had impoverished his soul. Johnathan slept to avoid thinking and feeling, but even with his eyes closed, his dreams murmured in the dark. What was a guy to do?

Eventually, he could sleep no more. Though his spirit was spent, his body was well-rested, and he grew fidgety. He roused, accepting that death would never take him (no matter how much he prayed), for immortality was his curse.

Reluctantly, he stood to his feet, wearing nothing but a white tee and pajama shorts. His bones crackled as he reached toward the ceiling, and he remembered that he wasn't as young as he used to be. But what did that matter?

He went to the closet to get his shoes—designer sneakers from France (Lanvin given to him after some photoshoot or fashion show or boutique launch). Gazing blankly out into the bright, blue morning, Johnathan decided he would take a walk. Perhaps the sunlight touching his skin would invigorate him (although, this was unlikely).

Outside, the taxis were whiffing between lanes, the cyclist ringing their bells. The sunlight leaked through the spaces between the tree leaves, breaking up the long expanses of shade along the sidewalk.

Zombie-like, Johnathan trudged along the path until he arrived at a newsstand set up near a playground at the edge of the park. He found the usual assortment of candy, bagels and fruit, along with a regular multitude of magazines and newspapers.

Johnny could hear the children over at the playground laughing and toying around. But there was one vile little child sitting on the swing by himself—not swinging, just sitting. A little black boy. The kid had a sinister look in his eyes, and Johnathan's flesh began to crawl. He was staring at Johnny with the most relentless gaze. That wasn't terribly odd. He always got noticed in public. That was the life of Mr. Johnathan Peacewood.

However, Johnny detested children, and this one was the most detestable. There were flies crawling on the kid's face and swarming all around him. He likely hadn't bathed in a week (but then neither had Johnny). The child had on a red hoodie, and it was filthy with mud stains. Thankfully, Johnathan stood at a distance so he wouldn't have to smell the little creep. He probably reeked! The kid looked like one of the African children you see on the charity commercials. You know, the ones where celebrities talk about these poor kids in the developing countries? And they tell you how you can feed them for just one American dollar a week?

The other children played around him as though he were a ghost. But he had locked eyes with Johnathan, and he was an eerie little thing.

"I'll take *The Gazette*," Johnny said to the man at the stand, slapping a dollar and fifty cents down on the counter between them. Quickly, before his own thoughts had time to come and whisper in his ear, he took a newspaper from the rack, hoping the headlines would distract him.

Johnathan was probably the last man in the world under forty to still read a physical paper. He liked the feel and the smell of real paper and ink. In fact, he typed his stories on a typewriter because digital editing felt too sterile. Johnny thought himself to be an old-fashioned American writer; after all, Faulkner never had spell-check.

Just a bit curious, Johnathan looked back out toward the playground. The creepy kid had gone. The swing where he had been sitting was empty (and he had taken the flies with him, thank god).

Oh well. *Just another strange little human*, Johnny thought, shrugging as he glimpsed down to read the paper. Luckily, the headline gave him just the distraction he had hoped for too: *Mother of Three Found Slaughtered in Her Northside Home.* Apparently, a newly divorced young mother had been found mutilated. According to the story, her sons—ages seven, five, and three—were standing over the body when the police arrived. Chicago PD entered the home, finding numerous puddles of water on the floor in the living room. The youngest boy was soaking wet in his clothes. According to neighbors, the boys' father had moved back to France after the divorce to be closer to his own parents, but he was now sending for his sons. Chicago PD had no leads or suspects. The victim had been a stay-at-home mom with no real enemies—just a nice lady with three young boys to raise.

"Don't you think it's a shame?" the man at the news stand asked, lamenting. "A young mother killed in her home, and her own children discover the body. Judgement day is upon us! I hope you believe in something! Oh, the spirits will haunt the streets! That's what *Revelation* says."

"Is that so, bud?" Johnny asked, not remotely interested in receiving a response.

"God knows," the man replied, biting into a bagel.

Life was funny that way sometimes. One minute, you're celebrating Christmas in July with your wine and your carols and your fist full of pills. The next minute you're reading the paper and wondering why the hell anyone ever bothered to have kids. One thing was for sure: the spirits were certainly haunting Johnny. Day and night. Night and day.

Chapter 2

It was a full moon and the boys were screaming. Mother was mad, and the boys were screaming.

Life had punched her in the teeth, you see? Long ago, she had graced the stage of the Met, radiant as a gem. Her legs were strong, her feet were powerful, and she had the bones of a bird soaring in the moonlight. Her momma had given her the genes of a prima ballerina, and so her path was certain. Her purpose in life: to dance—to float effortlessly in and out of the proscenium—as lithely as a lynx, as brightly as the North Star. Nothing had made her feel more alive than counting off steps: *One two three four five six seven eight. Two two three four five six seven eight.*

But love makes a mockery of fate sometimes, doesn't it?

See, Daddy wanted a family. He was the dominant type— big arms, big mouth, big ego. He couldn't have her out there prancing for the upper classes, traipsing off to Europe with those Bohemian boys. Imagine him holding her trophies and her bouquets as she posed for the cameras. What life would that be for a man? So Mother could dance in the next lifetime. This life would be about Daddy and homemaking. He made sure of that.

He was the get-in-there-and-cook-my-meal type. And he had a way of making her feel inferior. She was never pretty enough, never thin enough, never funny enough to deliver the punchline with the right zing. And unfortunately, masochistic dancers became batterable wives (in this case, anyway).

So she ditched dance. And eventually, Mother and Daddy had three boys. She raised them while he watched—stretch marks and breastfeeding and all the world entirely on her shoulders. Daddy didn't lift a finger. Macaroni Tuesdays and PTO meetings and special ointments for the middle boy's eczema? All her. After all, children were a woman's domain. His realm consisted of drinking scotch and playing tennis and chasing skirts. He had all the fun while she raised his boys. And the boys were screaming.

And it aged her so quickly. By twenty-eight, she looked forty. Her figure had gone, and her dreams had evaporated like puddles in the summer sun. But tears were an inefficient use of water in hell, so she held them in her face, keeping them secret. And those boys just kept on screaming.

And then? Daddy left. Went over to Europe chasing tail. He sent them money—in accordance with the court order, of course—but that was fatherhood to him: write a check, send a birthday card, never call.

Now, Mother lay on the patio, smoking a cigarette, dreaming of her youth. She had lost her dance, and the boys were screaming. And that little one looked just like his daddy, didn't he? Yeah, that was Daddy's pride and joy. The narcissistic little bastard was just like his pop, making the whole world revolve around him. That's why he was screaming.

So what? Let him scream. Let him shout until his spirit gives out. Hers certainly had. Now, when she exhaled, blowing smoke up into the starry night, she remembered herself. Her old self. Her true self. And as the smoke blossomed out into the navy expanse, like a ballerina dancing the saga of her youth, she went mad. She imagined herself dancing happily. But love had changed the hell out of that, hadn't it? And that little one screamed one scream too many this time.

She tossed the cigarette out into the night, storming back into the house to grab the little crybaby. He was filthy from the inside out and needed a good cleansing. "Quit that crying, you bastard!" she shouted, carrying him into the bathroom. She sat him atop the vanity and turned to fill the tub. "I'll give you something to cry about," she said. "I'll give you and your no-good daddy something to cry about." And the boy was screaming. And the other boys heard her. And they ran to see. And she took the littlest one and put him in the tub. And she held his head down beneath the water. And the other two started screaming. So Mother was mad, and the boys were screaming.

And the screams awakened a monster in the shadows. He had started creeping around outside the house some weeks ago, watching Mother. Some nights, he would watch her through the window as she got undressed. He enjoyed her body—that smooth, brown skin of hers—and could sense the spirit within it. He could feel her dance, and he loved it. So this night he had come looking for it again, looking for her dance. But the boys' screams were shrill, and they woke him from his trance. Then, through the window, as he hid out in the bushes, he saw her pressing the boy's little body down beneath the water.

Quickly, he climbed in. He climbed right through the window. He raced to her, grabbing her by the shoulder. The boys were too afraid of him to shout. And as the littlest one came up to breathe, he saw the monster slapping his mother hard. He slapped her once, twice, three times a lady. Then, she hit the floor crying. "Please!" she screamed. And the boys were silent. "Please!"

He kept a cool countenance as he dragged her into the living room, the boys following in terror. All her beauty and all her grace had faded. She had been stripped of her dreams, of her motherhood, and of her humanity. But he wanted to know her, to understand her—to breathe her essence. And so he cut her open, and she died.

And as the boys watched in terror, he searched for her dance—for her spirit—taking her apart. He longed to see it once more. But it had gone. And he and the boys would thirst for her life force forever more.

$$\triangle \ \triangle \ \triangle$$

North Avenue Beach, Chicago.

The air was warm and balmy; the water: cool and free of melancholy. A few stratus clouds streaked across the sky, but not a raindrop was in sight—not this day. This was paradise!

All the seagulls whisked and weaved through the wind in choreographed chaos, and the breeze was scented with hickory and hotdogs. A perfect day!

But Johnathan Peacewood wasn't writing anymore. He had plenty of ideas, but Johnny refused to avail himself to that inspiration. Writing had tortured him for long enough. For all he cared, Somerset could eat shit. He wouldn't pen a single word. Instead, he would lie on the beach languishing in the summer sun, with Ray-Bans on his nose, a newspaper in hand, and chilled pinot grigio in his canteen.

To be clear, Johnathan still felt that heavy weight of depression upon his chest. The suicide had failed, but he still felt entirely broken and unyieldingly lonely. Not even the warmth of the summer sun could raise his spirits. The beauty of the day was lost on him. Johnny believed that this pain would never relent, but he lacked the ambition that a second suicide attempt required. It took too much effort. A nice, passive declension would be the way to go this time. Skin cancer would do it if he kept sunbathing—or, if he kept gulping the pinot, cirrhosis of the liver.

"Aren't you Johnathan Peacewood?"

A gangly redhead loomed over him in a crimson onesie, holding her flip-flops and smacking savagely away at her mint-colored chewing gum. She had quite the sun burn, her skin glowing a bright red. In fact, her whole body looked like one giant, irritated, pulsating zit. She seemed to come out of nowhere (as zits do), but Johnny also hadn't really been paying attention; he was mildly drunk and falling into the headlines on the cover of his newspaper. But now here she was, just another annoying fan. She had seen him on a late-night television show—not *The Tonight Show* or *The Late Show*, but another one—promoting his last novel, which was being turned into a television miniseries. She wanted to talk about Somerset, of course. They always did.

"What are the odds!" she exclaimed.

This lady sure was homely with that freckled skin and those offensive red curls. What on earth possessed her to come out the door looking like that? And what on earth could she possibly want?

"I just need you to know how much your book inspired me," she told him. "I was thirty-five and becoming an old maid. My parents had given up on me ever having kids. My little sister married before me, and I never thought Mr. Right would show. Hell, I was about to get on one knee and propose to my vibrator! Ha ha. Was that an overshare? I can never tell."

Johnathan was hardly listening. He was playing connect the dots with the multitude of freckles on her crooked little face. And when he wasn't doing that, he was looking down at his newspaper. Truth be told, he had gotten sick of his single female fans begging him for love tips as if he were qualified to give advice on the subject.

"But Somerset gave me hope," the freckly zit of a woman kept yapping. "She waited hundreds of years. Hundreds! So I just kept hope alive, because if she could do it, so could I. And now I'm engaged!"

Bling!

Johnathan winced as the sunlight beamed off her prismatic engagement ring. It was as if a lighthouse was shining its beacon right into his face. And she was smiling the most ridiculous smile, as though this engagement had saved her life, as though she were the last single woman on the planet waiting for marriage. She kept looking down at that ring like it was the cure for cancer or the face of God—or anything else Johnathan didn't care about.

"I found him, Mr. Peacewood! I finally found him!" she celebrated.

"You're getting married?" Johnathan asked, bewildered— not because she was an ugly, gangly thing (although she was), but because no person in her right mind would get married. Marriage was to Johnny as Christmas was to Scrooge. Humbug! Wasn't marriage just a patriarchal institution and a death blow to sex, adventure, and happiness?

"Did you hear that ISIS blew up a church in Turkey?" Johnathan asked, gazing down at his paper, hoping to change the subject. "Isn't that awful? Terrorism is getting out of control. I think there's another war coming, don't you?"

"Yes," she said, smacking away at the mint-colored gum. "All because your books inspired me to keep going."

Johnathan felt more bewildered now, wondering what his books had to do with terrorism. They didn't, did they? No, not at all. Then, he realized that this giant, red zit of a woman was just an implacable fan wanting to talk about love. Humbug! Women were crazy and far too obsessed with love and marriage. Bah humbug! Right?

"I was going to just adopt a puppy or a baby or a cactus or something and never date again," she said. "But then I read *Somerset of the 1930s.* Somerset survived the KKK, World War I and the Great Depression. The Great Depression! And she just kept going. She left her little farm house in Texas after her boyfriend was murdered and moved up to Chicago, where she met a man named Al Capone. This Al guy really had a thing for her, you know, even though that type of love was forbidden in their time. Racism, you know? So Capone took her to Europe where they wouldn't be judged. Oh, Al would sing to her in Italian and write her beautiful sonnets, and I thought she would die because she had finally found her one true love. She was close. She was really close. Unfortunately, though, they had to come back to America because Al had business. That was the trouble, Mr. Peacewood. Al always had business. It was the one thing he cared about more than Somerset. So they came back. But then, he was arrested for tax evasion. At least I think it was tax evasion."

"Yes," Johnathan replied wearily. "I know the story well. I wrote it, actually."

"And because of that," she continued, "Somerset was never able to explore her feelings more deeply. But it would have happened. I just know she would have found love had Al not been arrested for tax evasion or whatever. But she lost him and just kept going, you know? She said at the end of the book that she would not stop living until she was able to find her true love. Oh, Mr. Peacewood, I remember her words exactly: 'Though I have failed, I am not deterred; for true love will soon be mine.' It made me believe! It made me believe, Mr. Peacewood. It made me keep going. And now I've found the one!"

Now, if there was one thing Mr. Johnathan Peacewood hated, it was the idea of "the one." As if there existed one person in this whole, wicked world who could make him complete. That was poppycock. Romance didn't make anyone complete, did it? No, of course not. This zit lady was so naïve. In fact, all of his fans were a bunch of dreamy-eyed nimrods, but he wrote for them anyway. He gave them exactly what they wanted: false hope.

Johnathan was no better than a shifty car salesman selling lemons to unsuspecting old ladies. But if they wanted to buy lemons, who was he to stop them?

"I'm thrilled that you found the one," Johnny replied, desperately wanting to take a nap. "Did you know a woman with three kids was murdered in her house last week, right here in Chicago?" he stated inquisitively. "Right in front of the kids. Poor gal."

"It was all you, Mr. Peacewood," she went on, entranced by her own romantic musings. "You may get this all the time, but you really did save me. I was so depressed thinking I'd never marry. I know I'm not much to look at. Hell, my face is shaped like a question mark. But this guy is the real deal. He's a neurosurgeon! A surgeon, Mr. Peacewood! He proposed in Paris underneath the Eiffel Tower, and I love him to death. We love each other to death. His name is Paul. He's amazing! Hell, I threw my vibrator away! Was that an overshare? I can never tell."

"I'm thrilled," Johnny said, still hoping she would walk away. Why was she still standing here yacking? Didn't she have a fiancé to pester? Weren't there bridesmaids' gowns to select? What about the venue? Weddings are all the about venue.

"We would be honored if you'd come to the wedding," she said. "It's here in Chicago."

Oh, dear. Now, he would have to feign enthusiasm as he kindly declined her offer. But pretending took so much energy.

"I'm flattered," Johnathan sighed, "but I wouldn't want to impose."

"You can even bring your girlfriend," she added.

Suddenly, there was an uncomfortable pause—the kind of awkward silence that always precedes laughter or crying or nausea.

"I'm not attached at the moment," he replied. "But according to this newspaper article I'm trying to read, the mayor of this city buys his cocaine in Colombia. Can you imagine?"

Although Johnathan's agent and his publicist had led his fans to believe he was dating a different Victoria's Secret model every other week, no one really knew how lonely he was, and they certainly didn't know he was gay. Johnathan kept it bottled up. Sometimes he wanted to go up to the Willis Tower and shout from the roof that he was going to die alone, a miserable, sulking queen. But he knew he'd never sell another book in that case. So he kept it secret. And it was his cross to bear. Johnathan Peacewood gave the world a reason to believe in love, even though love was a constant stranger.

How ironic.

How poetic.

How pathetic!

"Oh, I'm sorry. Well, you can bring your significant other," she replied with a sneakily probing tone.

What could he say? He couldn't let her in on his big secret, right? If the press got word of that, the headlines would ruin him. He could see them now: *Peacewood, Gay as a Rainbow!* or *Peacewood Single as a One Dollar Bill, and Now He's Worth That Too!* What a scandal it would be! But the loneliness was palpable. He had pushed it down as much as possible, but it was bubbling up to the surface. Johnathan found himself praying to God for the second time in one week, a new record. One more time and they'd be best friends. *Please, God, let this woman disappear,* he thought. *Just wash her away. Send a tidal wave!*

"And did I mention that the mother was murdered, and the kids found her body?" he asked.

"I don't believe it! I'm surprised you're unattached," she continued. "You're such a catch. Surely, there must be someone?" She looked over her shoulder out to the lake, her crooked little feet firmly plotted in the sand. She was searching for his companion. "Aren't you seeing some German actress? Didn't I read that? Oh, I could have sworn I read! Am I mistaken?" she asked. A partner? A special friend! The barrage of questions blasted Johnny, dizzying him until he finally started to see little purple spots—or maybe it was the pinot. No, these were definitely little purple spots.

A fortune teller had once disclosed to Johnathan that his aura emitted a radiant, purple light. He had always imagined that this light guarded him—protected him from ignorance and danger (and fans). Closing his eyes, Johnathan Peacewood surrounded himself in a ring of purple light and felt that he would soon explode with the energy of a thousand suns.

"Of course, I'm seeing someone!" he snapped, opening his eyes again. "I was just..."

"...Just waiting on me to get back from my swim!" a man in a speedo said, walking up to the two of them. The redhead touched her heart as her jaw dropped. And with that, her gum fell from her mouth down onto the sand.

His beauty stunned them both as he stood tall and tan with the face of a young Montgomery Clift. His torso formed a perfect V from his broad shoulders down to his narrow waist. And he had those annoying, rippling abs that you only get if you have the genes of a demigod or the diet of someone allergic to sugar, dairy, and fun. He looked like one of those shirtless heroes on the covers of the cheap paperback romances that you find in the grocery store.

"I'm back now," he said.

"Oh, Mr. Peacewood!" the annoying redhead screamed, fawning and slightly surprised "He is beautiful! You are a very lucky man. And you," she said, pointing to this Montgomery Clift-looking beauty. "You have a star on your hands. I hope you're good to him."

This hunky lad walked over and flopped down next to Johnathan on his beach towel, giving him a kiss on the cheek. Snatching the canteen of pinot from Johnathan's hand, he took a swig, grimacing as he realized that it was wine instead of water.

"The lake was a little too cold for a swim, I think," he said, laughing.

"Oh, well, I'll let you two get back to your *business*," the fan said, giggling and fanning her face, which shined with a glean of iniquity. "It was lovely to have met you, Mr. Peacewood! Wait until I tell my fiancé about this! Oh, I mean, wait until I tell him that I met Mr. Johnathan Peacewood! That's what I meant! Paul will die! He will just *die!*" Then she trotted off, leaving her gum in the sand and Johnny with his new friend.

"Um—thanks for getting rid of her, I guess," Johnny said, feeling a bit uneasy as he watched the red head scamper away. Truly, Johnny wondered whether this were salvation or the beginning of the end. The fan seemed a bit too excited to run off with her tidbit of celebrity gossip.

"I heard her talking, and I knew you were in trouble," the man replied, running his fingers through his thick, black hair. "It's really none of her business. I'll bet your fans think they own you, don't they? Never respecting your personal space?"

"Everyone owns me, yet I belong to no one," Johnathan sighed.

"How could the famous Johnathan Peacewood not belong to anyone?" the man asked. "How is it that no man has swept you up?"

Then, Johnathan became more unnerved. He found the fellow somewhat cavalier and uncouth. "Do you have any idea what you may have just done!" Johnathan asked, offended by the man's presumption. "How—how did you know?"

"I used to be closeted," the man replied. I know that look of dread for fear of being outed."

"Who are you?" Johnny asked, cautiously, looking over his shoulder to ensure that the fan had gone. And she had.

"The name is Harvey. Harvey Marcus," the man replied, speaking with more emphasis than necessary, as though his name deserved some special recognition. Maybe he was someone important.

"Well, Harvey Marcus," Johnny replied. "I usually keep my private life private! I rarely even speak to fans because they ask too many questions. What happens in my bedroom is my business only. I have a career to think of. I can't afford to wear my heart on my sleeve."

"Can't you?"

"Furthermore," Johnny continued, "you need to get me some more pinot grigio, since you pillaged the last of mine."

Chortling a bit, Harvey grabbed the canteen. Placing his open eye right up to the lid, he looked inside to see that it was completely empty.

"Oops," Harvey said, grinning bashfully, although remorse wasn't easily shown by a face so beautiful. "I guess that was the last of your wine. What do we do now?"

"If by *we* you mean *you*," Johnathan replied, "then *you* should get your gorgeous ass up and get *me* a bottle of pinot grigio. Please hurry. I'm sobering up, and we can't have that."

"You're cute," Harvey said, laughing.

"I'm aware," Johnny replied, gruffly—but not out of anger.

"Cute for an alcoholic! Ha!"

"Now, there's a liquor store two blocks from the beach. And get the good stuff," Johnny said. "Johnathan Peacewood will not drink cheap wine. Not today. Not tomorrow. Not ever!"

"Well," Harvey said, grinning enthusiastically, "if by some fluke of nature, the illustrious Johnathan Peacewood is actually unattached, perhaps I will get you that wine. But we will have it with dinner. I will cook for you!"

"You cook?" Johnny asked. "You don't strike me as the domestic type. But, I'm sure your boyfriends and girlfriends and sex friends enjoy that quite a bit. But about that wine . . ."

Johnathan found the banter amusing though he would never let it show. He hid behind the façade of hostility, but deep down, he hoped this Harvey would stick around and play a little longer. Johnny did, after all, like pretty things.

"Oh, I see. You think because I am a famous model, I could not be loving and faithful?" Harvey asked. "You think that because I have graced the covers of many magazines, I cannot be kind? You think that because I have strutted the runways of Paris, Milan, and Tokyo, I cannot be sensitive. You think that because I have had my picture taken by some of the most noteworthy photographers on Earth, I cannot..."

As Harvey blathered on about his accomplishments, Johnathan smiled and nodded, mostly admiring Harvey's good looks (and barely listening). He did, however, find Harvey's language a bit stilted—like cheesy dialogue from a tawdry romance novel. And of course, Johnathan knew that language well. Maybe this Marcus character was another big fan here to put on a show?

"...I have a heart!" Harvey continued. "Being a model does not mean I cannot love!"

"Who said anything about modeling?" Johnny inquired. "I honestly didn't know you were a model. Are you?"

Harvey paused.

Johnathan awaited his reply, but there was only silence. Awkward, embarrassing silence. Harvey grimaced a little in response to Johnny's question. Then, he turned his head away with unspoken disappointment and began to pout.

Suddenly, Johnny threw his head back, erupting into laughter. Poor Harvey was deflated. Sure, he hadn't worked in a while. But some years ago, Harvey was the face of a major campaign for a fashion line and had co-starred in a fragrance commercial—not for Chanel No. 5 or Obsession by Calvin Klein, but another really big one. Back then, he was rapidly becoming famous for his Montgomery Clift jawline. Women wanted him. Men wanted him. Even the animals wanted him; birds and rabbits and deer used to follow him around singing, as though he were a Disney princess, like Cinderella or Snow White (but not really).

However, his fame was short-lived. After his face hit the dashboard in a car accident, a permanent scar formed on the corner of his lip, ruining his career and leaving him an ogre (in his mind anyway). Cinderella had become Drizella. Harvey attempted to segue into acting, but he just had no talent. Dancing? No grace. He was now giving painting a shot, but nobody bought his work. Some fashion houses requested him still, but he couldn't bring himself to pose for the cameras anymore. His only gift in life had been that perfect face. And now, the perfection was gone. Worst of all, people like Johnny no longer recognized him.

"I guess I haven't worked in a long time," Harvey laughed with a tinge of shame. "I wish I had real talent. Writing novels seems like hard work. All those characters and motivations."

"I've had a lot of practice," Johnny replied, grinning proudly. "I was a lonely, lonely kid. I used to make up friends for myself, who then became characters. As I got older, their lives became more complex, until I just decided to write about them. Have you read any of my books? You talk like you have."

"Not even one," Harvey said. "But I promise to read them if you'll see me for dinner sometime."

Johnny had had models before, but they were always so stupid and clingy. But mostly stupid. And above all, just one-night stands kept secret. And this Montgomery Clift fellow was a little too slick and gorgeous to be trusted. Weren't guys like this a one-way ticket to heartbreak and betrayal? Furthermore, Johnny was altogether apprehensive about openly dating a man. He still wondered if that zit of a fan would run off and tell her book club she had seen him with this Harvey fellow. What would Charlotte say? How would the rumors impact sales?

But what did any of this matter, really? Johnny anticipated nothing but a life of lonely nights ahead of him anyhow. To hell with his career! Maybe a little tryst would do him good.

"Dinner may be impossible to manage. I'm exceedingly busy these days," Johnathan said, with the typically Peacewood pomp. "But what did you have in mind?"

Harvey was the most beautiful thing he'd ever laid eyes on, but a true cad never let himself seem too vulnerable. Johnny had a reputation to uphold. So while Harvey described to him what would likely have been a perfect first date, Johnny re-opened his newspaper, nonchalantly perusing the headlines. Baseball season was in full swing, and the Cubs were actually winning. The mayor had decided to run for re-election next year, despite that little scandal with him and his mistress in Bogota.

Sons of Northside Mother Traumatized after Mother's Gruesome Murder. The husband of the slain woman had arrived from France to collect his sons. The boys were traumatized and barely speaking, and the father was sending them to a psychiatrist. The Chicago Police Department still has no suspects or leads.

"All the world is insane," Johnny sighed, reading the paper as though Harvey were completely irrelevant (and wasn't everyone irrelevant to Mr. Johnathan Peacewood?).

"I don't like stories like that," Harvey snapped, snatching the paper from Johnathan's hand. "These papers always point out what's wrong in our world. Look at this," he hissed, slapping the front page with his knuckles. *"ISIS Bombs Church in Istanbul. Civil War in Tunisia Takes Several Lives.* Isn't there any love in the world anymore? Doesn't anybody want to be in love anymore? Where is the love? Where?" Harvey spoke with passion, throwing his arms about, conducting the choir that was his own pretentious voice.

"You think love is the answer?" Johnathan asked, snatching his paper back. "Bah! Shows what you know." Though Johnathan feigned disinterest, he truly wanted Harvey's opinion. He kept his guard up, but, behind his misanthropic exterior, he harbored just a hint of curiosity.

"Love is always the answer!" Harvey replied, even more impassioned now. "Love is all we need to fix these messes that you read about—to stop the terror and the bloodshed!"

Then, they both paused, gazing into each other's eyes for a few seconds. What a heartfelt moment upon which to stop and reflect. Harvey seemed refreshingly sanguine, didn't he?

Then, suddenly, Johnny threw his head back, once again erupting into uncontrollable laughter. "You're a regular John

Lennon, baby," he quipped, grinning. "And also, an unbelievable idiot."

"Ah!" Harvey exclaimed, with indignation and piety. "I see."

"Oh boy!" Johnathan continued, laughing and shaking his head.

"So you write about love, but you don't believe in it. Is that it?" Harvey asked, most sincere. "A false prophet!" he was roiled up—understandably so. Who likes being called an idiot? "You're no better than the silly television preachers, peddling their books and pushing their videos in Jesus's holy name, Amen—just for fame and money. The biggest atheists are the best preachers. Is that your game? Is that your shtick, Peacewood?"

"Actually," Johnathan started, but it was no use. Harvey intended to give him a good haranguing.

"Well, I have no interest in that, mister bigshot writer!" Harvey carried on. "You peddle love, but you're unloving. That's really sad. Warped and sad! I rescind my offer. Make your own damned dinner!" Harvey handed Johnny the empty canteen and stood to leave. "I'll keep this in mind the next time I'm on Amazon shopping for a good read."

"Wait!" Johnny said, realizing he had gone too far. "I'm not like that. I'm just having a bad day—or really a bad year. I'm sorry. You seem like a nice guy, Harvey."

"I am a nice guy!" Harvey snapped. He stood over Johnathan waiting for a more abject apology, maybe even some groveling. "The papers are right, I guess. If our writers and poets have stopped believing, then our generation is doomed. Soon, the entire world will be overrun by lunatics abducting children and killing mothers."

"I didn't mean to upset you," Johnny said, looking up with a gleam of contrition. Johnathan rarely ever apologized for anything. He spilt champagne on the president's daughter once—not Chelsea Clinton or Sasha Obama, but another one. It happened during her wedding reception in Los Angeles, after she married that financier who later cheated on her with the transgender hooker from Cambodia. Anyway, after spilling the champagne, Johnny joked that the dingy yellow stain was appropriate because she shouldn't have been wearing white in the first place. She didn't laugh. But she did hand him a new glass. Then, after raising a toast to him for having written the greatest love stories of all time, she walked away. That was the life of Mr. Johnathan Peacewood.

"I was rude. I'm sorry," Johnny said. "I'm really terrible sometimes."

Harvey stood fuming for a second more—just for drama's sake. Then, he relaxed his face and crossed his arms. Staring intently at Johnny, it seemed that further reprimand was on its way. Johnny sat anticipating. Suddenly, Harvey threw his head back laughing hysterically.

"Your wine was ok," Harvey said. "It's an Italian 1987. I can tell by the taste. That was an ok year, but 1985 was better. You were drinking something subpar. Imagine that! Mr. Johnathan Peacewood, drinking a mediocre pinot grigio. Wait 'til the paparazzi gets a load of that!"

"My wine choices will be the least of the paparazzi's concern by tomorrow morning," Johnathan replied, still wondering how quickly the gossip would get around. Maybe no one would believe the redhead. Or maybe his sexual orientation wouldn't matter as much as Charlotte thought it would. It was 2015, after all.

"Oh, forget about what people say," Harvey told him. "Let her go off and tell everyone she knows! I think a scandal might be good for your reputation—and even better for mine! Now, if you'd like to show me that you're not such a bad guy, what say we go for dinner?"

"Guilt-tripping me into a date. Good game!" Johnny replied.

"You think you're the only superstar in the world? I'll show you some things," Harvey remarked.

Showing confidence with Mr. Johnathan Peacewood? Now that was something you didn't see every day. Harvey didn't play around. He would speak his mind and push back if he had to. And his gravity was powerful enough to pull a rogue like Johnny out of unloving space and into steady orbit around him.

Harvey certainly looked like love to him anyway. He was everything Johnny had always imagined a perfect man to be—tall, handsome, and challenging. That was good enough, right? So what if it meant his career was over! It had been a good run. Charlotte had no right to stop him anymore.

Perhaps it's time to live, Johnathan thought, smirking as Harvey gazed into his eyes.

Meanwhile, as Johnny basked in the glow of his own ego, a long, gorgeous waif of a girl lay fifty feet away, watching the two men flirt. She found the goings-on to be delicious and intriguing. *How precious! How absolutely precious*, she thought, grinning and taking notes as Harvey scooted closer to Johnny on the beach towel.

This girl's name was Sasha, and she would become a central antagonist in Johnathan's story. She was slender and blond and beautiful, yet entirely sinister. Sasha wanted nothing more than the destruction of Mr. Johnny Peacewood, and she would stop at nothing to succeed. She was fifty percent jealousy and fifty percent ambition, and her plan was to bring ruin to him forthwith. She had been following him and studying him so that the attack would be effortless. And as the green waves of Lake

Michigan beat upon the sand, Sasha contemplated every detail of her diabolical plot to ruin Johnny. And there would be blood. Oh, there would be oodles of blood.

Chapter 3

Peacewood Mansion, Lake Forest, Illinois.

Mr. Johnathan Peacewood was floating in his pool, resting atop an inflatable dragon as he pondered the meaning of life. It was cliché. But he pondered, nonetheless.

He sensed the power within him, and, indeed, Mr. Peacewood was a universe teeming with spirits. Holding his arms out, he saw the purple lights surging through his veins up to his fingers. He was life. He was creation. And in the palm of his hand, a tiny galaxy formed, spiraling over his life line. He was a god.

Johnathan closed his eyes for a moment. Swishing his fingers through the water, he imagined himself on the back of a giant sea horse. He was the Don Quixote of the sea, and naturally, the mermaids encircled him, singing beautiful songs, worshipping him. And when he opened his eyes, he saw brilliant, rainbow-colored sea horses arching over him, emerging from the ripples to jovially ascend to the heavens before bursting like a bubble, raining droplets down on his face.

Harvey too emerged from the ripples. As he lifted himself from the pool, Johnathan admired his backside, watching as water dripped from his speedo. Instead of grabbing a towel, Harvey just glistened wet in the moonlight—his olive skin aglow beneath the stars.

"Are you going to lay there all night, Peacewood?" he asked.

"What would you have me do?" Johnny replied phlegmatically. "Movement is so proletariat. I'm more the sedentary type."

"How bout we go for a spin in that Lamborghini of yours!" Harvey suggested.

"The one in the garage? Oh, I never drive that thing," Johnny replied, shooing the notion. "It's a stick shift. I can't drive a stick."

"Then, why'd you buy it?"

"It was pretty," Johnny replied. "I like pretty things."

"I'll bet you do, Peacewood," Harvey remarked coquettishly. "Let's go for a ride!"

"I told you," Johnny groaned, "I can't drive that thing."

"Oh, but I can," Harvey replied, grinning coyly.

"Oh? You can, can you?"

"I can! And you're about to learn," Harvey said. "What's the point in having a pretty car if we can't drive down Michigan Avenue and make all the kids jealous?"

"People are already jealous of me."

Harvey shrugged. "There's always room for improvement."

And with that, Mr. Johnathan Peacewood sighed the most acquiescent sigh, rolling off the back of his dragon and splashing into the pool. He sank slowly to the bottom, holding his breath and pressing his feet to the floor. This was his sanctuary—his quiet place. Only dreams existed down there. Soon after, Harvey was down there too, pushing bubbles out his nose and playfully swimming in circles around Johnny. Then he came right up to him and pressed his feet against the floor too.

The two men stood face to face underneath the water, and Johnny could again feel the power surging through his body. The purple lightning shot though his arms, illuminating his every artery and vein until his body was a cloud of star stuff and magic.

Reaching out, he extended his hand to Harvey, and Harvey could see all the stars in the universe swirling in Johnathan's palm. And so he placed his hand in Mr. Peacewood's. And of course, Johnathan's lightning shot into Harvey and went into his blood, illuminating his arteries and veins too. Then, Harvey became his own underwater nebula, expanding and bursting with energy. And he could feel the stars burgeoning inside of him. And as comets and asteroids orbited them, Harvey could see Johnathan's heart glowing in his chest. A heart! Imagine that! He had one after all.

And then—just then—Harvey leaned in and kissed Johnathan on the lips. Now, life had become a work art. And there at the bottom of the pool, Johnny and Harvey created their own little universe.

Chapter 4

Bada bing, bada boom! In a short time, Mr. Johnathan Peacewood fell over the edge and plummeted deep into that murky abyss we call romantic love. He granted Harvey access to his very private life, giving him keys to his penthouse, his Lamborghini, and the world. The process was quick and insidious. It started with Harvey meeting him a few times a week for dinner— with good wine, of course—over which the obnoxiously cutesy pet names came into play. Darling. Baby. Honeysuckle Ice Cream Cake. That's when the dinners became cuddles on the floor and the wines became martinis. Suddenly, the good-nights disappeared and were swiftly replaced with good mornings. It's not clear when Harvey planted a toothbrush in Johnny's bathroom, but it happened somewhere between "baby" and "honeysuckle ice cream cake."

And Johnathan felt more alive than ever! He felt like a doting teenager on an endless cycle of somersaults, tumbling through a dream. It was nice to have someone there—someone with whom to share dinners, someone with whom to hold hands in the park, someone to pull the pesky nose hairs out of his nostrils when he couldn't get at them with the tweezers. Johnny could never get at those damned nose hairs, so finally having a companion was a miracle.

However, this new affair further distracted Mr. Peacewood from his writing. He hadn't written much more than a few paragraphs in weeks, and Charlotte, his agent, was pissed to the highest point of pisstivity. She had lied to the publisher, first about him having pneumonia, then about him having a death in the family, then about him being in mourning in Indonesia. Johnathan did, in fact, miss the writing. But he didn't give a single damn about Charlotte's deadlines. He was in love, damn it!

"It'll get done," Johnathan told her. He stood yapping with Charlotte over the phone down at the lakefront. Johnny was alone on his early, meditative walk. He took these walks all the time to keep a practical perspective on life. They didn't really work though, because Johnathan Peacewood never had any type of practical perspective toward anything. Delusions of grandeur were not delusions at all to someone rich and famous, as flashing lights and red carpets and limousines were mere banalities. Any other perspective than this was the wrong perspective.

"You're becoming a thorn in my side, you little pickle kisser," Charlotte told him. "And this is very unprofessional. Just finish this book so the publisher can get off our backs. They've been calling me non-stop. They interrupted my pedicure this morning with their damned phone calls! We have a contract, Peacewood!" Charlotte had negotiated a deal with the publisher so that Johnathan got a five million dollar advance with the expectation that he would have the book finished by midsummer. Now, the deadline had passed, and Charlotte had to answer for it.

But Johnathan didn't care about contracts. And he didn't care about Somerset anymore. Besides, Harvey hated when Johnathan wrote. It reminded him of his lack of talent. Harvey preferred his new boyfriend to just languish in the world—like a bird that never takes to flight because the ground is safe and comfortable.

"I've gotta go, Charlotte," Johnathan said. "Stop pestering me. The book'll get done. I'm almost there."

But that was a lie. Johnathan had stopped writing about Somerset and Clifton, just as they were beginning to fall in love in chapter six. What an awkward time to stop a romantic tale: just as the first buds of love were blooming. So Somerset and her new beau were left without resolution, and they were being denied the love that Johnathan himself felt for Harvey. Ah, love was heaven! Love was heaven?

"Oh hell, Charlotte!" he groaned, continuing to argue with her as he strolled up the lakefront with the phone to his ear. Summer was fading, and the leaves were falling into the water, one by one—languishing like Johnathan. "You want me to email you a few chapters? What? Well, I'd rather send them to you all at once. That's how I like to have them read: all together," he said.

Then, suddenly, Johnathan halted in his tracks because something ghastly had caught his eye.

Charlotte was still blathering away—as she often did, even when no one was listening—but Johnathan was petrified. Here that kid was again: the little creep from the playground. The dirty little black boy from the swing. He was wearing the same muddy, red hoodie as before, and flies were swarming around him like electrons around an atom. He had become his own little universe of unsightly filth. It was disturbing, really. He was up on the hill looking down at Johnny with a mean gleam.

"Are you listening to me, you narcissistic numbat!" Charlotte shouted, but Jonathan was entranced by the boy's sinister face. The child was mouthing something—whispering some spell or hex—but Johnathan was too far away to hear any of it. He could only see the boy's wicked little lips opening and closing around his words.

"What?" Johnathan called. "What are you saying?"

"You hear exactly what I'm saying, you cocaine-craving capybara!" Charlotte shouted. "I'm telling you that if you don't get to writing, the publisher will sue the hell out of you! That's what I'm saying."

"Not you, Charlotte," Johnny said. "There's a boy! A little boy is over here saying something to me."

"A little boy?" Charlotte asked. "Children are the worst, really. Never liked them. Quite frankly, I find their youth to be offensive and unnecessary."

The boy was mouthing more energetically now. He seemed to be saying the same thing over and over—chanting something. Johnny felt himself being tugged toward the kid by some irresistible force. Every cell in his body reacted to the boy in the most uncomfortable way, as if the child were a black hole sucking him in. Johnny was being beckoned. The boy pointed toward him, piercing him with some dark magic.

"Charlotte, I'll call you back," he said, drone-like.

"Oh, no you don't, you crooked little turd!" she shouted. "You're going to tell me when you'll have that book, you self-centered serpent of a—"

Click. Johnathan hung up the call.

"What's that you're saying? 'Can't be'?" Johnathan asked. The boy did, in fact, look to be mouthing the words "can't be." But as Johnathan got closer to the child, he could hear exactly what he was saying. This was no incantation. No magic. No spell. It was a directive. And the message was harrowing to Johnny.

"Claim me!" the boy said. "Claim me!"

"What are you saying?" Johnathan asked again.

"Claim me! Claim me! Claim me!" The boy kept repeating—with flies buzzing about his face. "Claim me! Claim me! Claim me!"

The words gripped Johnathan's heart, stopping his breath. This child was a wicked little spirit. Wicked.

Check, please! Johnny ran as quickly as he could away from the little creep. The morning meditation was over. He ran up the hill and out of the park, dashing without caution into the street. Cars honked, and drivers cursed. A cab almost hit him! But Johnathan ran without turning back. He could still hear the boy's words. "Claim me." And he knew exactly what they meant. But for now, he would run home where it was safe to hide. And maybe he would finish that damned Somerset novel.

△ △ △

Upon arriving home, Johnathan discovered that he had a new neighbor. Surprise, surprise! And how annoying! Johnny had enjoyed the peace and quiet of being the only top-floor resident. The adjoining penthouse apartment had remained empty the last year.

The previous neighbor, some old software inventor, had died suddenly of throat cancer or a coke overdose or murder or whatever, and his kids fought over the estate. Who gets the mansion in Napa Valley? Who gets the ranch in Wyoming? Who gets the old guy's seat aboard the space shuttle to Mars? The brats must have finally decided to sell this place, split the proceeds, and move on with their precious, trust-funded lives.

He hoped they didn't sell it to anyone friendly. God, wouldn't that be awful! The last thing he needed was some congenial little white homemaker baking him cookies and sending him Christmas cards. She'd probably invite him over for supper to meet the hubby, kids, and cocker spaniel. Or even worse, what if it was one of his fans? The kind who would want him to join a book club and nibble finger sandwiches and chat about Somerset all the damn time. Christ! That would be more annoying than herpes, wouldn't it? Of course, it would.

The new neighbor had left his front door wide open, so of course Johnathan peeked in to snoop. Wow, what a sight! A myriad of paintings adorned the walls. This place looked more like an art gallery or a museum than a penthouse apartment. It was a bit much, actually—the frames were practically touching each other. It must have been some old rich lady spending her deceased husband's fortune on cultural artifacts. There was a Lichtenstein and a Salvador Dali, a couple of Jackson Pollocks, and of course a Warhol. And Johnny recognized some of the paintings as Simon Sargent originals. Those must have cost a fortune. Whoever could afford a Simon Sargent original must have been loaded, maybe even as loaded as Johnny. (But probably not—let's be honest).

Simon Sargent had become famous for his beautiful, minimalistic abstracts. The shtick was that Sargent was blind and only painted with his sixth sense and psychic powers. The world was captivated by his work. A European monarch—not the queen of England or the king of Denmark, but another famous one—had discovered him while on a trip to Chicago years ago. Known for his discerning taste, this fastidious royal had commissioned Mr. Sargent to paint an entire collection. Soon thereafter, anybody who was anybody was buying a Sargent original. His most recent piece, "The Invasion of the Stars," had sold at auction for ten million dollars to a famous Hollywood director. (Unfortunately, his wife got it in the divorce—too bad, really. Love stinks, doesn't it?) Sargent told the press that the painting depicted the end of the universe. According to his visions, the universe would end by expanding too much. All the atoms would pull themselves into smithereens, and every tiny object would vanish into blissful oblivion. Poof! Gone.

"But the universe will be much different by then," Sargent once told a famous television journalist during a live interview. "Humans will eventually have to leave the earth because of the sun's expansion. By then, our species will have evolved quite a bit, and we'll have the technology to fly through space at the speed of light. Finding a new planet and even a new universe will be easy."

"This is all very hard to believe," said the famous journalist.

Johnathan remembered that interview like it was yesterday even though it was years ago. He remembered tuning in with morbid curiosity.

"Oh, but it's all very true!" Sargent said, pushing his point. "I can see the past, the present, and the future. It's really quite amazing!"

"So you're psychic?" the journalist asked, incredulous.

"We're all psychic—all of us," Sargent said. "But I'm far more psychic than you. Sargent went on to tell the journalist that she would continue having success and that she would one day have lunch with a Dalai Lama—but not the current Dalai Lama. And that she would marry three times but only be loved by the second.

"Johnathan Pots!" a voice called from inside the apartment.

Johnathan hadn't heard that name in years. Just then, a tall black man with a silvery beard emerged from around the corner. He was wearing dark shades and wielding a white cane so as not to bump any of his beautiful paintings off the wall. "Come in!" the man said. "Won't you come in and sit with me for a minute, Mr. Pots? We're neighbors."

"I don't really go by that name," Johnathan told him. Johnathan Pots didn't have the same romantic ring as Johnathan Peacewood.

"Won't you come in and have a cup of tea with me?" the blind man asked. He wasn't really dressed to Johnathan's liking. He had on one of those loose Hawaiian shirts—the kind your uncle wears during the summer barbeques, when the weather is all muggy and gross, the kind that fit like circus tents. You know that kind? But this guy was blind, so what did his appearance matter?

"You're Simon Sargent," Johnathan said.

"Of course, I am!" the blind man responded. "But, you can call me Sargent, neighbor! Won't you come in and have some tea?"

Waving his white cane back and forth across the floor, he walked toward the front door where Johnathan stood. "You look like you've just seen a ghost, Mr. Peacewood," Sargent said.

"You can see what I look like?" Johnathan asked. "So you're really not blind? I get it. Every artist needs a gimmick."

"Oh, I can't see you with my eyes," Sargent said. "But I can sense your aura. But it's trembling around you. You're shaken up. You've seen something just now that disturbed you."

Clearly, the creepy little kid had disrupted his aura—according to Sargent, that is. Johnny didn't even know he had an aura. He didn't believe in all that metaphysical psycho-babble. He was a stone-cold atheist and thought humans were just apes in fancy clothes who had learned to use weapons and tools to keep themselves artificially planted at the top of the food chain. There were no spirits or auras. That was all poppycock, wasn't it? Of course, it was.

"You're being haunted!" Sargent said. "And it's not going to stop until you finish what you've started."

"What are you talking about?" Johnny asked.

"Come in!" Sargent beckoned. "Come in. I have a jar of hydroponic weed I keep in the cabinet, right next to the Frosted Flakes and Oatmeal. We can smoke and talk—and smoke some more! I've got pot brownies and magic mushrooms too, if you're hungry."

"You're old enough to be my father!" Johnny shouted.

"So I am! But I'm not your father!" Sargent said. "Your father was a user. I want to be your friend."

Johnathan's father had been a user, a cocaine addict, in and out of prison all throughout Johnathan's teen years. Johnny never talked about his family to the public. So who had told Sargent? Was there some documentary circulating out there? Some tabloid gossip? Some Youtube video? No, Johnathan never talked to anyone about his family—not even to Charlotte. And certainly not to the press.

After making his first millions from *Somerset*, Johnny took the old guy in. He let his father stay with him in Chicago. He even sent him to treatment to get better. But the old guy had serious problems, and one day Johnathan came home to find all his belongings gone. His apartment was empty—no furniture, no rug, not even a damn toaster anymore. Johnathan hadn't seen him or heard from him in two years. He figured the old guy was dead, and, quite frankly, he was better off that way. The last thing Johnny needed was another father figure getting him high and betraying him.

"I don't think that's such a good idea," Johnathan said.

"Well, pooh," Sargent pouted. But he quickly re-inflated. "If you change your mind, I'm just across the hall. But please be careful, Peacewood. Things in your house are not as they seem. There are shadows around you! I see them diming the light of your aura. And if you're not careful, your gifts will turn against you!"

"Excuse me?" Johnathan looked quizzical.

"They'll turn on you!" Sargent reiterated.

"Turn? Like sour milk?" Johnathan asked perplexedly.

"No, like a scorned lover! Your gifts will turn on you," Sargent told him. "If you don't' use 'em, your gifts will turn on you and kick your butt. They may even kill you. Murder you! Shoot you dead! You have to do what you're destined to do, and if you keep going on like... "

"Well, thank you!" Johnny interjected, hoping to drown out Sargent's impertinent familiarity. "Your parlor tricks are impressive. But I don't believe in psychics. You're a fan. Thank you for reading. It was my publisher's idea to release the series in braille last year. I'm glad you're enjoying it. I'll be sure to get you an autographed copy. But I think I should be going home."

"Let me know when you want to stop by!" Sargent continued eagerly. "I've got some good green! It's Jamaican! They grow it right down there, you know! I think I'll go roll a joint right now."

"I have my own stash," Johnny said. "I'm Johnathan Peacewood! I can get anything I want—anything except a floor to myself in this building, it seems. But it was nice to meet you, Mr. Sargent. I've got to run call my real estate broker about finding a new place. Welcome to the building! If you ever want to chat, please feel free to call anyone but me. Have a good one, now!"

Then, Johnny went to his apartment. When he turned back to close the door, Sargent was still standing there in his doorway, smiling and holding his white cane. He was unyieldingly cheerful. How annoying! If there was anything Johnny hated, it was unyielding cheer. So he slammed the door.

What an eerie life this is, Johnny thought. What an eerie and exhausting life! Then, he walked into the kitchen and made himself a morning martini. A morning martini is no different than a regular martini—except you drink it in the morning, after you've been hassled by a creepy kid, a bitchy agent, and crazy-assed blind man.

$$\triangle \ \triangle \ \triangle$$

Johnathan had a date with Harvey at seven, so Harvey rang the doorbell at exactly 7:36 p.m. He was always at least thirty minutes late. It was uncanny! It was as if he planned it that way. He likely did it to demonstrate to Johnny that he had his own life (even though he didn't).

Johnny sprang to his feet, eagerly racing toward the door. He had put on his new designer tunic, which a famous Italian designer had sent him—not Miuccia Prada or Donatella Versace, but another one. Johnny's dates with Harvey had become the highlights of his weeks. The rest of the time, he was either jet-setting, snorting cocaine, or avoiding Charlotte's calls. And rarely, he'd write. Rarely.

He opened the door to see his new love. "How are you?" Harvey asked, walking in with a bottle of merlot. Grabbing Johnathan, he kissed him and waltzed him across the floor to the unheard music in his heart. "I missed you!"

"You were just here yesterday!" Johnny replied, laughing a bit.

"So what? I still missed you!" Harvey replied, playfully puckering his Montgomery-Clift lips. "I miss the bliss of being with Peacewood! Ha, I rhymed!" Harvey twirled Johnathan around in his arms and kissed him again. This was always Harvey's entrance: a dance, a kiss, and a few clever quips. This was everything that Johnathan had ever imagined a perfect romance to be—well, except for the incessant tardiness. But maybe he was imagining that, too.

"Well, you're late as usual!" Johnny said.

"What does that matter?" Harvey snapped, letting Johnny go quickly enough that he nearly fell to the floor. "I have a life. I know this may come as a surprise to you, but the world does not revolve around Johnathan Peacewood!"

Harvey had a terrible temper. His mood commonly switched from hot to cold at the drop a hat, and the slightest things ticked him off. Johnathan hated to fight, so he walked on eggshells to keep the peace. And the truth was, when he and Harvey got along, they were like childhood friends. So why not try and preserve that at all costs?

"It's absurd! You're so used to being pampered and calling the shots," Harvey hissed. "I'm not one of your servants. I'm your boyfriend!"

"I'm sorry, Harvey. It just seems to be a habit of yours," said Johnathan. "At least that's what I've noticed."

"Well," Harvey replied, calmly but with austerity, "I'm beginning to regret coming at all." He walked over to the kitchen island, sitting the merlot on the granite. "Maybe I should just go. I definitely didn't get all dressed up and drive across town to get bitched at. I hate when you're like this."

"Sorry," Johnny apologized, deflated and ashamed. He went over and gave Harvey a hug, hoping to mend the wound. "Let's have dinner. I'm sorry."

Harvey rumpled is brow, looking as though he was about to give Johnathan another good haranguing. But he didn't. After shrugging his shoulders, he began to smile. All was forgiven for now.

"Yes, dinner," Harvey said. "And then I'll give you a massage and run your bathwater."

Johnathan hesitated, but he knew he had to tell him. "No massage tonight. I'll have to do a little writing after dinner. Charlotte negotiated a new deadline, and it's coming up. And I can't miss this one."

Harvey hated when Johnathan took time to write. He didn't understand why Johnny had to work at all. Didn't he have all the money in the world? What use is work when you have everything you need and want already?

"You just don't love me at all!" Harvey pouted.

"Why would you say that?" Johnny asked.

"You care more about your work than you do about me," Harvey moped. "I know you do. You have millions—maybe billions! You could throw that manuscript away and never write again if you wanted. You don't have time for me because you don't want to. That writing is what you love, Peacewood. Not to mention, you won't even hold my hand in public. You won't even kiss me in the park for fear that some parasitic paparazzo is going to snap our picture and ruin your career. I'm sick of hiding in the shadows with you for the sake of your job, Peacewood."

"There's nothing I can do about it," Johnny said.

"Nothing?" Harvey ask, coldly raising his brow. "There is nothing Johnathan Peacewood *cannot* do about it! You're making excuses for yourself, Peacewood. In that case, I think I should go."

"I have a contract, Harvey!" Johnny attempted to reason.

"You're Johnathan Peacewood! What's a contract to you?"

Harvey's misery needed company. Now that he was done modeling, he was as useless as a plane with no engine. Harvey felt that he had no purpose but to languish about, waiting for death to take him. And maybe this romance distracted him from his own demise. But at least it was a distraction. He uncorked the merlot, pouring it into a glass while he stared angrily out the window.

"I'm glad to see you're not going," Johnny spoke wryly. But Harvey had no response. He sat drinking his wine. But he was boiling under the surface.

Jealousy was a cantankerous bitch, and Harvey knew all this contract business was hogwash. If Johnathan Peacewood wanted out of a contract, all he had to do was wag his magic little finger. Johnathan had become a god in the realm of publishing. He had become a god in every realm, actually; whatever he wanted became so. To Harvey, it felt like Johnny was cheating on him with Somerset. Or maybe Harvey was the other woman. Hmm.

The two sat and had dinner, neither speaking a word. Generally, Harvey was an expressive man (a bit of a drama queen, one might say). Johnny interpreted Harvey's reticence as a sign of worse things to come. He must have been livid if he wasn't talking. He wasn't even making eye contact. Johnathan couldn't stand the thought of a break up—not now. He had finally met the love of his life after years of longing. But it felt unnatural not to write.

"Harvey, you know I've always loved to write," Johnny said.

Again, Harvey said nothing. Instead, he sat at the table pushing little bits of pastry around his plate. He would look out the window from time to time, but never would he look directly at Johnathan.

"I am who I am because of it," Johnny continued, pleadingly.

Harvey didn't like that Johnathan had something to live for that wasn't him. Picking up his glass of merlot, he walked over to the desk where Johnathan kept his antique typewriter. Johnathan had bought it right after college in some old thrift shop in Pilson, and it was his most treasured belonging. He had written all his novels on it.

Inside it was a single sheet of paper, on which a few paragraphs had already been typed. And next to it, on the desk, was a thick stack of pages from Johnny's yet-to-be-completed manuscript. The final story of Somerset, in beautiful prose.

Harvey felt wicked, indeed. Hawking up some phlegm from the back of his throat, he spat onto the manuscript. He actually spat from his mouth onto those papers. Then, he flung them off the desk and watched until they zigzagged down to the floor like white feathers falling through the air. Harvey spread them over the hardwood with his foot, smirking. The beautiful prose was now covered with dirt marks in the shape of Harvey's Farragamo wingtip soles. What did he care about silly old Somerset? What did he care?

"Harvey!" Johnny called, standing to his feet. "Don't!"

Harvey held his glass of merlot over the typewriter, looking back at Johnny. "You've got a new love now, Peacewood," Harvey said. "His name is Harvey Marcus, and he's never playing second fiddle—especially not to some bitch named Somerset." Harvey tipped the rim of the glass, preparing to destroy Johnathan's typewriter. But boom! Before a single drop fell, the power went out in the penthouse. Must have been a blackout downtown.

"Claim me!" a voice rasped through the darkness. "Claim me!"

And then, a flash of purple lightening shot through the room, and Harvey was lifted from the floor and thrown twenty feet away. His body hit the wall, knocking the pictures down as tiny, purple sparks exploded in the air like miniature fireworks before quickly vanishing into ethereal nothingness.

The lights came back.

Wine was all over Harvey's shirt, but not a single drop had hit the typewriter. Johnny ran to Harvey's rescue, helping him up from the floor.

"What was that?" Harvey asked, stupefied and struggling to stand. "What did you do? What was that flash?"

He was stunned. The poor guy was like a deer in the headlights—or a man who'd just been tossed across a room like a softball by some strange purple light force. "I've been drinking a lot," Harvey said. "Yeah, it—it was the wine. The tannins in the wine always mess with me. I need to go to sleep. This is a nightmare. Yeah, I'm just dreaming. Yeah, yeah! That's it. I'm just having a nightmare." Harvey hugged Johnny around his neck, burying his face in his shoulder. Poor, pathetic Harvey was shaking like a frightened little boy. But who cares? The typewriter and the manuscript were all right.

△ △ △

After Johnathan put Harvey to bed, he sneaked back out to tidy up the living room. He picked up the loose pages that Harvey had scattered, carefully placing them back in order on the desk. Then, he examined his antique typewriter, making sure the wine had not touched it. All clear—every key was bone-dry. Johnathan looked back at the bedroom door. Harvey was still asleep. Good! He could sit and write a few chapters.

He had already started a new one, and the first page of it was in the typewriter. This was that page that Harvey had been about to ruin with the merlot, until that strange purple light threw him against the wall. Johnathan didn't know what had happened, but it didn't matter. He was thrilled that it hadn't been lost. Smiling triumphantly, he leaned in to read his latest work.

"Holy shit!" Johnny shouted. In the center of the page, in bold Times New Roman font, someone had typed the words *claim me*.

Chapter 5

September in Chicago.

The air was mild and jubilant, and the sunset had painted the clouds an amorous blend of orange and pink. Oh, the sky was radiant with so much love. The air, the trees, the streets—even the bricks looked and smelled like love. And our heroine Somerset found herself on the L train platform, elevated high above Division Street while the breeze lifted her sundress. Somerset was Marilyn Monroe in *The Seven Year Itch*, trying to keep that dress down over those smooth-to-the-touch legs of hers. She hoped the boys wouldn't look. But of course, the wind was the wind, and boys were boys.

She was a beautiful woman with the type of brown skin that never aged. After all, black don't crack. It helped that she was also locked into an eternal youth by a wondrous spell. She was now five hundred and fourteen years old. Somerset had seen war and famine and colonialism and slavery and emancipation and suffrage and prohibition and jazz and swing and atom bombs and Agent Orange and disco and AIDS and 9/11, but she had never found true love.

She had re-invented herself more times than Madonna. Somerset had been a princess and a slave and a suffragette and a singer and an actress and a writer and a spy and a courtesan and an assassin. She had triumphed again and again, in century after century, in struggle after struggle. She had worn cornrows and finger waves and bouffants and afros and Brazilian weaves and lace-front wigs. Now she had shaved her head so that she was completely bald, and had gotten a red rose tattooed on the side of her scalp so that she would never have to wear one behind her ear again. Her round, black head glistened in the sun more regally than a crown. After all these centuries, she was bold and confident. And she would just keep going until she found exactly what her heart had sought these last five hundred years: love, damn it! Love!

However, Somerset noticed that society was undergoing a tectonic shift in the twenty-first century. Europe and the Americas had lost much of their dominance, and Asia began to rise. It wasn't enough to simply be in the West anymore—that would no longer grant her the keys to the world. She had to become *of* the world. So she did something she had never done: enroll in university. It took her over a decade to get it all in, but she managed it. She was now pursuing her PhD, trying her best to understand race and classism. Somerset wanted to understand and love all people, even though, quite frankly, people and their ridiculous hang-ups had started to irk her like crazy. Everybody had some issue, be it race, religion, or class, that gave him or her an excuse not to love. Truthfully, Somerset had become a bit cynical. She had cared for men of every ilk, and each one had disappointed her, running away from love when she made it so available. So here she was—in 2015, perplexed by society and struggling to believe in love.

"That's a dope tattoo," a man said from behind her on the platform. He was tall with shoulder-length blond hair.

"Thanks," Somerset replied, disinterested. She was in no mood for small talk—not in this century. There was too much injustice in the world—too much to understand—too many problems to address. It distracted her. And she had certainly met her share of distracting characters.

"Almost as beautiful as your face," he continued.

Here goes another one, Somerset thought. Next, he'd ask for her number and try to get her to join him at some seedy sports bar for more small talk over a Bud Lite. Then he'd assure her that she was the most beautiful woman he'd ever seen, which Somerset knew was code for "I want to sleep with you." He'd summarize his resume, reciting his credentials and perquisites, his membership to the yacht club, and his key to some condo in yuppie Wicker Park—which was all code for "I'm a man who's extremely and unyieldingly impressed with myself." Finally, he'd ask her to accompany him home, where he'd show his true, disappointing colors. And after twenty-four more hours, he would vanish and never call her again. Somerset had been down this road before.

To know Somerset, you must first understand that the woman wore her heart on her sleeve. She had sewn it there many times, only to see it stabbed again and again, in century after century. Faithful to her pursuit of love, she wrapped it in bandages and never stopped living. The fates, however, threaded her life with betrayal and abandonment. Of course, a heart is resilient. But each wound left thicker scar tissue than the last. And eventually, Somerset's heart became as calloused as the soles of a dancer's feet. The muscle fibers had grown so hard now that she wondered if anyone would every break through again.

To top it off, this era was the worst! Men of the twenty-first century had neither charisma nor romanticism. Hemingway—now there was a real romantic! Langston Hughes had charm for days. Hell, even Napoleon wrote love letters. Men these days were lazy. They didn't even try. And the girls gave everything up too easily. Somerset hated the modern era. She was determined not to focus on romantic relationships for the next hundred years, or until the human race had come back to its senses. Somerset would boycott romance until men were men again. And why not? Hell, she had all the time in the world.

"Thank you again," she replied. "And the answer is no—to whatever it is you want."

The man laughed with unwavering confidence, tucking his hair back behind his ear. "I didn't really have an agenda, miss," he told her. "Just think you're gorgeous is all. And I love tattoos! I like the one on your head. I have fourteen myself!"

"Well, again," Somerset said. "Thank you very much."

"You're welcome," he said, placing his hands in the pockets of his jeans.

Somerset looked up the track, bouncing on her heels as she searched for the train. And when she wasn't checking for the train, she was trying to keep that billowy dress down over her legs. The wind was blowing, and the boys were being boys.

"It'll be here in two minutes," he told her, grinning with confidence. Somerset refused to acknowledge him. Not this century. She wanted nothing to do with the men of this contemptable era.

"You must have someplace important to be," he probed teasingly. "A date perhaps?"

Somerset looked down at her wristwatch again. She was in fact late for a dinner with one of her professors. But why would she tell him that? She didn't know him. He was just some pretty-boy flirt wanting to add a notch to his belt.

"I see you around here all the time," he said. "I'm sorry that I've never spoken until now. Sometimes I get caught up in my own thoughts. But I think I first noticed you early this summer. I remember thinking you were more lovely than a firework on the Fourth of July. Do you live in this neighborhood?"

"No," she said. "I have some friends up here. And I hate the Fourth of July."

"Oh, okay. I see," he replied.

There was awkward silence. What do you say to someone who hates the Fourth of July? Did she also hate apple pies and babies?

"Do you ever wear denim?" he asked, watching her sundress billow in the wind. She held one hand over her delicate area so that the skirt of it wouldn't fly up.

"Excuse me?" Somerset replied.

"Denim," he repeated, "Do you ever wear denim? You know, like the jeans I'm wearing right now. It's the material used to make jeans. It's really thick and—"

"I know what denim is!" Somerset snapped. "Why do you ask?"

"Well, I own a denim store," he replied, still grinning.

"And here come the credentials," Somerset mumbled, rolling her eyes.

"We specialize in vintage denim," he said. "We have denim from every era since the invention of the blue jean back in 1873. We have a pair on display said to have belonged to Billy the Kid."

Somerset knew Billy the Kid—or Henry McCarty, as she called him. And never once had she seen him in denim. He wore wool trousers. So those jeans in the store were imposters, and so was this blond fellow most likely.

"Here, take a card," he said, tapping one on her shoulder. "Come by sometime. I'm sure we can find you something special. We get lots of beautiful pieces in all the time. I would love to help you."

To Somerset, that was code for "I want to have sex with you in my store, on the counter, after closing, and then tell all my friends about it so I can be praised for yet another dalliance." But she took the card just to be polite. And to shut him up.

"I'm Clifton, by the way," he told her.

"Jeanetics?" she sneered, reading the business card.

"That's my store!" he cheered. "My pride and joy! You don't like the name? Speaking of names," he continued, "I didn't get yours."

Suddenly the train rumbled into the station. The planks on the platform rattled, and a surge of wind swept the trash from the ground up into the air. Somerset had to try harder than ever to keep her sundress down, but she didn't mind. It was just the distraction she needed to keep from talking to this guy. He was kind of cute, but he was one of those twenty-first century men— no charisma and no romance. She prayed he wouldn't follow her onto the train when the doors opened.

But he did! Of course, he did! And the car was empty, so it was just the two of them. She dreaded having to listen to him talk any longer. Men of this century lacked good conversation. What did they have to talk about? Reality television? Which celebrities were cheating on their wives? Somerset had shared dinners with Tennessee Williams and Josephine Baker. She had even had a drink with Mata Hari. Now those were interesting people!

"Sorry," Clifton said to Somerset, following her into the train car. He sat right behind her. "I'm sorry. I couldn't hear what you were saying. The train was making too much noise. I'm afraid I didn't get your name."

"Somerset," she gruffly replied. "My name is Somerset." Lord, he was implacable! She hoped the train would go as fast as possible. God forbid it stopped underground because of construction again. That would be annoying—to be stuck underground with a man talking about reality television. Somerset would rather have her eyes gauged out with a spoon.

"Wow! What a name!" he replied. "It's timeless. If I ever have a daughter, her name will be Somerset. Better yet, when I write my novel, the female protagonist will have the name Somerset."

Oh boy. "So now you're writing a novel?" she asked, incredulous but also just a wee bit curious. If there was one thing Somerset appreciated, it was a good read. She had read all the classics—everything from Voltaire to Toni Morrison. And of course, she had met both of them. Somerset immersed herself in literature, and she thought novel writing was a true sign of genius. She loved experiencing the unexplored, and novels were an exotic expedition that required no passport.

"What's it about?" she asked. She figured she may as well make polite conversation. At least Clifton had something about which to discuss. And he was a little cute, right?

"It's gonna be based roughly on my time in Iraq," Clifton told her.

"You fought in the war?" she asked. Well, that's interesting, she thought—a man who believes in something, unlike the other men of this sad, sad century. Somerset found them all to lack passion. Nothing was a greater turn-off for her than showing up to a conversation without passion.

"I did! 2005 and again in 2007. I was in the army. Craziest years of my life," he went on. "Those guys were crazy. But they became my best friends. And I shouldn't say this, but I had a shitload of fun over there. I know it was war. It's not supposed to be fun, but it is! So there! I said it!"

"I see," she replied. "Why'd you join the army?"

"I was pissed off!" Cliff said. "See, I lived in New York City on 9/11. Had just moved there for college in August. To me, New York was the capital of the galaxy. She was my maiden. But in September, damned Al-Qaeda ruined that. They ruined my dream. The attacks shook me up so much. The sound of the steel stabbing the pavement. The blood in the avenues. Somerset, the streets shivered. And the city exhaled a cloud of asbestos."

"My maiden had become a fire-breathing dragon. I didn't recognize her anymore. So I had to leave. I had to move back in with my family in Iowa, where it was quiet and boring. I suffered PTSD for months, and I was sensitive to any loud noise. The slam of a cabinet. The rumble of a passing truck. Even a late-night thunderstorm would set me off."

"Eventually, I awakened from my nightmare. And, honestly, I was ashamed. I had run from my love when she needed me the most. The real New Yorkers stayed and endured. They rebuilt. But I couldn't take it. I wasn't the real New Yorker I had hoped to be, and Al-Qaeda's the ones who showed me. Al-Qaeda ruined everything. So I went over to Iraq to blow the bastards up!"

He was blunt yet sincere. And as the train rumbled on and Clifton brooded, Somerset could feel her heart starting to race. It was fascinating—as fascinating as the stories she had heard in Studio 54 and the Kit-Kat Club, that's for sure. This guy spoke like a regular Robert Frost, who, of course, Somerset had known. How poetic of him to describe his relationship with New York City as an affair! He had gone off on a campaign to avenge his aggrieved lover.

At least he had passion, right? Not like the other lifeless drones overrunning this sad, sad century. And he was a little cute, right? She felt guilty about having been so short earlier. She liked the name of his store—it was actually a cute name for a denim store: Jeanetics. Wasn't that funny? Wasn't that creative?

"And tell me," she said. "How will Somerset play a role in this novel of yours?"

Cliff had her now. He grinned a sly grin, tucking his hair back behind his ear. "Well," he started, "she would be the strong type, like a World War II kind of woman. She would get up and work in her man's honor while he was away in Iraq. Her man—based on me, of course—would be the hero of the story, but she would go to school and work for justice. The twist would be that she'd detest bigotry. So she'd fight racism and Islamophobia in the US while her hero fought terrorism in the Middle East. She'd be defending the very people that her man would be fighting. And she would vehemently oppose the war, while still supporting her man. They'd bicker over their ideologies, but their love would keep them together—even while he was away in Iraq."

"I can't wait to read it!" she replied, smiling. Clifton was interesting. And definitely cute.

"Well, I'm glad to know I already have a readership," he said. "Pretty soon, I'll be as famous as that Johnathan Peacewood."

"Don't push your luck," Somerset said, rolling her eyes to the heavens. "Peacewood is a genius. He's the Faulkner of our generation—no, the Shakespeare! He's everything an artist should be. When he dies, I will stop reading. But your book sounds like a good idea too."

"Well, maybe I could tell you more about it over dinner," he said. "I would be honored if you'd join me sometime—even for just a drink."

Clifton certainly had a depth to him that she hadn't experienced since meeting Salvador Dali in Barcelona. It was a strange, magnetic duality—a warm light but also a fascinating darkness. When it came to light and dark, most people were about seventy percent one and thirty percent the other. But Clifton was half and half, which—to Somerset—made him a perfectly balanced whole. And perhaps his heart could be a home, a stable home on which to lay her bald, rose-tattooed head.

"You know what?" she started. "Call me crazy, but I'll join you for a drink. And maybe you can tell me more about Iraq."

Iraq.

Iraq indeed. And as the train chugged along—*chug chug chug chug, ch ch ch ch*—Clifton fell, then, back in time—as he often did. He fell into a time of camouflage and combat boots, when he flicked the heavy desert dust from his brow. And he saw the whole thing over again.

"No! Please!" a middle-aged man with a beard pleaded with Clifton, who was holding a rifle to his forehead. The man was down on his knees. His hands were tied behind his back. He and his son had been detained while walking through the hills with their family goat. The command was to let them go. They were harmless and in no way connected with Al-Qaeda. But when no one was looking, Clifton had gone back and kidnapped them. He didn't trust any of these Muslims. They were all bad. So this guy was down on his knees. His son was also tied up, and was being forced to watch his father's torment from twenty feet away.

"Not in front of my son, sir," the man pleaded. "He's only eight years old. He has done nothing. Please let him go."

"Now, you know I can't do that," Clifton told him, looking gracefully sinister. Clifton's eyes were the lightest of blue but harbored a frightening darkness. There was no logic in his gaze— only an obsession with destruction.

"But your commander said we could go," the man pleaded. "I don't understand. Why are we being detained again?"

"You sure do speak English well, boy," Clifton said. "Must be all that Al-Qaeda training. They teach you English, boy? Did Osama bin Laden teach you English?"

"What?" The man asked, trembling a little now. "No—no, my family does business with English speakers. We have contracts with British merchants. I have spoken it since I was a boy."

"Lies!" Clifton hissed.

"Papa!" the son screamed from the over in the corner. He was beginning to cry.

"Shut up!" Clifton shouted at the boy. "I'll handle you in a minute."

"Please," the man pleaded. "Do what you will with me, but let the boy go!"

"Did you see the towers as they fell?" Clifton asked.

"What?" the man asked, tears streaming down his face.

"Papa!"

"Shut up, you little sand nigger!" Clifton shouted. "Shut up, or I'll pop you right in front of your papa! Little terrorist bitch!" Clifton looked back down at the man now. "Answer me, you Al-Qaeda garbage. Did you see the towers fall?"

"I—I saw," the man said, trembling. "The whole world saw. It was terrible. But I was not involved. I don't believe in murder of the innocent. That's not what Islam is. We are a peaceful people. We respect life."

"Well, I saw the towers fall, Osama," Clifton said. He had drifted miles away from reality now. These delusions—these descents into unspeakable horror—had become very common for him. "I hear the hijackers were given virgins in paradise for attacking the U.S.," Clifton said. "They were promised some decent snatch—good virgin snatch, you know? Tell me, do you think you'll get virgin snatch in paradise?" he asked the man. "And your son, too? Does your sneaky little sand nigger of a son want virgin snatch in paradise?"

Clifton saw the Twin Towers falling over and over again, heard the bending of the steel and felt the trembling of the asphalt beneath him as they crashed, collapsing into a thick, gray cloud. And people were leaping from the windows to escape the flames. They'd rather plummet to their doom than burn alive. New York was on fire. The world was over. New York was on fire, and the world was absolutely over. And Clifton remembered all those men his mother used to bring home. And he'd watch them do things to her for money. She'd let them. Sometimes they would get too rough in the sack, and they'd leave her with bruises all over her body. He was in the East Village when the first tower fell. He studied at NYU. He wanted to be a writer. He was at a bookstore in the East Village. And his mom was being beat by some trick she turned. And the world was ending. And so he started killing animals to put them out of their misery. Cats and little dogs and even squirrels. Why should these innocent creatures have to suffer the fire and the brimstone of the end of days? He would catch them and cut their throats. An eight- year-old boy—whose mother was a despicable whore—was cutting the throat of the neighbor's cat. And New York was burning. And the world was coming to an end.

"Please," the man pleaded once more—the rifle still pressed to his forehead. "You can do what you want with me, but the boy is innocent. He's an innocent, eight-year-old boy!"

But Cliff was killing little puppies at eight. Frogs and snails and puppy dog tails. He ripped those puppy dog tails off and hid them from his whore of a mother. But he had done well for himself by getting into NYU. He had left Iowa behind, and none of that mattered anymore. None of that mattered because he had New York. New York would be his new mother. But what was happening to New York now? The towers were falling, and New York was burning. And nobody was innocent. Not after that. Nobody. So he had no mother.

Bang! Bang! The man fell backward into the dirt, bleeding out in front of his son. The blood and brains trickled out across the dirt floor, spelling the word revenge. "Papa!" the boy cried, seeing his father die before him. Bang! Bang! Two bullets into the boy's head too. So now everything would be right. Two less terrorists in the world. Two less towers, so two less terrorists. That's how Clifton saw it anyway.

Clifton drifted off like this more and more these days, especially when people asked him about Iraq. But if Somerset wanted to talk about it on their date, he would. He probably wouldn't mention the nine innocent Iraqis he murdered though. That was not first-date conversation. Certain things were just off limits on a first date: religion, politics, talk of marriage, and any mention of homicidal tendencies—and don't ask her if she wants kids.

"Where do you live?" Clifton asked Somerset as the train stopped. "I can pick you up."

"Oh, I live in Hyde Park," she replied. "I'm at the University of Chicago."

△ △ △

That Friday night, Clifton showed up at Somerset's door wearing a new suit that he'd had made on Savile Row, and new shoes made in Venice. Everything fit to a T, and he was so handsome—so very handsome. Clifton reminded Somerset of her finest lovers of yesteryear. He had a James Dean face with a Harry Belafonte charm. And of course, Somerset had met both of those fellows. Clifton brought her a pink corsage, too—a lovely pink corsage. What a 1950s classic! And of course, Somerset had known the 1950s well.

"You are just full of surprises, Cliff!" she said, slipping the pink corsage onto her wrist. She had definitely been wrong to prejudge him; he was not of this century at all. "Just full of surprises!"

"Oh!" he replied cheerfully, grinning with unarrogant triumph. "You have no idea."

And it was true. Somerset had no idea. No, really—she had no idea.

Chapter 6

Lincoln Park, Chicago, Illinois.

It was midnight on a Thursday. And what a crisp November evening it was! Fog enshrouded the treetops and the high-rises while a slight breeze scraped the leaves across the sidewalk so they pecked percussively against the concrete. The streets were quiet, and the air was almost lulling.

An elementary school teacher was strolling home, caught hopelessly in a trance. You see, she had just come from a fantastic downtown date with a fantastic uptown man. He had been a little older than what she typically considered appropriate. But he was well-established and very, very charming. Well-spoken. Cultured. Didn't want kids from her. Hell, what'd he need kids for? He already had two. She thought she may have found the one—that this time she may have actually snagged a winner. He had taken her to a fancy new restaurant in the Loop. The prices were astronomical and the portions were infinitesimal. They ordered lamb with very little mint sauce. What a treat! She had never had lamb with mint sauce, and she had never eaten in a five-star restaurant. This guy kept her pages turning—introducing her to new things, like escargot and crème brûlee, like trips to Monte Carlo and San Tropez. And, of course, riding crops and slings and kinky shit like that too.

He had given her his most abject apology for not driving her home this night, but he had received an emergency phone call during dinner. "It's my daughter," he said. "She's been rushed to the emergency room, so I need to get there now."

The hospital was in the opposite direction, so that was okay. She understood. Besides, she liked taking the L. It was full of characters. The Nigerian woman shouting to her little boy for picking his nose in public. The homeless man wearing the piss-stained stocking over his face. The gay couple making out rapaciously in the corner. There was nothing wrong with taking the train home. Or maybe she was just okay with being a doormat for this guy. He was so very handsome and so charming, after all. That may have been it. But he was oh so romantic too. He even brought her a pink corsage—like something out of a 1950s sitcom. What a dream! This was the first man she had dated in years not to treat her like an inconsequential little whore. *He's the real deal,* she thought, looking at the corsage glistening on her wrist. It was so lovely and pink against her soft, brown skin. And it matched her soft, pink dress so impeccably. How did he know she'd wear pink tonight? They must be soul mates. She knew they were. Every time he touched her, she became a giggling, swooning teenage girl again.

He was a champ in the sack too! In fact, she had become addicted to his sex and had to have it three times a week. Oh yeah, baby! Give it to me good! She wanted it tonight. She'd call him on his cell later, begging him to come nail her, except she wasn't allowed to call his house. She'd let him off the hook this time. Besides, he would have just been distracted thinking of his little girl the whole time; the poor thing had a heart murmur. So it was okay to take public transportation back to Lincoln Park. It was a nice evening anyway. Not too cool.

Quiet.

Safe.

But walking in those damned high heels was murder. What made her wear five-inch stilettos? They accentuated the calves and lifted the butt, that's what. They made her a hot tamale. Hot. Tamale. But she still had five blocks to go on this hard pavement.

Luckily, she knew a shortcut through an alley that would get her home in half the time. And she needed to get back soon. She had a lesson to plan, and there was that field trip to the Lincoln Park Zoo tomorrow; the hyenas were on special exhibit or something. So she had to be up extra early. She cut into the alley.

It was dark. One of the lamps had blown, leaving shadowy patches along the path. The lights that were lit were half-dead, so the walls glowed a menacing shade of orange. The shadows on their surface shifted and bent like ghosts on a death march.

She had taken this path many nights, but this night was different. Something here made the little hairs on the back of her neck stand.

She heard the rustle of plastic or something. Maybe there was a racoon in one of the dumpsters. Then, bump, bump, bump! Something was moving. Must've been a cat. She decided it was wise to get back out onto the street. It was late on a weeknight. Everyone was asleep, so nobody would notice her screaming if some lunatic snatched her. She picked up the pace—her heels clacking against the cobblestone in the alley.

Clack. Clack.

Then she heard something else. Bump! It sounded too big to be a cat. Maybe a stray dog? A cayote? No, not at all! But then she thought she heard a voice. No, a grunt. That was definitely a grunt. It was a manly grunt too. This schoolteacher was into kink and very familiar with the sound of male grunts, that's for sure. This fellow she had been seeing always grunted when aroused. Maybe this was some creep getting a blowjob behind the dumpster, yes? But wasn't Lincoln Park a family neighborhood full of nice, boring white people? Wasn't it?

"Who's there?" she called, looking into the shadows.

No answer. No sound. Just blobs of orange light creeping up the walls. So she moved along, walking fast again. Clack. Clack. Clack. Her heels beat against the cobblestone until she heard a second pair of footsteps behind her. She turned to see. And the footsteps stopped.

"Who's there?" she called again. Nothing. No answer. No one was there. Just jagged shadows crawling across the pavement. So she took off her shoes this time and turned to run. *Run*, she thought. But before she could, the foreign footsteps started to run behind her. These were not the clacks of a stiletto but the thumps of a heavy men's shoe.

Thump, thump. Thump, thump, thump! Thump, thump, thump, thump, thump!

"Come here, girl!" a guttural voice howled. And a shadowy figured snatched her and covered her face with a chloroform-dowsed napkin. She struggled momentarily. But it was no use. The chloroform was too potent, and her assailant was too strong. Definitely a man. He had her tight in his arms, so there was no getting away. And with her heels in hand, her corsage on her wrist, she passed out cold. And all was dark from then on for the kinky little schoolmarm.

△ △ △

Beethoven blasted from the speakers as Johnny twisted and twirled, newspaper in hand. He was barefoot and buoyant, dancing across the deck of a yacht in the Caribbean. He and Harvey were visiting a good friend, an Italian fashion designer—

not Armani or Valentino, but another very famous one—who had arranged a private fashion show of tuxedos for Johnny. As male models strutted up and down the deck in formal wear, the "Ninth Symphony" played with brilliant mellifluence. Johnny needed something to wear to a literary gala in Paris the next week. And it was late notice for the designer, but Johnny was a good friend, after all. "Anything for a good friend!" the designer said, tipping his champagne flute to the sky.

The sun beamed down upon Johnny's back. He was thrilled to be free of Chicago, where the first chills of winter were blowing in. To feel the warm sun right now was truly magical.

"This one is my personal favorite, Johnathan," the designer said, drinking his mimosa and reclining onto a chaise as a model strutted by in a black tuxedo and navy tie. "Navy is all the rage this season. All the princes are wearing it, you know!"

"You know I don't follow trends," Johnathan replied, wagging the newspaper at the designer—who was becoming a tangerine in the sun. "I'm Johnathan Peacewood, sir. I set trends! To follow is to fail. Winners lead. And I'm a winner." Johnathan tiptoed over to the model and slapped him on the rear with the newspaper. "Mmm," Johnny celebrated. "Firm as a new mattress."

The designer waved the model away and took another sip of his mimosa, giggling at the goings-on. "Peacewood, if you were anyone else, we'd throw you overboard. But you're you, so we just smile then praise God once you're out of our midst."

"Look!" Johnathan exclaimed, staring at the headline of his newspaper.

"What is it?" the designer asked. "The gossip columnists got your age wrong again? What'd they say this time? Thirty-seven? At least they got the decade right. They always guess I'm in my eighties, but I'm seventy-two. It's all the tanning. I look like a brown leather bag, don't I?"

"You silly little fag!" Johnathan snapped. "A schoolteacher has gone missing in Chicago. Listen to this. Mary Ann Bell, a Chicago schoolteacher, has gone missing. Bell was last seen on November eighteenth, leaving Chez Vous Restaurant with Donald Frye. Frye was the principal of Mary's school, as well as her reputed lover. Chicago PD took Frye into custody for questioning but released him on Tuesday."

"Oh, she's probably been killed," the fashion designer said, waving dismissively. "You Americans are so violent. Italians haven't been that brutal since we fed the Christians to the lions two thousand years ago. Chicago is becoming more dangerous every day. Come to Milan with me. It's safe there. You can stay with me and be my house boy, Johnny."

"You withered up little prune!" Johnny snapped, though he intended no harm. "I wouldn't touch you to scratch you! And you know I'm spoken for."

This was the first time in Johnathan's life that he had actually been spoken for; no one had been a brave enough man to claim him. But someone had now. And it felt good to admit that aloud. He was deeply in love. Finally.

"Well, you can't blame an old man for trying. At least I still have these boys," the designer said as a handsome model strutted out in a tuxedo with a white jacket and boastful black piping. "What about this one, Johnny?"

"Very 007," Johnathan laughed. Then, he looked back down into his paper. "The Chicago police suspect the disappearance of Bell to be linked to Cheyenne Cost, who was murdered this summer. This morning, the chief of police received an anonymous letter implying that the two women were somehow linked. The letter read in part, 'Bell is an imposter much like Cost, both barren whores with nothing for which to live. Now, they may both remain with me in eternal hell—beyond the reach of love.'"

"That's terrible!" the designer shrieked as another model sashayed past him in a slim-fit, gray tuxedo.

"Well, that would be fun to write!" Johnathan exclaimed. "I've always wanted to do a murder mystery."

"But what about Somerset?" the designer asked. "I love those books. She inspires me."

"Oh please."

"I'm just an old, leathery man, living alone in his mansion," the designer said. "The only men looking at me are these boys I keep on the payroll. Those books of yours give hope that even an old fart like me can find companionship. Like when Somerset is trapped on the island with Amelia Earhart."

"Yes, I remember," Johnathan grumbled. "I wrote the crap."

"The world assumed the poor girl for dead. But Amelia was a tough cannoli! She survived that crash and was stranded for years on a small island in the Pacific, living in isolation. She had no friends, no lovers—only the wind and the storms to keep her company. But she feared she was never to see another person as long as she lived. She got lonely—and sad. But decades after the crash, Somerset became stranded on the same island. If I recall correctly, she was aboard a tramp steamer that capsized during a typhoon."

"Amelia is nearly seventy when she first sees Somerset's beautiful brown face drifting to shore in that little lifeboat. Amelia is delighted! Finally, she has a friend! The two become close. They fish together and toss coconuts for sport. And Somerset tells her stories of her past lovers. Incredulous yet entertained, Amelia confides in Somerset that, despite her loneliness on the island, she was relieved to have escaped the burden of celebrity. In some ways, being stranded was Amelia's salvation. And Somerset was her angel. She loved her like a daughter and friend. And when Amelia's health declined, Somerset was there to care for her. Amelia died in Somerset's arms just as the sun set over the Pacific one summer night. She buried her in the center of the island, underneath the palm trees."

"Yes," Johnny sighed. "I recall. As I said, I wrote it."

"Two weeks later," the designer continued, "Somerset was rescued by a fishing boat. She never mentioned Amelia. She wanted her old friend to have peace and freedom from the limelight that she had hated so much, even in death. Reading that as an old man reminded me there is still kindness in the world. Sometimes I fear growing old alone, I do. But that story made me believe that I can still have love, even being the wrinkled suitcase of a man that I am. Johnny, you give us all hope with your stories. You can't stop now."

Before now, Johnny would have derided the concept of love. But not anymore. He had found it in Harvey. And speak of the devil, Harvey had just come out onto the deck to join the festivities. He waltzed over in his tiny black speedo, his rippling abs glistening in the Caribbean sun.

"How are you boys?" Harvey asked, kissing Johnny on the cheek.

"Johnny was just depressing us with the Chicago headlines," the designer said, waving dismissively.

"Ugh," Harvey grunted. "As usual." Then, he snatched the paper from Johnathan's grasp and brazenly tossed it out into the ocean. "Now we can all have a good time, yes?"

The designer smiled, taking another sip of his mimosa as a new model came out wearing a bright red tuxedo.

"Oh, Peacewood, that one is perfect for you!" Harvey cheered. "A red tuxedo!"

"I agree!" the designer delighted, lifting his glass to toast.

"You two must be joking," Johnny replied, looking bewildered. "I could never pull it off. I'd be on every worst-dressed list from here to Tokyo. I can't wear that to a literary gala."

Harvey laughed. "You are the most powerful man in the world. All you have to do is wave your hand and every star in Hollywood will be wearing a red tux by next season. You'll be on the cover of *Men's Vogue*! Wear the red."

Johnathan looked out at the blue patch of ocean where his paper was bobbing up and down on the waves. What was going on in the world when stay-at-home moms and elementary schoolteachers were being victimized and all anyone could talk about was what Johnathan Peacewood wears to galas? Apparently, red was Johnny's new color, and apathy was the world's new black.

"Johnathan is thinking about writing a murder mystery," the designer told Harvey.

"Ha!" Harvey laughed. "Shows what you know. Peacewood is retiring from writing. He's making the announcement at the gala next week with me by his side."

"Harvey!" Johnathan chided him.

"He's coming out publicly!" Harvey continued. "And it won't matter what his nosy, old agent says since he plans to retire. So let all his fans betray him for his being gay! Let them burn all his books if they want. It won't matter now. Johnathan made his millions. He doesn't have to write those silly books anymore."

"What?" the designer shrieked. "That's nonsense!"

"It's not nonsense!" Harvey snapped. "We've decided it!"

"*We?*" the designer asked, incredulous that the world's most famous writer—who loved writing more than he loved anything else—would consider retiring so early in his career. "Johnny, you haven't even finished your latest novel. Your fans demand a seventh book. And you're only thirty-three. You can't retire at thirty-three. A man doesn't even reach his prime until forty."

"Tell him, Peacewood!" Harvey insisted.

"Say it isn't so," the designed cried.

"It's—it's true," Johnathan said. "I've decided to travel the world with Harvey and not write anymore." He couldn't look the designer in the eye as he spoke. Johnathan felt a pang of shame and looked down at his feet touching the deck instead.

"You can travel the world and write!" the designer replied. "Johnathan, you have to write. We all have a purpose, and yours is to write. You know I've always thought of you as the son I could never have, and I just won't sit here and listen to this foolishness any longer. You are a brilliant writer. Like every great artist, you will retire when you die!"

Harvey had talked Johnny into coming out and retiring because he hated to see him work. He wanted his man languishing beside him—his mind rotting, his ego swelling—as the two of them blew Johnathan's millions on booze and boats and cars and whores. Johnathan was Harvey's cash cow now, and he intended to ride this coattail as long as he could. And Johnathan was so desperate for this love affair to continue that he would sacrifice his own divine journey for just another taste of Harvey's lips. Those lips! One kiss of those lips was like MDMA, sending Johnny on a euphoric high. Johnathan had become a junkie for Harvey's drug, and he didn't care who judged.

But Harvey hated that Johnny's friends discouraged the retirement. That creepy blind man who lived across the hall—

who always seemed to be there just as Harvey was getting off the elevator—was driving him ape-shit crazy. He always had something to say.

"I know what you're doing," Sargent told Harvey one day two weeks ago. "I can see into your soul, and I don't like what I see. You're a loser, and you want Mr. Peacewood to be a loser just like you. All you got is that pretty face, and you're losing that. God forbid, you have to follow Mr. Peacewood around and watch him get all the praise!"

"Shut up, you old fool!" Harvey snapped back. "You can eat my shit!"

"You are bad news," Sargent went on. "But I see you coming to a very bad end. I see you hanging by your neck. Just when you think you've triumphed, I see a noose of truth wrapped right around your dirty little neck and your legs swinging. Glory be! Glory be! I see the future! Glory be!"

"Oh really?" Harvey sneered. "And I guess you think you're Nostradamus?"

"No," Sargent laughed. "I'm better than Nostradamus—and I'll be more famous! You remember fame, right Harvey? You used to be."

"Good God!" Harvey replied, erupting into laughter. "You are certifiable!"

Harvey was certainly getting his way now because Johnny was retiring. And all was going according to plan. Harvey could tell that his love was like a drug that kept Johnathan in a haze, dangling beyond the reach of reality. Mr. Peacewood was high and refused to come down. With a champions glow, Harvey gazed across the water toward the beach.

And over on that beach, Sasha spied through her binoculars. What a fabulous treat! While she couldn't care less about the fashion show—she had seen enough of those in her lifetime—she had been following Johnathan and Harvey. And sooner than later, the havoc she had contemplated would certainly ensue. And the sanctuary that Mr. Johnathan Peacewood had imagined with Harvey was about to come crumbling down upon him. Yes, indeed! Yes, indeed! Glory be!

△ △ △

The monster had dragged Mary Ann back to his lair deep below the earth. She was sleeping as fairytale maidens do. After removing her blouse and bra, he tied her down to the bed. She was a vision—skin the color of copper and thick, curly hair. Spellbound, he caressed her forehead and kissed her cheek.

"Awaken, my love," he whispered. "Awaken for your prince."

And soon thereafter, Mary Ann opened her beautiful brown eyes. And for the first time, she could see her captor in the light. And of course, she did what any sensible hostage would do—she screamed to the top of her lungs.

"Please, God!" she shouted.

"Stop screaming," he hissed, slapping her hard. When she continued, he punched her in the mouth to get her to shut up. "I don't want to hurt you!"

"Ohhhh," she groaned, her teeth bloodied.

"I won't hurt you," he said, grabbing her face and kissing her on the lips. "You're beautiful even when you're scared. There is so much love in you. I can taste it in your blood." Then, he slowly licked the blood from her face like a mother cat cleaning her kitten.

"My boyfriend will come," she cried, shivering and weak as he tickled the insides of her thigh.

"Boyfriend?" he asked. "I thought I was your boyfriend. Didn't we agree on that?" Then, he slapped her again. "Are you cheating on me? Are you," (he slapped her again), "cheating on me?"

"Ohhh," she groaned!

"Now, you cut that noise out!" he said, laughing as he wiped her blood from his hand with a cloth. "You've always liked to play games, haven't you? Whether it's pretending you love me or playing the damsel in distress. You're not really scared, are you? Hmm?"

He leaned in to kiss her again, but she bit his lip.

"You always were feisty," he laughed and then started to pout. "Now, baby is thirsty for milk. Is Mommy weady to feed baby? Hmm? Can baby have a dwink of milk, Mommy?"

And then, the monster grabbed her breast and began to suck at the nipple. But nothing came out. He just kept sucking, but nothing came out. And this pissed him off.

"Now, you cut that out!" he hissed, leaning in to suck again. But nothing came out. "I will not be denied by you!" he shouted, starting to punch her. "I want your milk!"

She lay there in agony, her tears mixing with her sweat and blood as they ran down her cheek. "Ohh," she groaned.

He was a monster—a monster thirsty for milk. And if he didn't get it, there would be blood. There would be oodles and oodles of blood.

Chapter 7

December.

Harvey and Sasha were in bed watching the sunrise. They made wild, crazy love—the type of love you make when there is no tomorrow. Now, Sasha was smoking a celebratory cigarette, rejoicing the rapid rate at which her plot to destroy Mr. Johnathan Peacewood had progressed. Everything was going as planned, and now Sasha was envisioning herself sitting atop Peacewood's cold, dead body. She sits right on his chest, counting his money. In fact, she wipes the sweat from her brow with a twenty-dollar bill, before stuffing it into his cold, dead mouth. Then she goes back to counting.

Sasha, like Harvey, was a former model. She once graced the runways of Paris, New York, and Milan, and quickly became well-known for her heroin-chic look—shockingly waif-like with pale, white skin and short blond hair. But Sasha had a little drug problem. And all the cocaine and the booze had landed her on the black list. She yo-yoed in and out of rehab, but it was a farce, really; she hadn't tried to improve. But she thought if the world believed she had tried, the designers would pull her from the reject pile and let her work again.

She had shown up stoned out of her mind to a show during New York Fashion Week once. She fell twice on the runway, passed out backstage, and urinated in her couture. After that, she was escorted off the premises for attempting to strangle the fiancé of a very well-known American designer. That debacle and three DUIs later, and she was off the A-list. But that was years ago. Now, no one even remembered her—no one except her lover, Mr. Harvey Marcus.

Harvey loved Sasha to the moon and back. She was a beautiful train wreck who had only wreaked havoc on the world, but that's what he loved about her. Harvey knew that, underneath all the couture and self-loathing and narcissism and spitefulness and syringes full of God knows what, there was an angel who had lost her way. Harvey had appointed himself Sasha's shepherd, and would never leave her. Never! And there was nothing he would deny her. If it made her smile, Harvey would do it.

"What are you thinking?" Harvey asked, kissing Sasha's shoulder as she sucked her cigarette. He watched as the bright orange end faded into dull gray ash. It reminded him of his own meteoric fame—one minute, he was on a billboard in Times Square; the next, he was working as a go-go boy in Chelsea, grinding his backside on some old banker's lap. Life was cruel that way. Had it not been for the car accident, he'd be more famous and powerful than anyone, even Johnathan Peacewood.

"I'm thinking about all that money," Sasha replied. "All that delicious money that we are going to gobble up. We'll move to Mexico and build a big house. And we'll open an art gallery in Mexico City and display all those hideous paintings you did when you were—what were you doing, darling? Expressing your inner pain?"

"You don't like my artwork?" Harvey asked.

She puffed on the cigarette. "You have no talent, Harvey. You and I were born beautiful. Our faces are our contributions to the world. We were put here to give the human race something to which it can aspire. I keep all those fat teenage girls running on treadmills and throwing up their brownies, and you keep all the zit-faced boys thinking they have a shot at banging the head cheerleader. That's why we're here."

"Do you really believe that?"

"Oh, I know it. You never stood a chance at painting. All your talent is in that perfect jaw line of yours. That's your moneymaker."

"Oh, I don't know, Sash," Harvey replied. "I thought some of my later paintings were pretty good. What about the one I painted for you? The bouquet of roses?"

"That was a bouquet?" Sasha responded, erupting into laughter. "All this time I thought it was a house on fire! Or a woman covered in canker sores. All those red patches of paint! Oh, Harvey, it's a good thing you're pretty. If you were ugly, you'd be a waste of space."

"You're cruel," Harvey moaned, pulling away brusquely. "You said you liked it!"

"That was because I thought it was a burning house, Harvey," she told him. "I thought you were painting me a picture of the House of Peacewood burning. You know that's what I want to see."

Harvey groaned and fell over into his pillow. "So we're back to that now, are we?"

"We never left it!" Sasha snapped. She was a sinister thing, this Sasha. Nothing she ever did had any good in it. Once she walked in a charity runway show to benefit autistic children, only to be caught backstage giving one of the autistic kids a line of coke, claiming that, "The coke'll fix his warped little, autistic brain." The child's parents were not amused. Lucky for her, they dropped the suit—after the fashion label dropped her, that is.

"As I was saying, Harvey," Sasha continued, "people like us— beautiful people—should never work. We should marry people like Johnathan Peacewood. The mistake that you and I have made is that we fell for each other. You can't support me. That's why you're marrying Peacewood. You'll inherit all his money, and you can take care of us."

Harvey had heard all of this a thousand times. Sasha loved to rehash every detail of her plot to ruin Johnathan. "And then?" Harvey sighed, shaking his head with exasperation.

"Then," she continued, "we will live happily ever after! But you can't inherit the money until he dies. I know the law. I read treatises. As long as he's alive, your relationship only benefits you! But I want yachts and penthouses and private jets too, Harvey. And I deserve them!"

Then, she stopped, noticing that Harvey was rolling his eyes to the heavens. "Harvey!" she shouted. "Don't I deserve yachts and penthouses?"

"Yes! Yes, my love. You absolutely do!" Harvey replied, sort of exhausted.

"And so what are you going to do?" she asked.

"We've only had this conversation one million, nine hundred and thirty-seven times, Sasha. I am going to marry Johnathan then leave the city and let you kill him. We'll make it look like a robbery. And I will inherit his empire, Somerset and all. And we will move to Mexico and disappear before anyone suspects a thing. Yada yada yada."

Harvey recited the plans with disinterest, but he knew Sasha meant business. He knew how evil she was. But he loved that—it exhausted him, but he loved it. Evil was such a turn-on, especially in a beautiful girl like Sasha. Everyone in the world associates beauty with goodness, but that's a flaw. Sasha was as beautiful and as bad as they came.

"And I won't miss the bastard anyhow," Harvey said, shrugging his shoulders. "I was teasing him—pretending I would pour wine on his beloved typewriter—and he flung me against the wall. I don't know how. I didn't even see him coming toward me. But that skinny bastard flung me up against the wall and got wine all over my custom-made shirt. So he's already dead to me anyway."

"Good!" Sasha said, puffing one last diabolical puff. "Now be a lamb and order me some breakfast."

"What do you want, my love?" Harvey asked. "I was thinking waffles."

"Waffles?" Sasha laughed. "Do I look like one of those plus-size, waffle-loving bulimics to you? I don't eat waffles. I want breakfast, you brainless twat!"

"Yes, dear," Harvey replied, deflating a little and getting out of bed to retrieve his cellphone. Sasha grinned. She had Harvey wrapped around her corrupt, perfectly-manicured little finger where he belonged. It was possible that she actually loved him somewhere deep down in her wicked heart, but what did that really matter?

As Harvey dialed, she blew him a kiss. And he smiled coyly, catching it in his hand and pressing it to his cheek.

"Hello?" Harvey spoke with someone over the phone. "Yeah, it's Marcus. Yeah. I'm looking for the white girl. And maybe a bag of dro."

Sasha cleared her throat intently.

"Oh, sorry, babe!" he replied. "Make that two bags. Yeah. Yeah. I've got you covered. Yeah. How soon can you be here? Okay. Yeah. I'll meet you downstairs. Text me where you're here."

And so, on this chilly December morning, in Sasha's apartment, Harvey and Sasha did what they did whenever they were together: they got high and languished, all while plotting to kill Mr. Johnathan Peacewood.

△ △ △

A few months had passed since Somerset and Clifton started their relationship. Make no mistake—Somerset was still terribly apprehensive. He was, after all, a man of this era. But something was very different about this one. He had a backstory from which movies could be made, and that made him anything but mundane. He was a thrill seeker with a poetic heart, and he made every meeting an adventure. She cared about him, all right. And boy, was he crazy about his Somerset.

They lay in bed at Somerset's place one winter morning, nude as newborn babies after an exhilarating session of lovemaking. Cliff caressed her bald head, kissing her cheek and singing in her ear. He still had a bit of her breast milk on his lips. He had been sucking it from her just moments ago, sucking it like there was no tomorrow. He always sucked her breast milk when they made love, and he was becoming addicted.

Now, the story goes like this. Just before Somerset was granted the gift of eternal life, she had delivered a baby boy into the world. But the delivery hadn't gone smoothly. It was grueling. The baby had ripped her apart so that she was bleeding to death. Somerset could feel the life draining from her, but she wasn't ready to go. She was only nineteen and had never experienced true love, so she begged a witch doctor to keep her alive and young until she could find it. And since she was lactating at the time the spell was cast, her breasts never stopped producing milk. That milk was enchanted; whenever anyone tasted it, he or she became intoxicated. The milk was as addictive as crack and as detrimental to the mind and body. Men couldn't get enough of it. Edgar Allan Poe went to very dark places after drinking half a liter, and it was said that English author Robert Louis Stevenson got loopy from tasting it a few times and was inspired to write his famed novel, *The Strange Case of Dr. Jekyll and Mr. Hyde.* Madness. It inspired unadulterated madness.

Clifton was no exception. He was now mad with love. She pretended to forget he was there with her as she sat reading her book, *Race and Politics in America.* Heavy stuff. She pretended not to like him. But truth be told, Somerset was very happy to have Clifton by her side, worshipping the beads of sweat on her shoulder.

"Should we go to brunch?" he asked her. "I don't know your neighborhood well. Are there any good places around here?"

Ignoring him, Somerset tossed her book onto the nightstand and stood to stretch. Then she walked over to the window and opened the curtain, letting the sunlight hit her naked, brown flesh, and as it did, it burst into a thousand grains of golden glitter. It radiated off her bald head, illuminating the rose tattoo on her scalp, and soaked into her eyes so that they became warm cups of coffee.

"Your neighbors are going to see you standing there naked," Clifton warned. But she didn't care. And that was what intrigued him—he had never met a woman with so few inhibitions. To him, she was as wild as the world was vast, but regal and refined too. Somerset's duality kept Clifton coming back for more. He never knew what to expect.

"What a magnificent day!" she cheered. The snow on the ground glistened in the sunlight, and the black-barked tree branches dug up into the sky. A terrible blizzard had just passed, but now the sky was beautiful and clear. And across the alley, Somerset's neighbors—the world's cutest elderly couple—were sitting on their couch and getting a perfect view of Somerset's naked breasts. They were watching television. *The Price Is Right* or *General Hospital*, or whatever old people watched.

Somerset knew them well. The old man always gave her dirty winks when she passed him on the sidewalk—especially when she wore those billowy sundresses that raised in the wind— and the wife would come and grab him by his ear to take him back inside. What was that like? Somerset wondered. What was it like to have a relationship where you put up with someone getting old and their wandering, cataract-covered eyes? She would never know. And that was her curse. And that's what men would never understand about her.

The little old man looked up at her. "Don't do it, fool," Somerset whispered, as though he could hear her. But he did it anyway—he looked at her and saw that she was completely naked. He grabbed his chest, and those two, cataract-covered eyes rolled back in his head until only the white parts could be seen. "I warned you!" Somerset said, chuckling and shaking her breasts so that they knocked against each other like the balls in a Newton's cradle. Somerset was a good person, but after five hundred and fourteen years, a girl gets bored.

The old guy fell to the floor, causing his poor wife to look over and shout before spotting Somerset in the window.

"Sorry!" Somerset shouted. She waved her hand apologetically, realizing she had been caught. The old woman shook her fist and seemed to be cursing. Somerset closed the curtains and turned back to Cliff, who was laying naked on his stomach, kicking his feet back and forth.

"I love you, Somerset," Clifton told her.

And here it goes again. "What the hell did you say?"

"I said I love you," he repeated proudly, rolling over and tucking his long blond hair behind his ears.

Somerset didn't want to hear that. She didn't want to hear that at all. He couldn't love her because he didn't know her. No man knew her. Ironically, the very magic that Somerset had asked for to find love left her feeling detached from humanity. She had become an alien in this human world—a beautiful, tormented anomaly. And, to be honest, after all these centuries, Somerset was a little afraid to fall in love. She wasn't ready to die yet. She still had things to do—get her degree, walk on the moon, eat fugu. This wasn't a good time to get all swept up.

"You don't know love," she told him. "You're just a stupid little white boy. You think you can say 'I love you' and get everything you want? Well, you're mistaken, mister. You won't get it! Not this time."

"What do you mean?" Cliff asked.

"I mean get out!" she shouted. "Get out before I kill you! Better yet, get out before you kill me!" Somerset still wanted to go deep-sea diving and see the *Titanic*. She had never walked the Great Wall of China. She had never been a Rockette. "You don't know me. You never will."

"Why not?" Cliff asked, earnest as ever.

"Because you're just a dumb little white boy," she yelled. "What do you know? You have no idea what I've been through. You don't know what makes me cry, what makes me sad. I've been around long enough to see through your nonsense." And it was true. Somerset had been fooled before. In fact, she had fallen for a pretty boy with blond hair and blue eyes long ago.

It was her slave captor. He had kissed her and given her liquor and painted a future full of love and adventure. She let herself belong to him for a night—mainly because she had never seen such pretty, light eyes and hair before—and had fallen asleep in his arms. But when she awakened, she was locked in a mildewing cell with slave ships docked just outside, their high, white sails blanketing the free sky. And those pretty eyes—those pretty blue eyes—were nowhere to be seen. He was down at the dock collecting the gold he had earned for kidnapping her.

"Well, tell me everything, Somerset," Clifton begged. "I want to understand. You can tell me anything."

"There is no man in this world who will ever truly understand me. And I'm sick of hearing 'I love you' only to be betrayed over and over again."

Suddenly, Clifton sprang from the bed, naked as a jaybird, penis flopping. He ran into the bathroom. "I will understand!" he told her, oddly triumphant before slamming the door and locking her out.

"What are you doing?" she asked as a buzzing sound came from behind the door. Either he was shaving or toying with her vibrator. What did it matter to Somerset? She wanted him out before he ruined yet another century of hers. Better yet, she wanted him out before he killed her. And locking the door? Honestly? Men were so dramatic. She would just wait until he came out. Then she would hand him his clothes and send him on his way.

Meanwhile, she wondered if her perverted neighbor had recovered from his heart attack. She walked over and opened the curtains again to see that the old man was sitting up with his face concealed beneath a breathing mask. "Well, good for you!" she said. The old wife was patting his little bald head. "I guess I'm not a murderer yet." Then, she turned back to the bathroom door, shouting, "I'm not a murderer yet, Clifton! But if you don't come out soon, that's going to change!"

When she faced the window again, she saw that the old man was pointing at her. "Oh boy. Here we go again," she moaned, rolling her eyes, but playfully shook her breasts to tease him again. As the poor old man passed out and fell to the floor—again—the old wife started flailing her fist. Old people were so weird but so much fun—weren't they?

Finally, the buzzing stopped, and she heard the door unlock. Click. Clifton stepped out, still very naked but also very bald. He had cut his luxurious golden locks so that he was as bald as Somerset.

"What have you done?" she shrieked.

"You don't have to go through anything alone," he told her, rubbing his scalp. "I don't know what you've learned dealing with other guys, but I'm different. I swear I am. I want to understand. I'm sorry for being a dumb white boy. But help me to be a smart white boy." Then, he ran over and gave her a great big hug. "Your neighbors can see us!" he said, looking out the window and laughing hysterically as the old wife gazed upon Clifton's beautiful nakedness. He danced so that his penis flopped back and forth across his thighs. The old woman became flushed with fever, fanning herself wildly, but it was no use. She passed out.

"You're crazy!" Somerset said, though she was intrigued. Who was this Clifton?

"I got you a gift," he told her, turning to retrieve something from his duffle bag. Somerset wondered if it was a body in there. She wouldn't have put it past him at this point; this guy was nuts. But then he walked back over to her and presented a beautiful diamond bracelet. Just like Somerset, it shimmered in the sunlight. She was still afraid, but these were diamonds after all. And Somerset was Marilyn Monroe in *Gentlemen Prefer Blondes*. Diamonds definitely were a girl's best friend! Smiling, she held out her wrist, allowing him to fasten the clasp around it. Yes, there was definitely something very different about this Clifton. Very, very intriguing.

"You'd better clean that hair off my bathroom floor, dammit!" she shouted, frowning at him. "You ain't got no maids around here!"

Chapter 8

Winter had finally arrived in Chicago, and the city was suffocating underneath nineteen inches of snow. But that didn't stop one hard-working young lawyer from treading her way to the office in the middle of the worst blizzard since '75. She was a smart little lady—graduated at the top of her class—and made a name for herself defending the elderly and the disabled. In her television ads, she calls herself a champion of moms and pops. She was one of the most successful black lawyers in Chicago.

But this evening, she was feeling particularly worn out. Her legal assistant wasn't in because the snow had stalled the commuter trains. Now, the lights in the office were flickering on and off. So the young lawyer decided to lock up her office and get out. It had been twelve hours since she got to her office in the Loop, and she needed to close out her briefs, kick up her feet, and sip a nice glass of whiskey. And, most importantly, she needed to get home before the snow got any deeper.

Downtown Chicago was silent. The only movement was the falling of silvery snow. Pristine flakes pranced across the black night in perfect rhythm, as though the sky had choreographed a brilliant ballet, the wind and the ice its orchestra. It was a lovely sight. But as the ice scraped her cheeks, this young lawyer remembered that winter was a black widow— beautiful but deadly. Many of the streetlights were out, and icicles had formed on the power lines.

She was almost to the parking garage and her warm BMW when she noticed a man had slipped on the ice and was lying on the snow-covered sidewalk. He was struggling to stand, so she ran to his rescue. This handsome man was young and white with long blond hair. His pant leg was torn, enough to see that his kneecap looked like an eggplant, all swollen and purple and covered in lacerations.

"Are you ok?" she asked, pulling him up from the snow, which was now crimsoned with blood. "Goodness, you're bleeding!"

"I fell down the steps from the L platform. I need to get to a hospital," he told her. He was shaking in agony. "I'm homeless. I was going to sleep under the heat lamp on the L platform, but the police made me leave."

"Good gracious!" the young lawyer said. "I think the nearest hospital is about two miles from here, up on Michigan Avenue."

"Oh, there's no way I can walk that," he said, moaning in agony. "Maybe you could call me an ambulance?" He clutched her arm, trying desperately to stand, but it was no use. His knee was too weak, and he fell again.

Again, she pulled him up. "It'll take forever for them to get here." The jagged ice flakes beat against her cheeks, and the wind cut into her side. While she was reluctant to say what she was about to say, the guy's knee was throbbing and he'd certainly freeze to death if she didn't do something. "Come to my car with me. I can drive you there."

"Oh, that is very kind of you," the man said. "But only if I wouldn't be putting you out of your way."

"It's fine. You'll freeze to death otherwise," she continued, putting his arm around her shoulder. She helped him to the garage, letting him hop along beside her. She trusted him. After all, he was cute, right?

The garage attendant had gone home early because of the weather, and her car was the only car there—a shiny, black BMW waiting in the corner. She had one of those fancy, keyless entry cars, and she started it before they got there, with just the push of a button.

"Oh that is very fancy," the man told her, seeing the headlights of the car come on. "You must be very good at what you do."

"I try," she laughed.

"I'll bet you do," he laughed too. "And that is a very pretty diamond bracelet you are wearing," he said, eyeing the shimmering bracelet on her wrist. It sparkled beneath the florescent lights.

Suddenly, he let go of her shoulder and stood on both his legs with the poise of a dancer. Bending over, he removed the purple knee, which was—as she could clearly see upon closer inspection—really a rubber prosthetic.

"What's this?" she asked. "What's going on?"

Tucking the fake knee in his coat pocket, he smiled. "I'm thirsty. Pull out your tit."

All those years of school, and the young lawyer realized she had fallen for the old injured-sociopath-in-the-snow routine. But he wasn't going to rape her tonight if she had anything to do with it. She dashed off, running toward the exit. But the blond trickster was on her tail.

"No you don't!" he shouted. "You're going to love me the way I deserve to be loved!" He was clearly mad, chasing her through the empty garage.

"Help!" she screamed. "Somebody, please help me!"

"I am giving you my heart!" he shouted, running after her still. "And how do you repay me? By running? You selfish bitch!"

He lunged forward, grabbing her and covering her mouth with a chloroform-doused napkin. All became a blur. And then all became darkness.

△ △ △

When the young lawyer awakened, she found herself inside a mildewed cellar. Her hands were bound in shackles, which had been bolted into the wall, and she was completely naked. The blond trickster was over at a desk to her right, looking at her diamond bracelet underneath the light of a lamp. And to her left, there was an eerie darkness, as if the cellar just faded away into an obscure black hell. She knew something was over there, something terrible, but she couldn't tell what.

"You can have that bracelet," she told him. "I don't care. Just please let me go."

"You know I can't do that," he replied, not turning to look at her just yet. He was mesmerized by the diamonds. "This is really beautiful. I think I'm going to give this to my girlfriend. She really is the perfect woman. In fact, she's a lot like you: young, black, and impossible to control." Then, he threw the bracelet onto the desk and stood to face her.

Walking in her direction, he continued. "Why are you women so hard to control? I keep trying to figure out what makes you bitches tick. I cut you open to figure out how it works, how love works for you. But I still don't understand it."

"Please let me go!" the young lawyer pleaded. "I'll give you anything. Anything!"

"All I want is love," he replied coldly. "Love—and a little milk from your tits." He was eyeing her breasts now with an ominous gleam, and he leaned in and began to suck her left nipple. But to his dismay, nothing came out.

"Stop doing that!" he shouted! "Stop being stingy!"

"Please!" she screamed as he twisted the nipple, trying to pull it off, before leaning in to suck the right one. Still, no milk came out. So he slapped her—he slapped her hard as hell. And he slapped her. And he slapped her again. He slapped her so hard that blood came out of her nose.

"I am thirsty!" he shouted, his voice echoing off the cellar walls.

"That isn't how it works," she pleaded. "I can't produce milk. I haven't had a baby."

"You want to lie to me just like the others?" the beautiful, blond man hissed. "Well, maybe I should do to you what I did to them."

He walked over to that ominous, dark corner. He kept walking until he vanished into the darkness and could not be seen. But he wasn't gone; she could still hear him breathing and fidgeting.

"I'll just do you like this," he said, flicking on a light.

And there it was: the mutilated body of Mary Ann Bell. Mary Ann's breasts had been removed.

"I tried sucking her tits too, but she didn't wanna share any of her milk," he said. "So I cut them off, hoping that would help. But she was a fake. There was nothing inside her boobs but blood and fat." He pouted a bit now, seeming very disappointed. "And then I realized I had made a mistake. She was not the girl for me. So I made love to her to apologize. But she didn't seem to enjoy that, probably because she had already bled to death." He walked back over to the lawyer, who was—by this time— trembling. "So I will ask you one last time before I rip you to pieces," he said calmly, smiling and caressing her hair. "Please give me some of your milk."

"I would if I could," she cried. "But I don't have any."

"Well, you are very disappointing," he spoke—still very calm. "But can I keep the bracelet?"

△ △ △

"It's outrageous that you're still not done with that novel, Peacewood! Contemptable and outrageous!" Charlotte shouted, looming over Johnathan, who just sat on the park bench reading his newspaper. She had followed him all the way from his penthouse, nagging him the entire time. He let her fume, as was typical. "And this cavorting about with that man—that Harvey! We talked about this, Johnny. You write for a middle-American audience of middle-aged women. They aren't going to buy your books if they find out you're gay! Listen, I'm hip to the times, man. I've experimented with a few women myself, but we're talking about dollars, Peacewood—millions!"

Charlotte paced back and forth angrily, pushing her glasses up on her nose. What a nuisance! "You're going to get me in a lot of trouble, Johnny. And when you do, I am going to put you over my knee and give you a whipping. You have to finish that novel!"

Johnathan still hadn't come close to finishing. In fact, he had thrown several pages of the manuscript into the fireplace one night to prove his love for Harvey after he threatened to leave unless Johnathan retired. Johnathan couldn't bear the idea of losing his newfound love, so he grabbed the first four chapters of his manuscript and hurled them into the flames. Just hurled them as though they were piles of shit. So it seemed that Clifton and Somerset would have no resolution at all. Pity

"It's not just your reputation I'm worried about, Johnathan!" Charlotte kept yelling. "It's mine. The publishing company will have my neck. They'll never take a call from me again." Charlotte had renegotiated Johnathan's deadline once more, and she had very cleverly convinced the publisher to give Johnny a two-million-dollar bonus for meeting it. So now, she wanted her agent's slice of the pie. "Besides, you're a writer, man! It's what you do! It's your purpose in life!"

"There's been another murder, Charlotte," Johnathan spoke calmly, completely ignoring what she was saying. "Listen to this—last night, the Chicago Police Department recovered the body of Marilyn Gouche, a well-known plaintiffs' attorney. Gouche's body was found in a rail yard on the west side of the city. Authorities say it was badly mutilated. The breasts and the uterus had been removed. This is the third murder of its kind to take place in Chicago this year."

"How terrible!" Charlotte shrieked, her voice as loud as it had been before.

"Two weeks ago," Johnathan continued, "the CPD recovered the body of one Mary Ann Bell, who was mutilated in a similar fashion but badly decomposed. Mary Ann had been reported missing earlier this fall by her sister. Given the nature of the two crimes, investigators suspect that they were executed by the same person."

"You mean a serial killer?" Charlotte asked.

"Something like that," Johnathan replied. "It's a little terrifying, isn't it?"

"All the world is falling apart. And I'm going to lose my reputation because, rather than finishing your novel, you choose to sit here in the park, reading the paper," Charlotte said. "And it's so cold out! Why come to the park at all?"

"The cold wakes me up in the morning better than coffee," Johnathan said, flipping the page. "And if I never write you another book, you've already made millions off of me. Who cares if Somerset ever finds love?" He laughed.

"What is so damned funny, Peacewood?"

"I'm reading the funnies," he replied.

"You have a contract with the publishing company, Peacewood," Charlotte said. "You want to go to court? Is that what you want? You owe them that novel! Things will get very ugly for you if you don't finish it. I don't care if it's garbage at this point—Johnny! And by no means should you be out and about with that man of yours. You're going to destroy everything I've built for..."

She was turning red with fury because Johnathan was still chuckling.

"I'm sorry, Char," he laughed. "It's Garfield. He's just so funny. That silly little cat! He's always giving Odie a hard time, you know?"

"All right, Peacewood," she said. "Have it your way. The publishing company is going to sue the pants off you. I've given it my best shot. You don't have to write, but you do have to pay. See you on Court TV."

Then, she stormed off, throwing her scarf over her shoulder in the most dramatic way. But Johnathan wasn't afraid of lawyers; hell, they were being sliced and diced by serial killers at this point. Johnathan wasn't afraid of anything. He was starting to feel invincible. At least until he glanced over to the playground near the lake.

It was chilly out, and snow was all over the ground, but one child was there. Good gracious! It was that horrible little creep again. The little black kid covered in flies. And he still had on that muddy red hoodie, even though it was much too chilly to be wearing it without a coat.

The child began to walk toward Johnny. And, of course, the flies followed.

"Don't you come over here, you little creep!" Johnathan shouted with strong intention. "I don't have anything for you!"

But the boy kept coming.

"No!" Johnathan shouted. "I said stay where you are!"

But the boy kept coming. And now Johnathan could see how frail he was. It was like the poor child hadn't been fed in days. Johnathan could see every bone in the boy's face. His cheeks. His temples. His eye sockets. All protruding knots and ridges under his skin. He was emaciated. Where were his parents? They had to have been dead.

"Johnathan Pots!" the boy called.

"Don't you call me that, you little creep!" Johnathan shouted.

"Don't you call me that you little creep!" the boy repeated.

"My name is Peacewood!" Johnathan shouted. "My name is Johnathan fucking Peacewood!"

And again, the boy mimicked his words. "My name is Peacewood then!" the boy said. "Johnathan fucking Peacewood!"

"No!" Johnathan shouted, as the boy got closer and closer. He was about forty feet away now, and Johnathan was terrified. "I said stop!" Johnathan screamed, holding out the palm of his hand the way a crossing guard does when she's signaling pedestrians not to walk.

Suddenly, a purple light shot from the palm of Johnathan's hand like lightning. Boom! And the light hit the boy, and he fell to the ground. Johnathan stared at his hand as though it were the Loch Ness Monster or a space alien or the Abominable Snowman while the boy lay helpless on the ground. Then Johnathan threw his newspaper on the bench and ran for the hills—or actually, he ran home.

You see, the universe works in mysterious ways. Yet there's a science to it. Again, Johnathan had spotted this unsightly, little creep in the park. And again, the curious, purple light had saved Johnathan from either total destruction or some self-realization.

When he got back to his building, another familiar face was there, standing in the hallway. It was Sargent, of course, congenial as ever, just smiling away. Something big was at play here. Johnathan knew that, at least. Dazed and in desperate need of a distraction, he invited Sargent in for tea—and maybe a marijuana cigarette.

Chapter 9

"Want another hit?" Johnathan asked, passing the joint back to Sargent. The two had gotten high on Johnathan's couch while looking out at Lake Michigan. It was now completely frozen.

"This city can be ice cold," Sargent said, taking the joint from Johnny. "Women are being mutilated, dreams are being abandoned, and I'll bet the lake is frozen about now, isn't it?"

"It's amazing how you can see the world without seeing it," Johnathan told him.

"You don't need eyes to see," Sargent said, puffing circles out into the air. "We are more powerful than our bodies, Johnathan. They are merely vessels, but our spirits are powerful beyond measure. And it is the spirit that truly sees."

"That's some deep shit," Johnathan said, laughing. "What do you think about all these murders, Sargent? It seems like we have a serial killer on the loose."

"I think that when we don't raise our children—when we don't love them and nurture them—they grow up to be madmen. And they seek out nurture in this cold, cold world, but they never find it. And our dreams are the same way, Johnathan. Our dreams are the creations of our inner children. It's the youth inside us that allows us to dream. When a man ceases to dream, he has completely lost his youth. And when he has completely lost his youth, his dreams become monsters."

Sargent passed the joint back to Johnny, blowing a heart-shaped ring of smoke up into the air.

"That's deep. You should write something," Johnathan told him.

"Writing is not my gift, Mr. Peacewood. I'll leave that to you," Sargent replied, grinning. "That's your baby. That's the child that you should be nurturing. When we fail to nurture our dreams and our talents, they turn on us."

Johnny was listening to Sargent but not internalizing those words. Maybe it was the weed, or maybe it was Johnathan's stubborn intention to continue fleeing from the reality of all things (as he often did). Either way, Johnathan was ready to change the subject. To keep smoking—but change the subject.

"So tell me about yourself, Mr. Sargent," he laughed, coughing a bit. "Tell me something that I can't see on TMZ or read in the tabloids. I'm tired of telling the stories." Johnathan closed his eyes, letting his head fall back onto the couch.

"What do you believe in, Mr. Peacewood?" Sargent asked.

"Nothing. I don't believe in anything anymore," Johnathan replied. "Yet I believe in everything. And that is because I know nothing. Are you going to tell me a story now?"

"I'm going to tell you about me," Sargent replied. "And I'm going to tell you about the everything and the nothing that you think you claim not to know." And then, Sargent recounted his story: the years before he became the legendary painter everybody needed to know.

△ △ △

Sargent was a plumber in his late thirties—and still very much sighted—when he got the call on his work phone. He didn't really believe what the police were saying. Some officer was telling him that he needed to get out to Highway 40 just at the Nashville junction right away because his son had been involved in terrible car accident. A drunk driver had run the poor boy off the road and into a watery ditch. And things did not look good. Sargent called his wife Leanne but couldn't get a hold of her, so he rushed out to the scene right away, leaving Mrs. Cleary's drain clogged and his tools all over her kitchen floor. He didn't even wash the drain cleaner off his coveralls.

Trevor wasn't Sargent's biological son. Actually, he was his nephew. Sargent's degenerate little brother ran off to start some band just before Leanne gave birth, and Leanne's parents wanted nothing to do with their teenage daughter, who had given up a scholarship to Princeton to have some pothead musician's baby. Leanne told them she could never abort the baby of the man she loved, even if he had left her. Truth be told, she always hoped that Sargent's brother would one day come back. But of course, he never did, and he changed his number so she couldn't reach him.

So Sargent took them in and raised Trevor as his own. And he married Leanne to make a decent woman out of her, even though she never loved him. She thought Sargent was ugly, but she was the type to just need to belong to someone. Sargent loved her though, and he sure did love the boy as though he was his own. He took him camping and taught him to tie knots. And he taught him to swim and to treat girls like ladies. He saw him grow from a boy into a young man, and Sargent was very proud when that young man got a full scholarship to Notre Dame and decided to take it even though Leanne wanted him to stay close to her in Memphis. Sargent had encouraged him to go off and try something new. And Trevor was only a sophomore in college when this terrible accident occurred. So Sargent had to get there right away. Things did not look good.

If anything happened to the boy, it would be his fault for letting him go off to school way up in Indiana. That was too far for a boy to drive—all that back and forth. If anything did happen to Trevor, Sargent felt he would just die on the inside. Trevor had been the only person on the planet to love Sargent back. He certainly cared about Leanne, but she didn't give a hot damn about him. She had been stepping out since the marriage began— once with a waiter, a few times with a lawyer from Atlanta, but mostly with the football coach from the school at which she taught. He knew from the way she cried herself to sleep that Leanne always felt ashamed that she had allowed herself to marry a weird plumber with a crooked smile when she was capable of so much more. Trevor was her only solace. He just hoped that Trevor was okay. Things did not look good.

A circus of bright lights awaited him at the site. The cops had cordoned off the street, and red and blue lights reflected off the wet pavement. It was early evening, just around twilight, and a rain storm had just passed. Leanne was standing near the sheriff's car, her arms folded and her head hanging low. The ambulance was just beside her, but it was parked with the engine off and the siren off too. The sheriff seemed to be offering Leanne a bottle of water, but she pushed it away, turning to see Sargent as he pulled up. Her face was gray, and her eyes were beet red. When she noticed Sargent pulling up, her eyes became two balls of fire.

"Leanne," he called as she began to run to him. "Tell me our boy is okay."

He held his arms out, preparing to embrace the woman he had loved for so many years, but when she got to him, she punched him in face. And she punched him in his chest, over and over and over. He stopped her from breaking his nose, yet she continued to jerk and writhe in his grasp.

"You killed him, you bastard!" she shouted, swinging at him, tears rolling down her face. "He's gone! You told him to go to that school!"

Sargent wanted to let go and fall to the ground. But he knew Leanne would knee him in the face if he did, so he held on tightly. Staring over to the side of the road—where Trevor's car had been pulled from the watery ditch—Sargent began to weep. The front was completely crushed and covered in mud. "No, it can't be!" he screamed. He cried. He screamed and he cried.

Trevor had died upon impact. A drunk driver had crossed into ongoing traffic. Trevor swerved to avoid being hit, but his tires had skidded on the slick asphalt, hydroplaning into the ditch. The car ended up in four feet of muddy water. The drunk driver sat in the back of the sheriff's car while poor Trevor's body had been removed and lay lifeless in the back of the ambulance.

"I told you this would happen!" Leanne shouted.

"Leanne, I'm so sorry," Sargent cried. "I'm so, so sorry." Then, he pulled her into his arms, and she cried into his chest. He still wanted to fall to the ground and sob hysterically, but he knew that he had to be Leanne's strength. He had taken care of her all her adult life. She was seventeen and pregnant when Sargent was twenty, and he had put off his dream of art school to stay in town and take care of her. He had housed her and fed her and raised her child, but she always wanted more. And now the one thing in the world that Leanne was actually grateful for was gone. She would never forgive him. Sargent knew that Leanne would never forgive him, but he had to be her strength right now.

Sargent and Leanne had the boy cremated, and they scattered the ashes over the Mississippi River, where he and Sargent had loved to fish in the springtime. The next day, Leanne moved out of the house. She quit her job and moved to California or New

Mexico, Sargent wasn't sure where. He agreed never to contact her again after the divorce, but he never stopped loving her.

He worked for another year in his plumbing business before his eyes took a turn for the worst. He had always worn glasses, but now they didn't seem to be helping much. The world became dimmer and dimmer every day.

"I'm afraid you have glaucoma," his optometrist said. "It's only going to get worse. You may want to start making plans for yourself. You'll likely be blind within a year or so."

And Sargent did go blind. The world wasn't completely black at first— more patches and blurs—but he couldn't see well enough to find his way to the kitchen, let alone unstop Mrs. Cleary's pipes.

Within three years, Sargent had lost his son, his wife, his vision, and his career. And he had no one to love him, no one to even help him from the den to the bedroom. What was there left to live for? That's what he wondered. In fact, Sargent lay in bed pondering this very question for three days without eating or even getting up to go to the restroom. He would wet himself and just lay there, stinking in his own mess. What did it matter? No one ever came to visit. Who was there to be offended besides the flies? His life was meaningless, and Sargent had no vision of a happier tomorrow.

Eventually, he got up from his bed. Feeling his way down the hallway, he made it to the kitchen where he knew there was a bottle of drain cleaner under the sink if he could just feel where the damned sink was. He patted around, touching surfaces to determine what they were. Okay, that was the refrigerator. The oven. The toaster. The portrait of his family—former family, that was. And finally, after grasping through the darkness for a few moments, there was the sink. Bending down, he opened the cabinet and felt around for the bottle. There it was. Unscrewing it was easy. And he emptied all the drain cleaner into his mouth, swallowing every bit. He remembered the horrible taste. He remembered feeling sick to his stomach soon after. Aches and pains shot through his body before he passed out on the linoleum. But then, something miraculous happened.

Sargent awakened. He was naked, and it felt as though he were laying on a metal table. He thought he must be at the hospital. The doctors had inserted tubes into him, but he could feel no pain. They pumped all the drain cleaner from his body. And though he couldn't hear them speaking, he heard several clicking sounds. One of the doctors touched his arm, but the hand didn't feel human; it felt otherworldly, and a touch of that hand sent a warm hopeful feeling shooting up his arm. Then, suddenly, a flash of brilliant, purple light shined through Sargent's glaucoma-induced darkness, and he was able to see as he did before he had gone blind.

Several shadowy figures loomed over him, and, though he could see, he could not decipher their faces. One placed a hand on Sargent's forehead, and the fingers began to vibrate. Suddenly, Sargent seemed to be thinking thoughts and hearing words without intending to. The figures had taken control of his mind and were communicating with him telepathically. As the soft fingers grazed his head, Sargent felt the words rather than hearing them.

"We will not do you any harm," he felt them say. One of the figures was speaking to him by sending vibrating pulses into his brain, and the pulses were being translated into English.

"Who are you? Where am I? Why am I here?" Sargent asked.

"To be healed" the shadowy figure said. "You are to be a great visual artist. Your paintings will show humans the world as it really is, and it will teach them how it can be improved.

Eventually, you will come to foretell the future of the human race through your artwork."

"But," Sargent started, "My eyes—you've healed my eyes. Will they stay this way? I can see again!"

"No," one of them said. "Your eyes have not been healed. You are sensing our presence with your sixth sense—your intuition. You know that we are here because you can feel us."

"But I don't want to be blind anymore," Sargent cried.

"You are not blind," one of the shadowy figures told him. "Your eyes have merely failed. Vision is a sense that you will continue to possess, even when your eyes can no longer see. Let your intuition guide your hands along the canvas so that you may paint what you are destined to paint."

Sargent awakened, his belly to the linoleum. The amalgam of stomach acid, drain cleaner and tears had congealed on the floor after he had thrown it up. As he lay on the cold floor contemplating the meaning of all things, the warmth of the morning sun peeked through the window, touching his eyelids.

And on that day, Sargent realized that he was the most powerful man in the world—not because he possessed power, but because he knew of that power. You see, when a man knows the extent of his innate power, he becomes a bad motherfucker.

$$\triangle \; \triangle \; \triangle$$

"You know," Johnny laughed, sucking in what was the last of his marijuana, "I believe you!"

"Of course, you believe me, Peacewood," Sargent chortled, high as a kite. "You've seen them too, haven't you? I can always feel when they're near me now. I can feel their vibrations."

But Johnny was too private and too proud to confirm what Sargent was saying. He couldn't admit that he had also attempted suicide only to be saved. He couldn't risk having the world know he was just another cliché—just another melancholy artist, another Van Gogh. His ego wouldn't allow it. "I don't know what you're talking about," Johnny joked. "But I believe you."

"As long as you believe me!" Sargent said. "Well, I'd better get going. But first I want you to see something. If you could, come to my apartment with me for a moment. It won't take long. I promise." Sargent stood, all high and happy, and extended his white cane. He found his way to the front door quickly, as if he knew Johnathan's penthouse like the back of his hand (though he could not see any of it).

"I'm right behind you. I have nothing but time these days," Johnathan said, following him out the door.

"Now, how is it that the world's most famous novelist has so much free time?" Sargent asked, crossing the hallway. "My understanding is that your fans are waiting on you to finish the last novel in your Somerset series."

The two crossed the hall. When Sargent opened his front door (left unlocked, because he was a bad motherfucker and who would mess with him?) Johnny saw a very large painting hanging on the atrium wall. To the untrained eye, it would have appeared to be a bunch of red and brown blobs on a black background. The art dealers would laud it as another brilliant abstract by Simon Sargent. It could probably sell at some gallery for a zillion dollars. But this was not abstract—not at all.

"I call it *The Purpose*," Sargent told Johnathan.

To Johnathan, these giant, amorphous blobs looked like a writer sitting at his typewriter, diligently pecking away. There were bombs blasting all around him, but he could not be distracted from his task. He knew he was born to be a writer. And even if all the world fell from around him, he would write.

"It's beautiful, Sargent," Johnathan said. still a little high but genuinely very happy.

"Well, it's all yours!" Sargent said. "It's a Simon Sargent original just for Mr. Johnathan Peacewood."

And with those words, Johnny knew exactly what the painting meant. But he still wasn't quite ready to accept it. Languishing with Harvey was so much fun. And Harvey was so cute, right?

"I know what you're getting at, Sargent," Johnny said. "But I don't want to write anymore. I'm tired. I just want to lay on the beach with Harvey and spend all my money. I've worked so hard."

"But your work is not done, Peacewood," Sargent urged. "You think you've been writing romance novels, but any fiction contains a bit a truth, albeit dressed in elaborate metaphors. Your books are full of magic. You are telling us the truth about romantic love. It's not what people think it is. Love may be the most powerful force in all of creation. Most of us spend our lives looking for sensual passion and hoping it lasts forever. But love is so much more than that. Somerset has to discover that, Peacewood. And when she does, so will your readers. Your purpose is to show people what love really is. It is greater than the body. It is more than sex and infatuation. Love is the realization that we are all particles within the body of our creator. Love is understanding that you are connected to me and I am connected to you and that we work together toward one purpose. You have to tell us the truth about love, Peacewood," Sargent told him. "That is your purpose."

"It isn't fair, Sargent!" Johnny replied. "It isn't fair that I have to do all this writing about love when I never get to feel it myself. It just isn't fair, Sargent! My fans are always telling me how I help them to keep believing in love. They stop me in the supermarket to show me their wedding pictures, and they wake me when I'm napping on airplanes to tell me about their honeymoons. And never does anyone notice that I'm all alone. Never does anyone think that Peacewood might actually be the loneliest person on Earth. Nobody has ever really loved me, Sargent. And every sentence I write for Somerset is a reminder of that."

"It sounds like you and Somerset have a lot in common," Sargent laughed.

"She is me, and I am her," Johnny replied. "Honestly, I don't see her having a happy ending at this point. She's destined to die of betrayal and a broken heart. And I am destined to die of loneliness."

"You are wrong."

"Not to mention," Johnny continued, "I can't even tell the truth about being gay. I can't even go to a gay bar and make friends or go to the pride parade and wave a rainbow flag because one of my fans in Missouri will see it on CNN, and that will be the end of my readership."

"But you don't know that," Sargent replied.

"That's what my agent says," Johnny replied. "She says the publishing industry cares only about its bottom line, and middle-aged women are my bread and butter. They show up in droves to buy autographed copies of my books, and they need Peacewood to be straight. They need to believe that the men they're going home to—the men they wish they were going home to—think like me. They need to know that straight men have heart. I'm their beacon of hope. That's what Charlotte says anyway."

"But," Sargent interposed again, "what about all the people out there who *are* like you? What about all the gay men out there who need love? What about their loneliness? What about every gay kid who chugs a fist full of pills because he's being bullied and his parents won't let him go to the prom with his boyfriend. What about gays in rural Mississippi who have to hide in the shadows like you? Who can't kiss in public for fear of persecution? Who jump off bridges to escape the agony of loneliness. What about those people, Peacewood? Don't those people need a beacon too?"

"But Charlotte says..."

"What if she's wrong?" Sargent asked. "I've been having visions about you."

"About me?" Johnny asked. He was feeling pensive and somber now—and altogether less high.

"You will find true love," Sargent said. "But not until you have finished that novel, because that is the cosmic order of things. And if you're not careful, your gifts will turn on you. You have a mind like a goddess mother; whatever you imagine manifests in physical reality. That's why you're so successful. Peacewood—if you want love, all you have to do is imagine it," Sargent said. "You're very gifted. There is nothing you can't do!"

"Well," Johnny snickered, "I am sure that you won't remember saying any of this after that weed wears off."

"It's true!" Sargent continued. "I had a vision. You're going to finish this book of yours. And you'll later go on to write a book about me!"

"A book about you?" Johnny laughed, though the idea of writing about Sargent had intrigued him. A blind painter who'd been brought back from the dead. It would make him millions!

"Yes, you will write about me and my gifts," Sargent replied. "You're going to help me guide the human race to transcendence."

"You really want me to write about you, Sargent?" Johnny asked.

"Oh, you have to!" Sargent replied. "Don't let those precious gifts turn on you. I'll bet they've already started to, haven't they? I didn't pursue my passion as a youth, and so my gifts turned on me. I had dreamed of traveling the world and painting all the beautiful people and things, but I never did. I never allowed myself to. And so my gifts turned on me, taking my sight away so that I could no longer see those beautiful people and things. Peacewood, you are far more gifted than I, and I'm afraid for the world if your gifts turn."

"Harvey hates me to write," Johnathan told him.

"That Harvey is a disease!" Sargent shouted. "He is a herpes lesion on your soul, Peacewood! Our dreams are our babies. If we don't nurture them, they grow up to be monsters."

And with that, Johnathan realized that he was an integral part of this universe. He had a gift—hell, he had multiple gifts. And his work was in line with a cosmic purpose, whatever that was. Somerset was Johnathan's baby. But Harvey didn't want him writing about her anymore. So then, what did that say about Harvey? And what did that say about love?

Chapter 10

Winter in Chicago was an insufferable bastard. The temperature was so negative that not the world's most cheerful optimist could give it a positive spin. The wind cut like blades. And the sky was an army of gray ghosts, looming listlessly, singing all the saddest songs ever written.

Still, Clifton was thrilled to have Somerset at his side. As he caressed her bald head and kissed her soft, brown cheek, he whispered "I'm glad to have you in my life," in her ear.

The two lay so close together that Somerset could feel his eyelashes against her face when he blinked. But she paid him no mind. Rather, she gazed upon the yellow flames as they rose and crackled in the fireplace, lost in contemplation.

Something was not quite right about Mr. Clifton. She had thought she was falling for the one. But she wasn't so sure about old Cliff anymore. Sometimes he made dark jokes about choking or whipping her. He was into some kinky shit, all right. Somerset had met the Marquis de Sade, and not even he was this dark. And Clifton kept drifting off into stories about Iraq, which were not romantic at all. They were horrific. He had seen so many dark things over in the desert—like children blown to bits trying to throw pipe bombs at the Americans, like detainees being forced to sleep naked next to their own shit in the dark, like rape and sodomy. Some of it reminded her of her voyage to America on the slave ship. But Clifton didn't ever see it that way. For him, these were just commonalities of war—brutality had kept America free, after all.

And what about Clifton's capacity to love? He had said "I love you" much too soon. It didn't seem logical that his feelings had grown so intense so quickly. And he had become addicted to her breast milk. He would stop by late at night to have a suck, but then fall asleep before they could really even talk. Then, he'd want a sip or two in the morning before work. And he had started bottling it so that he could have some during the day while she was away. She knew she had to pull away soon. Otherwise, she would be trapped forever with a man she wasn't ready to love. She just hoped it wasn't too late to get out of this mess. The last lover of hers to get addicted to her milk died violently—stabbed to death while sleeping.

His name was Charles DeBerry. He was a six-foot-tall white man, awkward and gangly as they come. Somerset had met him while teaching grade school in Texarkana back in the 1940s. DeBerry was a drifter—he went from town to town doing odd jobs, working with his hands. He was trying to get out to California where his brother had recently purchased a farm, but he needed money. So he got a job as a farm hand just outside Texarkana in early '45. And one night, he ended up on the colored end of town, where he wound up drinking with the negroes and chewing tobacco and talking about how if he were more handsome he could marry himself a movie star. And the negroes laughed at that. They all liked this tall, gangly white fellow. He didn't act better than them. And he wasn't a racist at all; it was if he had been born white by mistake and regretted it.

"White folk are so boring, ain't we?" he'd joke. "And we smell like ham, don't we!" And the negroes laughed at that too.

And so one night, while he was spitting tobacco into a can and playing poker on a porch belonging to a negro carpenter, he saw Somerset coming along. And their eyes met. And he was in love. DeBerry's deep dark secret was that he couldn't keep his hands off black women. He knew he wouldn't keep a single one of his negro friends if they found out he had been sleeping with their kind, so he never discussed his sexual proclivities. But he loved the way his pasty skin looked next to what he referred to as that smooth, brown butter. And so he had to have Somerset. He just had to.

And DeBerry and Somerset did in fact have a clandestine affair. But she didn't love him, not really. She only loved his adoration of her, at least until he became addicted to her breast milk. He would stop by the schoolhouse when the children were eating lunch and ask for a drink of it out back. She was obliged at first. But then, Mr. Charles DeBerry started to act very peculiar. He began to talk to people who weren't around—Clark Gable, for example. He would talk to Clark Gable as though he were right there next to him.

"Mr. Gable, you are the finest actor the world has ever seen!" he would say, pointing to an empty corner or an icebox or a horse. The negroes would laugh at him, but the whites never did. To them, he was becoming a lunatic. "If I had a handsome face like you, Mr. Gable, I would not be scooping up horse shit in Texas," he said, thinking his boss was actually Clark Gable. "Look at this shit heap!" DeBerry jeered, referring to his boss's barn. "We should burn this shit heap, Clarky."

That comment got him canned, of course. And then there were the murders. Five people were mysteriously shot that spring. The killings happened in two-week intervals, and the culprit was never captured. Two potential victims did get away, however, and described their assailant as a tall white man who wore a cut-up potato sack over his face. The locals referred to him as the Phantom Killer, and these events would go down in history as the Texarkana Moonlight Murders. Of course, it was Mr. Charles DeBerry, drunk on Somerset's milk, who was doing all the killing. He would drink her milk, then go out into the streets wearing that ridiculous sack on his head. He thought he was an actor in a cowboy movie and co-starring with Mr. Clark Gable. He was the vigilante in a town corrupted by all sorts of nefarious white people. He thought the entire town of Texarkana was a movie set on some Hollywood back lot, and that he was shooting blanks.

"I'm gonna be a big star," DeBerry told Somerset one night after they had made love. He lay in her bed, running his hands across her silky finger waves. Black women had much thicker hair than white women, and he loved that.

"Of course, you are, baby," Somerset patted his head. But she would come to learn that he was dead serious.

"We're almost done with the movie," he told her. "We wrap next week."

"What are you talking about, baby?" Somerset asked him.

"I just have one final scene to shoot, girlie," he went on. "The school shooting scene."

"What school shooting scene?" she asked, pulling away.

"Mr. Gable and I have been vigilantes. We've been hunting the bad folk in this town. But we gotta wear masks so nobody knows who we are. And the little negro kids are plotting to rob a bank and kill the sheriff. Actually, they're full-grown bank robbers dressed up to look like little negro kids. So we're going to come in and take all the little bastards out. And then the town will be safe. And Mr. Gable can ride off into the sunset with his maiden. And I'll be a town hero."

As DeBerry stood and left the room, Somerset was terrified. She hoped that it was just the milk talking. Sometimes her milk caused men to hallucinate. But when DeBerry strutted back into her bedroom wearing that potato sack and looking like a scarecrow, she knew he had done it. She knew he had been killing people at night.

DeBerry stood there pointing his finger into the air as though it were a pistol. "Bang! Bang!" he whispered through the darkness.

"When are you filming the last scene with Mr. Gable?" she asked.

"Tomorrow morning," he replied, hopping around the room as though he were on a horse and was a cowboy vigilante. "The crew will be at the negro school. And Gable and I are gonna act out the scene."

Somerset could see it all now—this freak walking into her classroom with that horrible mask. Her babies would be terrified. And then—bang, bang—he'd shoot them all to death, spraying blood all over their little textbooks. And it would be her fault because her milk caused him to do it.

Well, Mr. Charles DeBerry got tuckered out after a few more bangs from his pistol. So he fell asleep in Somerset's arms. Then, she got up and went to the kitchen, where she kept the knives. She came back to the bedroom where the Phantom Killer was snoring and probably dreaming about Clark Gable.

First, she stabbed him in his throat so that he couldn't scream. Next, she stabbed his heart, then his stomach, then his heart again and again and again and again. She chopped his limbs off, cut out his intestines, and removed his head. She let her dogs eat most of the meat, and she buried the bones far out in the woods. Then she threw his head in a pond with that ridiculous mask still on it. Nobody was gonna shoot up her babies.

The Phantom Killer of Texarkana was never heard from again, and the Moonlight Murders ceased.

That was the last time a guy had gotten too addicted to her milk, and that was the last time she had had to kill one of her lovers. And that was awful. So she needed to get away from Clifton before things got carried away. And before he started asking one idiotic question too many.

"Will you marry me?" Clifton asked, pulling a diamond ring from his pocket. It glistened in the fire light.

"And there's the one idiotic question too many," Somerset muttered to herself. "It's just the milk talking, Cliff. Let the high wear off. Then ask me again." She laughed, hoping he was joking, although she knew he wasn't.

In five hundred years, Somerset had been married seven times. Of course, she had never been in love—love had nothing to do with marriage. But she couldn't marry Cliff. She didn't love him, and she really didn't even want to date him anymore. This was just another one of those convenient relationships that was becoming less convenient. Sure, he was intriguing at first, with his war talk and his poetic passion. But there was something about him that kept Somerset from going over the edge. His darkness had just gotten too dark. It was so dark that Somerset couldn't see anymore. She needed to get out and find some light.

"I need to be going now," Somerset said, laughing as she stood and reached for her coat. She was trying her best to go quickly.

And Cliff looked absolutely stupefied. In his mind, he had found his soulmate. He had shaved his head for her, and was keeping himself as bald as possible just so that she would feel comfortable. He had given her gifts—tennis bracelets, flowers, a pearl necklace, and now this engagement ring. Nothing was good enough for her.

"This was fun while it lasted, but I just don't want to marry you, Cliff," she said, wrapping herself up in preparation to go out into the windy winter night. "We aren't meant to be married. I like you. I really do. You're a great guy, but you're not for me."

"Well, why don't you just take a little time to think about it, Somerset?" he asked, standing to stop her from leaving. "You don't have to give me an answer tonight," he said. "Think a little."

Somerset opened the door. "Boy, please," she said, laughing as she left the room. "I am out of here! I haven't even known you a year!"

"But I love you!" he shouted. But Somerset didn't hear— she had already closed the door behind her.

Clifton couldn't lose his Somerset. She completed him. She was what he had been searching for all his life. Clifton was certain that living without Somerset would drive him mad—well, madder. So he did what any noble, romance novel hero would do. He went after his girl.

Clifton opened the door and. Clifton opened the door. And? Clifton opened the door and then what? And? Then. What? And then what?

Oh, hell, I don't want to write this story anymore. Who cares what happens to Somerset and Clifton? Do I care? No. Honestly, I don't even think Somerset wants true love. She keeps running away from it when it's right there in front of her. I've always personally felt that when people walk away from love, they don't deserve it. Well, my loving readers, I have finally found love. And I refuse to live my life like that bitch Somerset. I choose love. Choosing to continue in my writing would be to walk away from Harvey, the true love in my life. Therefore, Somerset is finished. My apologies to all my fans, but I have to stop now. I cannot do this anymore. Yours truly, Johnathan Peacewood.

Clifton walked out of his door, hoping to find Somerset. Instead he found a white space. Nothing was there. No walls. No streets. No people. No Somerset. No words. No story. It was if the entire world had been erased. Clifton looked down, but there was no ground beneath him. Just white space. Just limitless potential.

"Hello!" Clifton called. But no one was there. His voice didn't even echo. White space. Limitless potential. And? Purpose. And? Gone. And?

Chapter 11

Johnny Peacewood's Private Island (the exact coordinates cannot be disclosed)

Johnathan had had enough of the Chicago winter and decided to sweep his fiancé—yes, they were now engaged—off to a tropical paradise so far removed that no one could ever find them. Now Mr. Johnathan Peacewood was lying in a tub on the lanai of his bungalow, sipping a Mai Tai. Harvey was across from him at a table, cracking crab legs and slurping up the meat. Harvey was a beautiful man, even when he had garlic butter running down his chin. That thick, black hair and the perfect jawline. Who cared about that scar on his lip? Johnny sure didn't.

"You are the stuff that dreams are made of," Johnny told him. "I love you, Harvey Marcus."

Harvey sighed. "Yeah, yeah. I love you, Peacewood."

It was perfunctory, with no warmth whatsoever. Harvey was more interested in slurping down the crab than discussing feelings. But Johnathan figured the indifference was a sign of Harvey's newfound comfort level. That was how old couples said I love you, right? Elderly couples didn't really have to say it. I mean, after fifty years of marriage, it pretty much goes without saying. So of course Harvey loved him. That was obvious.

"I am grateful to know a man named Harvey Marcus who comes with me to my island and makes me feel anything but lonely," Johnny said, chewing on the fruit from his Mai Tai.

"I am grateful to know a guy who can afford a defense lawyer after I kill that chef of yours for not bringing me any lemon with my crab," Harvey replied, grimacing as he sucked the crab meat from its bright red shell.

"Gee. Thanks," Johnny replied. He had hoped for something a bit more poetic. A bit more romantic. A bit more emotional than crabs and lemons. "Is that all you have to say to me?"

"Actually, no," Harvey replied, putting his crab down for a moment. "I think you should know that I envy you, Peacewood."

"What for?" Johnny asked.

"You've got all that talent," Harvey said, "and that's why I have all these things. You think I don't know that? Well, I do! You make up all those stories, and people want to read them. And that's kind of amazing. And I'm a little jealous of that. I've never had any talent, Peacewood. Not at sports or art or anything. After I had the accident, I tried acting. But I suck at it. I was in one vampire movie back in 2011, but nobody went to see it. It was a big fat flop. I tried painting too, but I'm terrible. My roses look more like flames than flowers. The truth is, modeling is all I've ever been good at. And it's honestly all that I've ever liked to do. So when I was in the accident, it sort of ruined my life."

"Well, you could still model, Harvey," Johnathan told him. "You have a gorgeous face."

"Not with this scar," Harvey replied. "The fashion houses like perfection in their ads. Nobody wants an accident victim."

"Is that what they told you?" Johnathan asked.

"No," Harvey said. "I just know it. I just know that's how it would work. I stopped going to the walk-ins because I knew I would just keep getting rejected. They would give it to the guy with the perfect face standing next to me. And I can't bear to hear 'no' over and over again."

"But you really haven't even given anyone a chance to reject you. You've rejected yourself. The scar gives your face a touch of character. I'm sure you'd be fine."

"This scar makes me an unlovable troll, and you know it!" Harvey replied.

"That's nonsense!" Johnathan snapped. "I have never loved a troll!"

But Harvey couldn't hear Johnathan anymore. All he could hear was the sound of rejection from the fashion houses in New York, from the agencies in Paris, from the world. From himself. He didn't believe in himself anymore. Thus, he could no longer act on his ambitions. And this is why he was languishing. When Johnathan looked at Harvey he was a white space. Limitless potential. Purpose.

But none of that mattered as long as Harvey was blind to it. Suddenly, Johnathan was thrilled to have retired from novel writing. He needed to spend the rest of his life nurturing this poor, wounded baby bird. He had to show him that he was as beautiful as he had always been and that anything was truly possible. And most of all, Johnathan had to prove to Harvey that he was loved.

So for Harvey's sake, Johnathan would take all of the pages from all of the stories he had ever written and scatter them to the wind. The world could piece them back together as it wished, for they were no longer his responsibility. This was Mr. Johnathan Peacewood's chance to love and to be loved—yes, indeed.

Part II: Requiem

Chapter 12

The coast of central West Africa, about 1520. Somerset—or Sumi, as she was known in that time—is pregnant with the child of Taye the Beast. Taye's people were the victors in a war with Sumi's tribe, the Uti, and Sumi has been made an unfortunate trophy, forced into this marriage with a man she cannot possibly bring herself to love. Taye the Beast is a dreadful, ugly thing with the head of a crocodile (its wide, gaping jaw and beady little yellow eyes) and the body of a gorilla (its broad back and the wrists that dangle at his knees). Poor Sumi is only a girl, not even twenty, and she is terrified of him.

Their coital relations had been tearing her apart as he was nearly three times her size, with no rhythm and no romance. It was militant sex, free of passion and strictly for asserting his dominion. He would grunt with his throat and click with his tongue as he smothered her underneath his monsterish mass, every thrust more numbing than the last.

And she could tell this child inside of her would be huge and would likely rip her to pieces during the birth. Sumi could sometimes feel the little devil kicking and writhing within her, and she knew that she would die during the delivery. Taye's tribe, the Hootu, was mostly male because the females always died birthing their gargantuan warrior offspring. Those wide crocodile jaws and broad gorilla backs were torture on a birth canal. Taye's mother bled out on the floor and died moments after his birth, so he never knew her. He never understood women, and he never respected them. This was why most Hootu men lacked compassion. They were a band of men without mothers.

And now, here Sumi was, ready to deliver Taye's monstrous little baby—head of a reptile, body of primate, spirit of a warrior—and she was simply terrified. She could sense her own mortality.

The matrons gathered round her in the birthing hut, coming with incense and oils, praying to the spirits that she and the child survive. Sumi could feel her body tearing as the head passed through the birth canal. And she knew that death was imminent. The spirits had begun to haunt in the shadows of the hut.

Yes, Sumi saw a playful spirit prancing around her, making funny faces behind the backs of the matrons. In fact, several spirits had entered the hut. They were beautiful, transparent angels. The playful one, Wesse—the messenger—teasingly flapped his tongue up and down through the air, as though he were using it to wave goodbye. Another, a female—Ana, the mother spirit—came along and bopped the jokester on his head with a tree branch, warning him that this was a serious matter and that he should cut out the tomfoolery. Ana extended her hand to Sumi, offering her comfort as she pushed the child from her.

Then, a third spirit came. He was a male, wearing a golden mask so that Sumi could not see his face. A regal crown adorned his head. This was Wille, the father spirit. He was the most austere of all, and carried a staff. They were beckoning her into the afterlife. Finally, a fourth spirit came in. He was particularly handsome, with a chiseled musculature and the wings of an ostrich. This was Curta, the spirit of transitions, who ushered one through the aisle connecting life and death. And he was carrying the spirit of a baby in his arms. And that baby had the head of a crocodile and the body of an ape. And he was bringing the little monster toward her. It was tiny and crying, but most of all, it was terrifying. And all the time, she could feel the life slipping from her body as though it were leaking out the bottom of her spine. And the beautiful winged spirit threw the little baby spirit at Sumi, and it was absorbed into her body.

The pain eventually built to a raging fire in her loins, and Sumi felt as though she were being pulled open into a canyon. The little child was alive now, and he was crying—actually he was screaming, and the matrons cut the cord and gave him to Sumi. She saw him, but she did not love him because he was the spitting image of Taye the Beast.

"Give him a taste of your milk," one matron said. "Nurture that baby boy."

But Sumi didn't want to nurture this baby. It would certainly suck the life from her body. And it was the ugliest thing she'd ever seen—well, the second ugliest thing, after Taye. So the matron took the baby and put it in a little crib made of mud and sticks. And it screamed and screamed and screamed for love, but Sumi felt weak, lightheaded, as though she hadn't eaten in days. And the world was becoming a blur of light and shadows.

"Oh god!" one matron cried. "You're bleeding onto the floor!"

And Sumi was indeed bleeding out. There was a black puddle underneath her, where the monster baby had come out. The child had truly ripped her apart. This was the fate of a Hootu mother. And she knew that the presence of the spirits was a harbinger of her doom. The baby had come to Earth, nestled in Curta's arms, to take her place.

"Oh god, she's going to die!" a matron cried. "She's bleeding so much. Her body is going cold." And Sumi was cold. She was so cold and so faint. And the puddle of blood underneath her was expanding, drop by drop. And Curta was now standing right over her, caressing her head, running his fingers along her thick, nappy head. And his gigantic wings were outstretched, as though he were preparing to fly her away.

"I'll take you to paradise," he told her. "I will take you to your family—all of those who were killed by the Hootu. You brothers. Your father. They are waiting for you, Sumi."

"No, not yet!" Sumi cried. "I don't know what it is to love! I'm only a girl. I don't love Taye. I could never love a man who killed my people. And I will never love a man that ugly!"

"But you have your son," the spirit replied. "He is your love. Surely you love him."

"No!" she cried. "I don't love him. I don't. How could I? He looks just like his father. And he's killing me! The little monster is killing me!"

"Won't you give your baby a name?" Curta asked.

"She is not ready," Ana told the others. "Let her stay a while."

"No!" Wesse, the playful spirit, shouted. "I want to play with her," he laughed, flapping his tongue across his teeth. "Bring her into the spirit world so we can play! Titty titty titty!"

"Sumi!" one of the matrons called. "Who are you talking to?"

"The spirits!" Sumi cried. "They're all around you! They're here." By this time, tears were streaming down her cheeks nearly as fast as blood was gushing from her loins.

"No, my child," another matron said, wiping the sweat from Sumi's face. "No one is here."

And Sumi knew she could only see the spirits because she was dying; they rarely appeared to those anchored in the realm of the living. "Please don't do this to me," Sumi cried. "I just want to be loved. Please let me live to know what love is."

"Fetch the healer!" Ana ordered Wesse.

"You aren't the boss around here!" Wesse teased, tumbling over and standing on his head. "Titty titty titty!" Then, he began to sing a silly song about death: "*Thirty-one babies, a bottle of blood, and a Wesse in a pear tree—and a Wesse in a pear tree, and a Wesse in a pear tree—titty titty titty!*" Then, he stood back up on his feet, swaying back and forth because he was dizzy.

Ana picked up her stick and bopped Wesse over his silly little head. And suddenly Wille, the masked spirit, waved his staff, silently commanding Wesse to go forth and fetch the healer. And the playful one did go.

"You will soon be arisen, child," Ana told Sumi, leaning over her and kissing her forehead.

"Take him back!" Sumi shouted to Curta, whose wings were still outstretched. "Take him! I don't want him. Let me live instead."

"Hush, child," Ana said, "before you say too much."

Sumi felt the chilly breeze of death rolling over her as her spirit drained from her body. She could not feel her arms, her legs, her face. And the light, which had illuminated the matrons, had faded until their faces were dim, patched with shadows. But the spirits were no longer transparent—they had become solid and real.

"She's crossing," Ana said, rubbing Sumi's head.

"No, I'm not ready," Sumi cried. "I've never been loved—not truly. I've lost my entire family, and I have never been loved. This isn't fair!" she shouted. "That little monster cannot be the death of me!"

Just then, a shadowy figure loomed in the doorway. The face and legs were within the darkness, but the light fell upon his chest so that she could see his necklace. It was gaudy but brilliant, with triangular pendants of gold. In the center was a purple jewel, and it was majestic and dazzling. And the figure said something to the matrons in the shadows, though it was so faint that Sumi could not hear. The matrons stood to leave, but they left the newborn in the room, screaming to the top of his lungs for his mother—for nurture.

The figure came closer so that Sumi could see his face now. He stood over her, tall and mysterious, as Wesse followed behind. This figure was the healer of the tribe. He had many gifts and could speak with the spirits. He could hear their songs and their cries, and he could touch them and dance with them. Oftentimes, he could control them. And this day, he would do just that. Raising his hands to the ceiling, he called to the spirits.

"Wesse!" he called, and the playful spirt ran to Sumi's side, grabbing her hand and kissing it. He really was an impish thing.

"Titty titty titty!" he sang, thumbing at Sumi's breasts. Then he took Sumi's hand and placed it in his pants so that she could feel his privates.

"Wesse!" the healer shouted, and the playful spirit yanked her hand from his pants and placed it on his heart. "Curta!" the healer called, and the spirit of life and death came to Sumi, standing across from the playful one. He took her other hand and placed it on his heart. His wings rested at his sides with quiet veneration, but his face was the most sinister Sumi had seen, with a furrowed brow and eyes the intense red of a volcanic eruption. "Ana!" the healer called next. The female spirit placed both her hands upon Sumi's heart, her touch like a flowing water and her hair like the leaves of a willow.

"And you," the healer called, looking toward the masked spirit named Wille. "Come to me with your staff. I have a special request of you."

And the masked spirit did come, and he did embrace the healer as though he was an old friend. Then, the healer whispered into the spirit's ear, but Sumi could not hear the word. And the spirit nodded his head in acquiesce. Wille walked over to the newborn child, who was screaming in his crib. And Wille held his staff like a spear high above the baby's heart.

"What's he doing?" Sumi asked.

"If you want to live, you must give something," the healer told her. "A mother gives life to her child, forsaking her own so that he may thrive. That is motherhood. We gain immortality when we bear children. Our spirits linger with them and with their children and with their children's children. And we are passed into new generations by them. It is a great gift to bring life into this world, even when it means you must lose your own. But you want to remain in this realm, Sumi. You want to remain of this world so that you can find love. And if that is what you want, the child must die. He must not pull your spirit away from you."

"What do I care?" Sumi cried. "He's a little monster. And so is his father! Take him!"

"Think of what you're doing, child," Ana cried, still touching Sumi's heart. Tears fell from the spirit's eyes, becoming butterflies that fluttered across the room to the child's crib.

"I don't want him!" Sumi shouted. "Take him! Let me live!"

"I warn you, Sumi," the healer said, "the love you seek may not bring the absolution that you so desire. True love is the love a mother has for her son. True love is the love that a shepherd has for his sheep—that a griot has for his stories. Sumi, that boy is your story. Are you sure you're ready to abandon him this way?"

"Please, I'm dying. Kill the boy!" Sumi cried, watching as the butterflies formed a flying hoop around the lid of the boy's crib. And the masked spirit readied his staff, bracing himself for the fatal jab.

"But he is your child," Ana cried, "just as you are mine."

"Please let me live!" Sumi screamed. She wasn't really alive, but she wasn't really dead. She was floating now in the realm of the bardo, where there was no turmoil but also no harmony. Everything was even and neutral—a realm between the hell of Earth and the peace of paradise. This was where the soul came to ponder life and death. It was a peaceful space of temperance. But the soul must make a decision on where it wishes to journey next. It cannot languish in the bardo forever.

"Are you sure?" the healer asked.

"Do it!" Sumi screamed. "Give me the staff, and I'll kill him myself. I don't want to die until I've felt true love in my heart. Then you can take me."

"If that is what you wish," the healer said.

He nodded his head. And with haste, the masked spirit stabbed the baby through his little heart, killing him. As the healer's purple jewel began to glow, the spirits began to leave Sumi. Curta, the spirit of life and death, went to the child and pulled his spirit from the crib. Ana wept, but butterflies filled Sumi's wound so that it healed. The playful Wesse did a somersault and vanished in midair, while the masked Wille walked into a wall of smoke. Curta went out the door with the spirit of the child and flew away. Ana exploded into a billion butterflies that fluttered out the window and up to Heaven. Finally, all that remained was the healer, who stood over Sumi, holding her hand.

"I worry for you, my girl," he said. "I worry for you."

"Worry for me not!" she laughed triumphantly. "I will soon find true love!"

"Then, my girl," the healer spoke, "may you live to feel true love. And until then, may you never perish." This is how Somerset became eternal.

△ △ △

At last, it was springtime in modern day Chicago. Somerset was sitting in Lincoln Park reading a novel. The lake had thawed, and the city had come back to life. An old lady was feeding the pigeons as though they were her children. Two men were playing checkers over in the shade of a knurled spruce. And Somerset had found a park bench on which to rest and read her favorite novel: *Somerset Eternal* by Johnathan Peacewood. It was Mr. Peacewood's first novel, and it made him a star. And most importantly, it had made Somerset a star. She was amazed that Johnathan had gotten every detail of her story down so perfectly, as if he had been there to see it himself. And it was as though Somerset had not been real at all. It was as if she had somehow leapt from the pages of this novel and come to life. She had never met this Peacewood fellow, but it was remarkable the way he had depicted her—a love-deprived heroine, torn between sacrifice and desire. That's how she started anyway. Lately, Somerset was beginning to believe that she had been a fool to accept eternal life for the sake of romance. She had not found it in all these years, and would be doomed to live forever if it turned out that such love was only a farce.

And wasn't it? Wasn't romantic love just a notion invented by the Brontë sisters because those two bitches had nothing better to do in the 1800s? Until the twentieth century, hadn't marriage been about the exchange of property and the expansion of estates? All of a sudden, it was about love and passion, but wasn't that why the divorce rate is so high? Because isn't love fleeting?

Somerset read on about how she allowed the spirit of death to carry her first and only child into the afterlife before he could even touch her, before he could even speak, before he could even dream. She had been so arrogant as a young girl, believing that romance was worth such a sacrifice. And now, although her body was preserved in its original teenage state, she was over five hundred years old and had no love to show for it. So what use was the power of immortality when she couldn't even find what she was really looking for? She was trapped, for not even suicide could bring her death, and she was tired. Somerset was tired of looking and hoping and searching. She was ready to cross over and be with her child and her parents and her sisters.

"Do you have cancer?" a little girl asked, standing before Somerset and holding a baby doll.

Somerset put the book down for a moment to study this child standing in the grass and twirling her hair around her finger. She couldn't have been any older than six. Children were so precious—how could she have allowed her own to be carried off into the afterlife like that?

"Aren't you cute," Somerset remarked, smiling. "Is that your baby? Is that your little girl you have there in your hand?"

"Her name is Clarissa!" the girl replied, pulling the doll close to her heart.

The masked spirit of Wille appeared, standing behind the little child. He was holding his staff above her head and was preparing to stab it though her cute little skull. But Somerset knew that the spirit would not do such a thing. He was only there to taunt her; whenever her maternal instincts kicked in, the spirit would appear with his staff, reminding her that she had sacrificed her child so that she could live to find true love. What a farce!

"Clarissa is a lovely name for a little girl," Somerset replied, a little peeved. She frowned at the spirit, hoping he would hit the road. She was tired of him harassing her all the time. Didn't people make mistakes? Didn't she deserve another chance?

"Do you have cancer?" the little girl asked again, still twirling her finger through her hair.

Somerset did have cancer. A tumor had formed in her past and had metastasized into her present. And it was malignant and staff-wielding. But she replied, "No, I don't have cancer, little one. I just shaved my head. I was tired of my hair. Women like to change up their looks from time to time, and I got bored with my old look." And she was bored with this old life as well. Thirty-one Tylenol, a glass of zinfandel, and partridge in a pear tree would have been helpful right about now. If only she hadn't given up her ability to die.

The girl laughed, then ran away, carelessly swinging the doll by its arm. But the masked spirit remained.

"Yeah, I get the point. You can hit the road now," Somerset told him. "I'm reading a book about myself, if you don't mind."

A column of smoke blasted up from the grass, and the spirit walked into it, disappearing from the living realm and leaving Somerset to read in peace about how she had been tricked by that kidnapper who sold her off into slavery. Reading all this reminded her of Clifton. She had left him—just walked right off the page after hearing "Will you marry me?" and then ended up here. She didn't remember coming to the park. So how'd she get here? It made no sense. In fact, she hated the Northside—too many white people. And it was becoming dangerous with all those sad black women being murdered and having their breasts cut off. There was a serial killer on the loose, and Somerset wanted to stay clear of that. But she figured it was safe in the daylight. Nothing too creepy in the daylight—or that's what she figured.

Then, she saw him. That little creep. That little hooded creep.

It was the kid in the red hoodie who had been haunting Johnathan. He was there in the park again, this time staring at Somerset. And as usual, he was filthy and standing underneath a halo of flies. He clearly had not eaten in days—Somerset could see the bones in his cheeks. And she knew immediately who the child belonged to.

"This can't be!" she cried. "That bastard!" And suddenly, she understood everything. Looking at the novel in disgust, Somerset threw it to the ground and called out to see if the child was all right. But that creepy little kid was not all right. In fact, he was dying of neglect. He fell onto the grass, and the flies crawled along his little brown face and devoured it.

"No!" she screamed, leaping off the bench and racing over to him immediately. Her story would never have a resolution if this child died here and now.

"Get up, boy!" she shouted, slapping his face and shooing away the flies. Up close, this kid was even more a fright. Dried mucus stained his face from nose to mouth, and his lips were chapped and cracking. He hadn't had his hair cut or even brushed since God knows when. And the smell! The smell was the worst! Garbage and shit! "Wake up!" she shouted, again slapping his face. But the boy did not respond. She knew then what she would have to do.

Somerset picked the boy up and carried him into the arboretum down near the lake, to a spot where the perverts liked to do naughty things in the bushes. She would need privacy for this.

"Don't you die on me, child! You better not even try it!" A canopy of spruce and oak trees shaded the arboretum, and grasses grew wild until there was no clear pathway. Once hidden behind a wall of weeds and shrubs and trees, Somerset placed the boy on his back then pulled out her breast, putting the nipple in his mouth. "You better drink, boy!" she said, squeezing a bit of her milk out.

He didn't suck at first, the intoxicating nectar just trickling down his throat, but soon he began to cough. He loved the taste, so he drank until he awoke and became rapacious, feeding himself until high. The boy barked and moaned, constantly sucking, feeling this new rush of energy coursing through his body. Inspiration.

"No more languishing!" Somerset shouted, crying as the boy bit her and drained her. "Finish what you started, you bastard," Somerset cried. "Finish! Finish! Finish!"

And the boy sucked so hard that Somerset was sore. But that was a sacrifice she was willing to make if it meant keeping this poor child alive a little longer, for his sake and for hers.

On the other side of the tracks, Johnathan Peacewood was suddenly itching to write. Just plain itching.

Chapter 13

Extra! Extra! Grieve all about it. Famed novelist Johnathan Peacewood came out as a flaming queen and married short-time boyfriend, long-term parasite Harvey Marcus in the Bahamas. Fans are shocked; friends are relieved. How will this torrid turn of events affect the career that brought publishing back from obsolescence? Peacewood's fans respond:

Well, I certainly won't be reading his books anymore.

> *Who cares if he's gay. He's a great writer! And love is love, right?*

> *I feel I can no longer support him, being the Christian woman that I am.*

We certainly will not be stocking his books in our school libraries after this.

> *I think it's great! What a twist! Now, I want to read the books even more!*

> *I don't see what the big deal is. He's an artist. Aren't they all a little gay?*

When asked how coming out might affect his book sales, Mr. Peacewood responded with a resounding "Who gives a shit!"

The arts community is supporting Peacewood for the most part. The who's who were present at the nuptials. That famous singer who married that famous music mogul. That famous novelist who brought her husband, that other famous novelist. And of course, that silly heiress who drags her poodle onto every red carpet as though it's a fashion accessory.

The Peacewood wedding was the event of the century. There were fireworks and belly dancers and flamethrowers and conga lines and a giraffe named Gonzo that Peacewood had painted pink to match his tie. And above the gazebo where the two got hitched hung a banner that read *Love Lives!*

All the guests entered the gambling pool to bet on how long the marriage would last. Last year's Best Director nominee bet two thousand dollars that it wouldn't last a year. And that internet mogul, the one who started that famous social networking site, bet ten thousand that it wouldn't last three. But, nonetheless, the world's most famous novelist came out of the closet (finally) and tied the knot, and he and his honey have moved into the Peacewood penthouse in Chicago, Illinois, announcing to the world: they're here; they're queer; now deal with it. Extra! Extra!

$$\triangle \ \triangle \ \triangle$$

And Johnny was itching to write. His mind raced with ideas—new characters, new plots new motifs. Of course, he realized his next novel might flop because of his coming out. But what did that matter? What was another ten million dollars? Johnny was wealthy enough to retire. Finally, he had gotten back to his sweet spot—to the place where his writing had nothing to do with profit. He could focus now on artistic expression.

He had to get out of the penthouse. He had to go collect his thoughts—to communicate with these new ideas, these spirits, these brainchildren. He just had to or he would go stir-crazy. So one morning, he kissed his beloved goodbye and went out into the city to walk.

Truthfully, Johnny always got his best ideas during walks. He first thought of Somerset one day while walking up Broadway to grab a hotdog. He could taste her words in the sauerkraut and smell her scent in the mustard—though, to be clear, she did not smell like mustard.

△ △ △

Meanwhile, Harvey remained in bed. And as soon as Johnathan was out of the way, the sneaky little devil reached for the phone.

"Hey baby!" he exclaimed. "Oh, I know. I miss you already too! Yeah, I leave for NYC tonight. Yeah. A week. Yeah. Come by Thursday if you feel that's enough time. Do you feel that's enough time?" Harvey's eyes trailed along the bookcase on the wall, beaming with enmity as they gazed upon the beautiful hardbound books. All of Peacewood's creations along with his inspirations, everything from *Julius Caesar* to *The Cat in the Hat*. Everything inspired Peacewood, and his fertile mind had always vexed Harvey.

"Yeah, no worries," he continued, rolling his eyes. "The doorman always falls asleep. He's about ninety years old and completely useless after seven o'clock. Mmhm. Narcoleptic or something."

"The key is under the mat," he continued. "Yeah, he won't hear you. Yeah, I bet he'll be writing. He listens to music through his headphones while he's writing. What? Yeah, no. Yeah, babe, trust me, he's going to start writing as soon as I leave. I just know it. He's been dying to write lately, it's all he talks about anymore—new characters, new stories, new ideas. Yeah. Yeah, well, who cares if they don't buy it? He's got enough in the bank to feed an army. What? Oh, I don't know, almost a billion. So you'll shoot him in the back of the head while he's at the old typewriter. Yeah. What? Burgle? Yeah, that's a good idea! Take the Matisse in the living room or something. Maybe smash a few things. Break a vase. Make it look like a real burglary, ya know? Then, get out. I'll meet you in Mexico in a few weeks after I get back to collect my inheritance—and of course, after I pretend to mourn a little. Yeah. Yeah, of course I'm getting it all. He didn't have me sign a prenup, and he doesn't have any heirs. What? Yeah, no. No way would that narcissistic bastard leave anything to charity. I'm definitely getting it all. He's really in love! Go figure!"

So that was the plan. Sasha would come shoot Peacewood the next Thursday night when Harvey was off in New York, trying to sell his hideous paintings as an alibi. And he would need one, as he would be the obvious first suspect. A millionaire is slain in his penthouse apartment, and suddenly his new spouse inherits his fortune? The press would string Harvey up by his neck without a decent alibi. So Sasha had to come do it after Harvey had gone. Betrayal with a side of homicide on a sesame seed bun, please. Oh, now that would be delicious!

Harvey was revved up to inherit Peacewood's publishing empire. He would control all the book rights and have a stake in the future of the Somerset series. Now, instead of Johnny, Harvey would be the one hobnobbing with all the Hollywood directors and beautiful actors. He would be the one chatted up at all the galas, and he would be on the covers of the magazines. He would become the most powerful man in the world. This is what he really wanted. To Sasha, this murder was about the money. But Harvey had no intention of spending the rest of his life languishing in Mexico with the Peacewood millions. No, he wanted whatever it was that had given Johnny his power. Harvey envisioned himself standing alone on the red carpet—no Johnny and no Sasha. He no longer played the role of gorgeous arm candy escorting someone else to the ball. He was his own man who had sown the seeds of his own fame. The microphones were at his mouth, the cameras in his face.

Harvey saw himself taking an interview at the premiere of the latest Somerset movie— which he had directed and starred in, of course. It was magical. It was as if there was nothing in the world that Harvey could not do. And there was no one in the world who didn't want to meet him.

"Mr. Marcus," called a famous journalist. She held the microphone to Harvey's mouth as the cameras flashed and the crowd cheered. "Now that you've conquered the world of publishing and have starred in all of the Somerset movies, what is your next big move?"

"Well," Harvey replied, "next, I'm starting a charity to help widowers like me to get back on their feet after their bereavements. It's been a struggle for me these last three years, you know. Life hasn't been the same without my Peacewood." Harvey would then feign tears.

Click-click! The cameras flashed, blinding Mr. Marcus. Har-vey! Har-vey! And a starlet, the one who won the Oscar for best actress back in two thousand and it doesn't matter, came up and touched him on the shoulder. Harvey nodded, acknowledging her because they were good friends. Then, he whispered something salacious in her ear. She smiled and kissed him on the cheek, but as he continued with his interview, she walked away, the train of her gown following behind her like a golden shadow.

"I'm terribly sorry, Mr. Marcus," the journalist replied. "I can't imagine that it's easy. Tell us, have you thought about dating at all since you lost your husband?"

Harvey pretended to get all choked up. "Until now, I haven't. But I think I'm ready to try."

"Good show!" the famous journalist said. Then, taking the mic away from Harvey's face, she leaned in and whispered, "Take down my number and call me, handsome."

The cameras flashed more quickly than Harvey could blink. And that would be the life of the new Mr. Harvey Marcus when he got rid of Johnathan—once and for all.

△ △ △

Later that evening, just after Harvey had left for the airport, Johnathan sat down to Skype with Charlotte about this book that he would finally get to finish while Harvey was away. He figured that if he finished it while Harvey wasn't around, it wouldn't hurt anything. Of course, Harvey would find out once it was published. But by then, he could buy Harvey an I'm-sorry Rolex or a Please-forgive-me Tesla.

"I'm working on it, Char," Johnny said, rolling his eyes at the computer screen. "I've got a great finishing act lined up for the old gal. Somerset is going to find exactly what she's been looking for."

"Well, I'm glad you finally changed your tune, you little shit!" Charlotte laughed, sipping a glass of Pinot Grigio. "The publishing company has been up my ass about getting that last book out of you. I thought I was going to have to look for a new job. And perhaps your coming out was just the extra boost we needed. Now, I've set up about a dozen interviews for you. The whole world wants to know what it was like to have to stay in the closet for the sake of your career. People are applauding you as an LGBT hero. We should capitalize on this while we can. I told you! I knew coming out was the right thing to do!"

Johnny laughed. "Oh, Charlotte—you opportunistic little gremlin! I enjoyed my little break from Somerset. But I missed her, honestly."

"Good!" Charlotte cheered, pushing her glasses up her nose. "Why don't you tell me a little about the new book so I can get rolling on a pitch for it?"

"Well, you see, Somerset meets this ex-soldier named Clifton, and she thinks it's love at first sight because he possesses that Old-World charm she's been longing for."

"Sure," Charlotte said, nodding her head.

"But it turns out this dude has a serious dark side. I'm talking Charles Manson dark. This guy is into some fucked-up shit, Char. Like Nazi-level shit! And once Somerset gives him a taste of her sweet milk, it's done. This guy is obsessed with her. He gets nuttier and nuttier, drifting off into these dazes until one day, just a few months in, he proposes to her out of the blue. But she's like, "Boy, please!" and gets the hell out of there because she knows something isn't quite right. But it's too late by then because Cliff is already addicted and way too crazy to just give her up. In fact, unbeknownst to Somerset, the first sip he took triggered some repressed urge he had to kill. So Cliffy boy goes on a killing spree in Chicago, hunting down female victims who look like Somerset. You know? Black and beautiful. He goes around cutting off their breasts to get at that magic milk. But these women just aren't Somerset. He kills three or four girls. But nobody has that milk. Nobody has that magical milk except my Somerset."

"Oh!" Charlotte said, sipping her wine again. "A serial killer! I love it! Do go on!"

"Yeah!" Johnny said. "So he terrorizes the Northside of Chicago, looking for her. And finally, he discovers that Somerset has fallen for some middle-aged painter. And Clifton is enraged. He follows the guy on foot, all the way home, where he—"

"Oh, don't spoil the ending for me!" Charlotte shouted. "I'm going to read it. I just want a little taste, baby boy!"

"Fine!" Johnathan laughed. "You know I can get a little carried away."

Johnathan was more than just carried away. He was feeling swept away by his own writing, as chirpy and cheerful as he had been when he first kissed Harvey. Truthfully, writing about Somerset made his heart pitter-patter. Writing was Johnathan's connection to the universe. With every word he typed, he experienced a little big bang inside of him. With every chapter, a new star was born and was expanding. And it made him expand. And it made him better. Reuniting with Somerset was like gazing upon the sun without being blinded by its light. Quite frankly, it was better than sex.

"I'm so glad to have you back, Peacewood!" Charlotte told him. "I missed you!"

"I missed you, Char!" he told her.

"Now, if only I can get you to divorce that rancid Marcus bloak," she sighed, shaking her head and sipping her wine.

"Don't start with me about that!" Johnathan warned.

"Oh, darling, he's driftwood," she laughed. "He's a board of beech floating on the waves. You know it. I know it. Even the tabloids know it. It's only a matter of time before this little game of house gets old."

"Hold your tongue, Char!" Johnathan growled, actually showing his teeth a little. He hated when she attacked poor Harvey, who also made his heart pitter-patter.

"Why don't you date that nice rock singer who slipped you his number last week at the concert in Montreal?" Charlotte asked "You remember? The one who looks like Bono and sings like Ray Charles. He was very charming. Out to all his fans too. Just won a slew of Grammies, you know. It might be good for your sales if you're paired with someone who is actually famous—unlike Harvey."

"Charlotte, Harvey and I are married," Johnny replied. "Had you come to the wedding, you'd understand that."

Charlotte laughed. "But you invited that horrible comedienne friend of yours. The one you know I can't stand. What's her name? The skinny one? The one who's always making lewd jokes at the award shows."

"You just don't like her because she talks about your plastic surgery in her act," Johnathan replied. "What did she call you, Char? Fish lips? Speaking of which, you could lay off the collagen."

"Eat dirt, Peacewood!" she replied good-naturedly. "It really isn't her. I don't mind being made fun of. I've always had a good sense of humor. The truth is, I just couldn't stand to lose my baby boy to that dreadful Harvey Marcus. The boy has no soul. There's something about him I just don't like. Mainly that he will do nothing for your image. We need someone as famous as you. There are millions to be made, Peacewood!"

"Well, it doesn't matter if you don't like him," Johnny said. "I love him. He's my husband. We love each other now. So be nice!" he ordered, pointing to her through the computer screen the way a teacher points to an unruly pupil.

"What about that nice baseball player?" Charlotte went on implacably. "The one who was suspended for using steroids. He really liked you. Started blowing my phone up the moment you came out. He would let you handle his bat, I'll bet?"

"You're getting on my nerves, Char!"

"Or that attorney from Los Angeles?" Charlotte laughed. "The one who came to the wedding. The one with the antique car collection. He would take you for a spin in his Model T, I'll bet? I'll bet he would let you honk the horn."

"Okay, Char!" he shouted.

"Marcus is a leech who only wants you for your money. But I would rather you give it to me. Ha!"

"Enough!" he shouted.

"I wanted to see you with someone on your level—someone as rich and strong and talented as you. Marcus has no talent. I've seen those paintings. A kindergartener could do better. And he has the mind of a child."

"Char!" Johnathan shouted. "That's enough!"

But Charlotte could not be stopped: "What's the world to do with some silly..."

"Charlotte!"

". . . no-talent..."

"Charlotte!"

"washed-up..."

"Char-lotte!"

". . . scar-faced ex-model with no plan for his future!" Charlotte erupted into laugher. "He is driftwood, darling! Peacewood and Driftwood."

She clapped her hands triumphantly, applauding her own jokes. Charlotte cared for Johnny as if he were her child. She was always looking out for his best interest (his financial interest, anyway), even if her words were at times harsh and insensitive. That was just her style: unadulterated truth, dressed in Chanel.

"Well, Charlotte," he said quietly, though infuriated. "I guess we're done here. I'd like to get offline and go back to my writing now. I have a lot to cover."

"I won't settle for it," Charlotte went on. "You can't see it because you think you're in love. But that isn't love! He doesn't empower you! A real love would encourage you to do what you were born to do, which is write! He's stifling you so that you can stay down where he is: in the bardo, slumming it with the dead. Good relationships empower us and lead us to expansion. That garbage of a marriage is shrinking you! And I won't have it for my Peacewood! I won't!" she exclaimed. "I will get rid of that driftwood if it's the last thing I do!"

And then, Johnny had had enough. "Good night, Char. And goodbye. We're done. Forever. You're fired."

"Fired?" Charlotte laughed. "Charlotte Swanson has never been fired. I'm the best publishing agent in the country. I am the conduit to the stars."

"And you have fun being that, Charlotte," he told her. "We're done. You're out of my life. You're out of my story." And with that, he closed out the screen, and Charlotte was gone.

"Some people have no sense of humor," Charlotte laughed, closing her laptop and finishing what was left of her wine. But she refused to be done with Johnny. She had known him for over ten years now, and they were more than just an agent and an artist, they were friends. And she knew that that Harvey was trouble. She wasn't about to let her Peacewood fall by the wayside. She would march right over to the penthouse and talk some sense into Johnny.

But first, she would finish the next chapter of this fantastic little book that she had been reading. It was really quite the page turner!

Chapter 14

Harlem, New York—summer of 1926.

Our heroine had found herself once again caught within the bardo of love. This time, her lover was jazz music. Its highs and lows and irreverent improvisations kept her constantly in pursuit of her heart's desire. To Somerset, jazz was the theme to her love.

It is formless and frenetic, yet rhythmic and erotic. And she has taken it upon herself in this era to become a great jazz singer. "Miss S" is what the cool kids called her down at the Renaissance Club on 126th Street. From time to time, Miss S would take the stage—after a few drinks of course—and seduce the boys in the audience with her sultry contralto. And boy, could she scat! Scoo bee doo, bee doo bop—weeee! And when that sax played, the music tugged on her spirit and she would sway across the stage like a flame on a wick. She always wore a red rose behind her ear to set off her black, wavy hair and complement those raging red lips. And boys whistled. And she whistled back. Hell, why not? It was Somerset's time in the summertime.

This particular night, a very special friend of hers had dropped by the club to see her. He walked in, shy and unassuming, while she was up on stage, flickering like the flame that she was. The guy was a young poet by the name of Lang. And Somerset had fallen head over hills for this pretty boy with his dark, wavy hair and his high yellow complexion. And every time he came through, he'd try out some of that sweet poetry on her. And she'd sing him some of that smooth jazz, just knowing that he would be the death of her. But scoo bee doo, bee doo bop—weee!

Lang found a table right near the stage. The waiter brought him his usual as Somerset emerged from the silvery clouds of cigar smoke that had filled the room. She began to sing—to croon like no respectable woman back then would have crooned. And as the soft spotlight illuminated her dark skin, she could feel his eyes sinking into her. He knew that she was being undressed by him. And so she ran her fingers down her chest and around her hips as though her body was a saxophone and she was the player. Lang clutched his chin with intrigue before parting his lips and blowing a puff of air at her. He knew she was a hot flame and wanted to discover whether she would flicker or go out altogether. But it was neither. She just burned brighter the more he blew. That kiss of air he was blowing made Somerset expand until she exploded like a supernova—hitting a high note just as the song climaxed. Doo bop—weee!

Somerset was a flame inside a cloud. And when the music stopped, she got down from the stage and flickered over to sit in Lang's lap. And she took a sip of his whisky. "How was I tonight, daddy?" she asked.

"You were a vision," he replied. "And Miss S..."

"Now, don't you call me that!" Somerset stopped him. "That 'Miss S' nonsense is for boys I don't know. You're my main squeeze!"

"Aw, Somerset!" he replied, bashfully looking down into his drink. "I know you're just a girl, but I was taught to respect a lady."

"A girl?" Somerset threw her head back, laughing. "I'm older than I look. Sometimes I lose count."

"Well," Lang started. "I was just going to say that you sounded amazing. I've never really heard a voice like that before." Then, he took the rose from behind her ear and placed it to his nose. "You make roses smell better than roses."

"What smells better than a rose?" Somerset asked.

"Love," Lang replied.

"You are a smooth talker!" Somerset laughed, flirtingly tapping her finger on his nose. And she could feel that very special feeling that one feels when falling in love—that tug of gravity that implies adventure but foretells danger. Lang was a beautiful man. And she didn't care how much it would hurt. She deserved to have herself a piece.

But Lang hadn't really made much of a move yet, and Somerset didn't understand why. She knew he liked her. She could feel his energy—there was definitely more to this equation than sexual attraction. Horny men came and went, but Lang had been coming here for months now and had never even kissed her on the lips. He just flirted all the time. And she knew that he didn't have a girlfriend because she had asked around.

"Tell me what you like," she said.

"What I like?" he asked honestly, a little confused.

"Yeah," she said. "Tell me what you like."

"I like whiskey and jazz," he grinned, looking past Somerset into the silvery cigar smoke. It reached through the velvety darkness like ghostly fingers massaging the air.

"Don't be a poet, Lang," she replied. "I'm serious. You've been coming in here for months now flirting with me and playing with my old heart."

"Old heart?" he laughed. "What are you? Like twenty?"

"I'm a lot closer to twenty-one than I look," she said. "I'm serious. What gives? A girl gets insecure waiting on a guy to ask her out on a proper date. Now, everyone sees you coming in here making goo-goo eyes at me when I'm singing. People are starting to suspect a scandal. When are you going to take me out for a coffee, Lang? I'm starting to..."

Just then, a dark-skinned fellow emerged from the smoke, sucking on a toothpick. He was tall and fit—with the body of a dancer—and as handsome as he could be. He walked by Lang's table, eyeing him as though they had met a couple of times. And Somerset saw it all.

"...wonder," she finished. "I'm starting to wonder."

And Langston didn't like her wondering. "I have to go, Miss S," he said. Though, really, he was ashamed because he knew the smoke had finally cleared. Swigging down the rest of his beverage, he pushed her off his lap. She was just able to catch the edge of the table to keep from hitting the floor. "I need to go," he said nervously, then walked away.

And suddenly, Somerset felt that feeling she had prayed to never feel again—that nauseating depression that comes from foolishly falling in love with yet another imposter. If there was one thing Somerset had learned over the last four hundred years, it was that the world was full of imposters. And yet again, she had been a fool. And she really liked this one too. Damn it! She could remember the exact moment she had fallen for him. It was on a Thursday night. They sat at the bar joking about British literature and how silly and romantic it was, but how they both still wanted that Brontë-sister kind of love anyway. Somerset wanted to be a society lady who fell in love with the dirty farmhand—maybe a guy like Heathcliff from *Wuthering Heights*. And Langston joked that he could be that farmhand type for her, and they would become their own story. He would be her Heathcliff. And, at the exact moment, she knew that she had found the one she had waited to die for.

But that was all false. Her instincts had betrayed her again. And now here she was all alone and feeling foolish. This heartbreak was palpable; it would probably take her a century to recover. Or maybe she would never recover. Maybe she could never really trust her instincts again. Maybe the gut is nothing more than a silly inner child with nothing better to do than dream of British literature while the world falls around her. Somerset bolted out the back into a courtyard. It was here that she often liked to pray, but this night, she came to cry and to plead.

She fell onto her knees, kneeling in the grass. The crickets were chirping and the city was buzzing and no one could see her here. The courtyard was enclosed by the backsides of four adjacent buildings. So while the jazz was teeming, this sanctuary was relatively peaceful.

"Please, God," she said. "No more. I don't want to do this anymore. I don't want to! End this curse and just let me die!" And the tears were streaming down her face. "I'll give anything not to live another year. I made a mistake. Please."

Her tears molded themselves into black butterflies and green lightning bugs, and they fluttered and flickered all around her until they had pressed together to make the body of a female spirit. And the female spirit kneeled next to Somerset in the grass and stroked her cheek. Her touch was like that of water, and her hair was like the leaves of a willow. This was Ana, the mother spirit.

"Don't cry, my sweet baby," Ana spoke peacefully, pressing her head to Somerset's.

"I was a fool to have wished this upon myself," Somerset cried. "Why did you let me do this?"

"It was not my place to tell you otherwise, baby girl," Ana replied. "Your heart was enraged when you were dying. You wanted so badly to find true love that nothing could have killed you."

"You let that healer put his black magic on me," Somerset said, crying.

"It wasn't his magic that preserved you, child," Ana said. "It was your magic. Your passion has been your magical force all this time. Your heart simply refuses to stop beating until it finds exactly what it's looking for."

"But I don't want it anymore," Somerset cried. "I want to be at peace—with you."

"But don't you see, child?" Ana started. "You will never be ready for the next realm until you find your peace in this one. It is your purpose in this life to create your own peace, to create your own sanctuary. The butterfly does not forget the tears she cried as a caterpillar. If you cross over now, you will bring all your anguish into the next life, and your wings would be sullied and soaked in tears. And that would be tragic."

"But I'm tired," Somerset cried. "I'm so tired of looking and not finding. I've been alive hundreds of years. I don't think it's out there."

Ana hushed her. And the crickets hushed, and the city hushed. And Ana kissed Somerset's head. "Remember your purpose, baby girl. Remember why you are here."

"But—"

"Your purpose," Ana spoke peacefully. "Remember why you are here, and you can have anything that you want. Your purpose is your power, girl."

And then, Ana began to fade. But her voice still rang out. "Your purpose is your power." And she was gone. And Somerset was alone in the world again—but never really alone.

"Please come back!" Somerset pleaded. "Please don't leave me in this world all alone." But Ana was gone. She had come to Somerset many, many times in the past—always to comfort her through the agony of a broken heart, to be her spirit mother in times of need. But this time would be the last. The time had come for Somerset to learn her lessons on her own. And so Ana would never appear to her again.

△ △ △

"No, I don't wish to accept his call," Charlotte told the operator. She had finished reading her favorite novel and was now going out for a glass of wine. That's when she got the call from the federal penitentiary.

It was her son. Her flesh and blood. And the only child of hers that she had not aborted. Born when Charlotte was only seventeen, Charlie was a wild love child conceived with God knows whose sperm. Charlotte's sister raised the boy while Charlotte was off at NYU studying to be a writer; she wasn't going to put her career on hold for some bastard, even if that bastard was her own child. So she left him. She would see him from time to time at Christmas, when she would bring him little trinkets from New York: a snow globe one year, a paperweight the next. He never knew what to do with them, the poor thing, but he cherished them nonetheless. However, he always wondered why his Aunt Charlotte from NYC was always so aloof. She never held him or played with him. She was nicer to the neighbors' kids than she was to him. It wasn't until he was sixteen that he found his birth certificate while rummaging in the attic looking for things to steal. And there it was with Charlotte listed as his mother.

He confronted Charlotte's sister immediately. He demanded to know the meaning of it. So she told him everything—about how Charlotte was his biological mother but how she had raised him as her own because she had always wanted a child, despite her fibroids. She told him how Charlotte was too selfish for children and how Charlotte had aborted all his little brothers and sisters. She told Charlie that she was his real mother, not Charlotte—that she was the one who cared for him, even if she couldn't give him the milk from her own breast. She had done her best, and it shouldn't matter who his biological mother was.

But Charlie wasn't having it. He was furious. His real mother was a rich publishing agent while he and his aunt struggled to keep the lights on in their shotgun house in Arkansas. He had joined a street gang, selling drugs to make ends meet. And his life was a piece of shit right now because his real mother wasn't doing anything to help him.

He was twenty-five now, and doing hard time for armed robbery. What made him think he could get away with that? Maybe he didn't care whether he got away. Maybe he wanted to be caught. Maybe the street life was too much hard work. Pushing heroin one night and robbing schoolkids the next. Maybe he just wanted stability. He was getting it in the penitentiary, that's for sure. He would call Charlotte from time to time. Most of the time, he would call his aunt, but sometimes he'd call his mother, just to see if the old bitch would actually answer. But she never did. The call would always be rejected. Charlotte didn't want a child. It was hard enough keeping tabs on Johnathan Peacewood. What good did she have for some delinquent? And what could he possibly want? Money? But Charlotte wasn't going to hear of it. So she declined the call, and slipped her cell phone down into her purse.

It was a quiet night. Not a lot of people on the streets. And the clack of her heels against the pavement echoed ominously as she walked toward the train station, the wind whistling a subtle but menacing tune. The whole thing had an ungodly feel, as though the shadows were filled with spirits. "This night is a serial killer's dream," Charlotte laughed. "Jack the Ripper, where are you?"

"Excuse me, Miss," a male voice called.

Charlotte turned to find a bald-headed stranger holding his wounded leg. He looked very young and was handsome enough. But he was filthy—probably a homeless vet who had run out of medication.

"Where is the nearest hospital, Miss?" he asked, coddling his wound and grimacing terribly as he limped toward her. The poor thing looked young enough to be her own son. But what did that matter to Charlotte? She was on her way to wine night. And wasn't there a serial killer on the loose?

"Could you just give me some change so I can get on the train, Miss?" the bald-headed stranger begged. "If not, I'll bleed out."

"I'm sorry," Charlotte told him, "but I don't carry... Hey! Unhand me!"

"Shut up!" he hissed, covering her face with a chloroform-dowsed napkin. She struggled and kicked and scratched. But of course, that did no good for her. Poor Charlotte.

Somerset brought the creepy little boy back to her hotel, where she had checked in—where she had checked in for some reason. She remembered having an apartment, but couldn't find it. And she wasn't in possession of any key. So maybe there was no door. No door? But didn't she have neighbors or something? Somerset remembered something about old neighbors who would watch her from across the alley. She saw patches of memories that didn't seem real.

So she brought the little creep back. He had told her his name was Junior. What kind of a name was that? It wasn't a name, was it? Junior was what people called a kid when he was named after his dad. "So who's your father?" Somerset asked him, although she already knew.

"The same as yours," Junior said.

But Somerset's father had been dead for five hundred years. He was killed in the tribal wars, along with her brothers and her uncles. The little creep was playing games.

"Look, I want to get you home, but you have to tell me where home is," she said.

"You know where home is," he told her. And she absolutely did know.

This poor child needed a bath and a decent meal. Then she could take him to the police station or something. They would know what to do, wouldn't they? Maybe the police could help them sort this out –although Somerset knew they could not.

Junior needed to be cleaned up. The child hadn't bathed in what appeared—and smelled—to be weeks. His little red hoodie was covered in mud, and he had crust all along the side of his little brown face.

"Your milk was good," he told her, flopping down on the bed with the television remote in his hand. He turned on the set, searching for cartoons or sports or whatever kids his age watched these days. He looked to be about twelve.

"Go in the bathroom and take a shower," she told him. "I'll go out and get you some clean clothes, and we'll get you something to eat."

"I only wear these clothes," said Junior, smiling at Somerset's breasts and licking his chops.

"But they're dirty," said Somerset. "You need new ones."

"No, I'll wear these ones. You can't just throw away good clothes," he said. "Let the rain wash them."

"Okay," Somerset sighed. "Well, we should eat. What do you like?"

"I want more milk," Junior said, licking his lips and flipping the remote around from hand to hand.

"No!" she shouted. "That's perverse. I did that to save you, to save us. But you need to go back."

"Where is back?" he asked impishly.

Rummaging through the disconnected patches of memory, Somerset searched her thoughts to recall where and what back was. Where was back? Where was front? Weren't they exactly where they needed to be? No address had ever been written.

"This isn't funny!" Somerset screamed. But wasn't it funny? Wasn't it darn hilarious how he had gotten here the same way she did? It was that Johnathan Peacewood. He had brought her into this world. Well, first he had brought her into the literary world as a character. She could always hear him, telling her everything that would happen right before it happened as he guided her through the centuries. She could always hear his voice. And that voice was a comfort because it meant she always had some sense of direction—some sense of purpose. But that voice had stopped. And she found herself wandering, flummoxed. She was in a new world now, one where there was no voice and no purpose. And now here was this little creep who belonged to Johnathan. She had to get him back to Mr. Peacewood so that this would all make sense again—so that the voice would return, and so that she would once more have a purpose.

"We've got to get you back to Peacewood," she said.

"He won't take me," Junior replied.

"We'll make him take you," she told him.

"He doesn't want me anymore," Junior said, frustrated. "He's got that Harvey now."

"We'll see about that," Somerset told him. "Now get out of those clothes and get in the shower. I'll get you some food."

"I'll shower after you give me some more of that milk," the little creep replied, licking his lips again.

She yanked him up and pulled the hoodie off his body. He had on no undershirt, and she could see the little creep's freakishly smooth belly. He had no navel—nothing there at all. That little hole or nub that most of us have on our bellies? That navel? Junior didn't have one.

"Get in the bathroom now before I whip your butt," Somerset said, slapping the boy across his shoulder. "I said get!"

And the boy dropped the remote and scampered into the bathroom, grumbling, "Okay! Okay!"

Somerset followed him in, pulling the curtain and turning on the shower. She unwrapped a package of the mint-green hotel soap and handed it to him. "Now, you make sure you rub all that mess off of you!" she ordered. "You smell like you don't have a home."

"I don't have a home!" he snapped. "That Harvey took it from me."

"We'll see about that," she said. "Now, I'll go get us some Thai or whatever. You get cleaned up, and we'll figure all this out."

"I don't like Thai," the boy grumbled, tapping at the running water, feeling to see if it was warm enough. Steam started to fill the room, making things cloudier than they already were. Then he stepped out of his jeans and kicked off his sneakers.

"Well, what do you want?" Somerset asked, hoping he wouldn't say what he was about to say.

"Tit!" he laughed. "I want titty! Titty, titty, titty!"

"Absolutely not!" she snapped, slapping him on the shoulder again and trying to push him into the shower.

"I need it!" the boy said, grabbing rapaciously at Somerset's breasts. But she just slapped his hand away. "I need it, or I'll die. And if I die, you die!" he reminded her.

To Somerset, it all made sense. And she knew that she would have to feed him as he had requested. You see, Junior was Johnathan Peacewood's inner child. He was the spirit that had kept Johnathan writing, dreaming, and creating all these years. But Johnny had stopped nurturing that child, and without proper nourishment, Junior would die. And if he died, then so would all of Johnathan's creations. So Somerset knew that it was up to her to keep him alive until she could get the little creep back to Johnny. In the meantime, he would have to have that milk—that addictive milk that had driven men mad, that milk that had caused Van Gogh to cut off his ear, that milk that had caused the pilot of the Hindenburg to ignore the heat sensors. So Somerset pulled out her nipple and let the little creep drink. Then she went for pizza.

And Junior let the warm water pour over his filthy, brown skin. And it cleaned away all the lies—all the pretense—so that when he finally confronted Johnny, there would be nothing left but the absolution of their unity. He would reunite with Johnathan and bring him back to his purpose. We dream as children. And those dreams are messages from the divine. Those childhood dreams are our roadmaps into destiny. It is the inner child in all of us that shows us the way into a proper and healthy adulthood. But when we neglect those children, our lives become our nightmares, and our spirits wither. Johnathan had neglected his inner child to pursue the love that he felt had been missing— he felt that, without romantic love, he was somehow insufficient. And so he abandoned the route drawn out for him by his inner child, and he perused a new passion. But this new passion—this romantic love—had distracted him from his purpose, which was to write. Therefore, his inner child began to starve, and he began to languish. Just like driftwood.

Junior stepped out of the shower, clean and refreshed. The milk gave him confidence to go and jump back inside Johnny and make him write those books. Truth be told, he missed him. He missed whispering wonderful, inspirational stories into Johnathan's ear. Junior was already thinking of the next story he would have Johnathan write. It would be about his neighbor Sargent—the blind one who had been painting his psychic visions.

But a knock at the door yanked him from his thoughts. Why would Somerset knock? Had she forgotten her key?

"Room service," a voice called from the other side.

Somerset must have gone down to the front desk to request food. Junior didn't want pizza, and he certainly hoped it wasn't Thai. Maybe she had ordered fried chicken and macaroni. Truthfully, all Junior wanted was more of Somerset's milk.

"One sec!" he yelled, drying off and slipping on his dirty jeans and hoodie. He waddled over to the door. "Okay! Coming!"

But when Junior opened the door, room service was not there. It was Clifton. Junior knew him better than anyone else, of course. He knew that Cliff was the Northside Butcher. He knew he had been killing all those women because they reminded him of Somerset. And he suspected that he was here to kill her now.

"You're not what I came here for," Cliff said, "but you'll definitely do!"

Chapter 15

Somerset teared up as she read page six of the morning paper. Johnathan had married Harvey Marcus. And since she had lost Junior, she feared that the worst was yet to come. She had gotten back to the hotel room with a cheese pizza, but the little creep was gone. And she knew that Clifton had taken him. On the bed, there was a note:

Dear Somerset,

> *I still love you with all of my heart and soul and miss you. I have searched all of Chicago to find another like you, but it seems that you are irreplaceable. I accept that you do not love me and that I will never have you. But I cannot accept that anyone else will. So I plan to do away with us both by killing Peacewood. When he goes, I go. You, of course, being his finest creation, will cease to exist as well. Therefore, I will cut his throat and feel myself fade into nothingness as the blood drains from his body. You will soon fade away too. And the world will finally be rid of you and your lies. For it is not love that you desire. You want merely to live forever, relishing your immortality as you torment we mortal men. But I will not allow it, my dear. Therefore, I will kill Johnathan Peacewood to avenge my broken heart.*

Your Darling Sociopath,
Clifton
P.S. I've got the little creep too.

And so Somerset knew she had to warn Johnathan before it was too late. Her plan was to sneak into the penthouse and drag him back to reality, even if he put up a fight, but she needed to get past the old doorman downstairs first. So she got herself a maid's uniform from the hotel's laundry room and pretend she was from a cleaning service.

"I'm here to clean for Mr. Pots," she said, looking at the little old man. His eyes were barely open, and his chin rested upon his fist.

"What's this world coming to?" the doorman asked, pressing the buzzer to let her on the elevator while staring at her bald head. "Men are dressing as maids now?"

It did not surprise him that Johnny had a transgender maid—or maybe this was just a prostitute in costume. The little old man had let all kinds of characters upstairs to see Johnny. But he watched in amazement as her apple-shaped behind waddled onto the elevator. And he smirked a little with lustful delight.

"Thank you kindly," Somerset said.

"Fags!" the old man said, watching the elevator door close. "Hate em!"

"Old people are so weird," she laughed. "Good thing I'll never be old." And the elevator took her up to meet her maker.

When Somerset arrived upstairs, the hallway was quiet—long and quiet. Somerset had always wondered what the writer Johnathan Peacewood actually looked like. She had heard about him on campus as his novels were all the rage with the undergraduate ladies. A little Oscar Wilde and a touch of Stephen King, but completely romantic. That's what they said about him. And it never occurred to them that all those books were about her. They were about her, weren't they? She remembered working toward a PhD at the University of Chicago. And she remembered studying race. But where did she go to undergrad? Had she gone to undergrad? Somerset couldn't remember her alma mater. Or her undergraduate major. Minor? No minor had ever been written.

She had so many questions for Mr. Johnathan Peacewood, but first she had to tell him about the little creep named Junior and warn him that Clifton was coming. And she had to cover the blank space with words. But as Somerset began the march down the long corridor toward the Peacewood penthouse, she saw someone who would quickly become a new friend. He stepped out into the hallway, smiling gingerly. And she smiled back. And suddenly Somerset could feel her spirit expanding in all directions. And as she looked upon this man's face, peace washing over her, she forgot why she had come here in the first place.

△ △ △

The Northside Butcher strikes again! Publishing Agent Charlotte Swanson is the latest victim in a string of murders on Chicago's Northside. Officials say her body was found mutilated in the same manner as the killer's three other victims: Cheyenne Cost, Mary Ann Bell, and Marilyn Gouche. Swanson's remains were found early this morning dumped in the Lincoln Park arboretum. The mayor has issued a warning to all women to be watchful of their surroundings as the CPD has yet to name a suspect. Swanson was 59 and leaves one son, Charles. Swanson was best known for discovering famed novelist Johnathan Peacewood, author of *Somerset Eternal* and its many successful sequels.

"Jesus!" Johnny shouted, dropping the paper on the kitchen table. Then, he picked up the phone, his fingers trembling. "Darling, have you heard? It's Charlotte, Harvey." He dragged himself over to the sofa, where he collapsed onto his back, feeling sick. "She's dead! Yes, dead! No, Harvey, not during cosmetic surgery. She was murdered! Yes, murdered! The police are calling the killer the Northside Butcher! They've given him a name, like Jack the Ripper and the Zodiac Killer. Nobody knows who he is!"

Harvey was rambling on about something, but Johnny could barely process the words. He just kept seeing poor Charlotte ripped to pieces by that monster.

"What?" Johnny asked. "No. No, I'm not going anywhere today. I don't want to be out in that world. What?" He buried his face in the pillow. "Yeah, I'm gonna stay in. Yeah, babe. I promise I'll be safe. What? Yeah. Yeah. Just try to get back as soon as you can, please. I love you too. Be safe."

Johnny was an emotional wreck. Charlotte had been a sister to him—no, a mother. She was the only one who understood him, who knew his secrets, and now she was gone. A tight noose of anger and downheartedness wrapped around his neck until he could barely breathe. What could he do now? She was gone. And what's worst is that he had wished her out of his life, just because she encouraged him to do what he was born to do: write. She had always encouraged him to do his best. And how did he thank her? By telling her to get lost and drop dead. How could he ever forgive himself? How could he ever look himself in the mirror again?

Johnathan thought of Charlotte—her voice, her style, her sarcasm. What a gal! He recalled her showing up to the New York Literary Gala at the Met, wearing that sable coat and daring the PETA protesters to throw red paint at her. "Go on, cowboy! Throw the paint. If one drop touches my good fur, I'll ground you into sausage and feed you to my poodle. Oh, relax. The varmint didn't die in vain. This coat fits like a dream, darling!" And she once came to a Hollywood house party—hosted by a famous acting couple who shall not be named—and the wife asked Charlotte to put out her cigarette while in the house because she didn't want their son to get asthma. So what did Charlotte do? She handed her lit cigarette to the little tyke and told him: "Go and find an ashtray for your Auntie Charlotte, darling, since your parents want to be a killjoy. Feel free to take a few puffs along the way. Honestly, doesn't anyone in Hollywood have any personality anymore?" That was his Char. That was Johnathan's Charlotte Swanson. The two of them were quite an act. But now the show was over.

He wondered what she would be doing if she were here now, watching him languish on the couch. "Get up!" she'd say. "Get up, you lascivious lizard! Quit being a driftwood! Go over there and write my book." And that was it! That was his solace! That was his source of peace. Johnathan Peacewood only had peace when he was writing. Nothing else calmed his spirit and made him happier than writing. Charlotte had been telling him that all along. He was a goddamned writer, and when he did anything else, he was languishing. And now, with Charlotte gone, he needed peace more than anything else.

He rushed over to his typing table, where he had been slaving away at the manuscript for his next novel. And it was getting good. He picked up a page, and he began to read.

$$\triangle \, \triangle \, \triangle$$

Charlotte awakened in a dimly lit cellar. Her hands were tied to a beam on the ceiling so that she looked like Jesus at his crucifixion. Her breasts were hanging naked, as the assailant had ripped her blouse from her body—the expensive blouse from Yves St. Laurent. How dare he? That was good silk!

Along the walls were several jars, stuffed with what appeared to be human appendages preserved in formaldehyde. There were nipples on them. Breasts! They were human breasts! Cut from bodies. And in some jars, there were little pear-shaped organs, purple and smooth. Stomachs? No. Livers? Nah. A uterus—one, two, three of them.

Over on the other side of the room, there was a bed with a chain-link fence as the footboard. And a little boy—no older than twelve—was chained to it. But he was sitting up comfortably and didn't seem bothered by the confinement. He was shirtless, and on the ground next to him was a red hoodie. The little boy starting staring at Charlotte's breasts as though they were two prize hams. He licked his lips with an ominous audacity.

"You're going to die," the boy said. "He's going to come and rip you apart."

"No!" Charlotte cried. "What is this place?"

"It's Hell for bad girls," the child said.

"Who are you?" she asked.

"Junior. Just call me Junior."

"Why am I here?" she asked.

"Peacewood wants you to die," the child said. "What'd you do to him?"

"Help!" Charlotte shouted. "Help!"

But it was no use. Clifton emerged from the shroud of shadows, his facial hair scruffy even though his head was shaved completely smooth. He moved toward her slowly, holding a machete at his side, until he was so close to her face that his nose nearly touched hers.

"I've missed you, Somerset," he said, kissing Charlotte on the lips. "Mm. You taste different."

"Please don't hurt me," Charlotte pleaded. "You can have whatever you want. Just please don't do to me what you did to the other girls."

"It's not too late. We can still be together, Somerset. I miss you, babe. Have you missed me?"

Charlotte looked over at the little boy, who was still grinning at her breasts. She could feel the cold metal of the machete blade against her side as Clifton lifted his hand to caress her nude torso. She grimaced as he kissed her neck and squeezed her breasts.

"Have you missed me, baby?" he asked, nibbling at her earlobe.

"Yes! Yes, darling!" Charlotte cried. "I've missed you quite a bit!"

Junior was laughing hysterically now. "It won't work," he told her. "He's still going to kill you."

"Shut up!" Cliff shouted at him. "I'll deal with you in a minute."

"I've missed you so much. Let's be together, my love," Charlotte said.

Clifton pulled back from her, smiling. "I've waited so long to hear you say that, Somerset. You changed your mind? And marrying me? Can we, Somerset?"

"Yes, I'll marry you!" Charlotte shouted. "Let's do it now!"

"It won't work," Junior told her. "You'll see why."

"Yes, let's get married, Somerset," Clifton said. "Right after you give me some more of that sweet milk."

"Milk?" Charlotte asked.

"I told you it wouldn't work," Junior said. "It has to be her."

Clifton leaned back in, putting his mouth to Charlotte's nipple. And she grimaced again as he began to suck. "Ouch!" she shouted when he bit her, trying to get the milk out. He sucked and sucked and sucked. But nothing ever came. Finally, he gave up, pulling away deflated and disappointed.

"You tricked me," he groaned. "You tricked me! You pretended to be my Somerset. You pretended!"

"No!" Charlotte shouted.

"You're a liar!" he screamed.

"No!"

"I hate liars! You know what we do to dirty girls who lie and abort their babies?"

"No! Please!"

"He's going to kill you now," Junior said, still smiling.

"What do we to mothers who erase their children?" Clifton asked. "Who pretend that their sons don't exist? Who tell lies about who they are? Who abandon their little boys and their boyfriends and their husbands?" He was so enraged that veins were bulging in his forehead, his eyes as cold as the bluest ice. "Do you know what we do with mothers who abandon their sons?"

"I know!" Junior said, giggling.

"Please don't do this," Charlotte pleaded.

"I know!" Junior said, cheerfully dangling his feet off the side of the mattress. "We erase them!"

"We erase them!" Clifton shouted.

Then, he grabbed her left breast and sliced it off with the machete, blood spraying his face. Charlotte's screams were louder now, and they echoed from the walls. Junior watched on with feverish delight as Cliff proceeded to rip her to shreds. Junior liked Charlotte well enough, but he didn't like it when mothers mistreated their sons. After all, he was a child, abandoned by Johnny. And it was not a good feeling. So maybe Charlotte had this coming.

When Johnathan abandoned his post as writer—as father to these characters—they continued to exist, emerging from the pages of the book to roam the world like bastard children with bad upbringings. Johnathan had used his powers to bring characters to life, but had abandoned them to the world. Junior understood all of this because he understood Johnny. But he could not have been prepared for what was coming next.

After Cliff has finished slashing poor Charlotte to bits, he placed her breasts and her uterus in jars and put them up on the shelf with the others. But then, he decided he needed more blood. So he came over to the bed, wielding the machete. "I think we need to call our daddy," Cliff said.

"Get on!" Junior told him, but it was no use.

"This'll only take a minute," Cliff said, laughing. Then he knocked the boy over the head with the handle of the machete so that he was too weak to fight. "Let's send him a message, shall we?" Clifton kneeled down and, with the very tip of the blade, carved the letters W-R-I-T-E into the boy's navel-less belly.

△ △ △

Johnathan was sitting on the sofa, editing his manuscript, when he felt a sharp pain in his abdomen, like a knife cutting through his skin over and over again. At first, he thought that something must have bit him. A millipede? A spider? Brown recluse spiders were beginning to be a problem in his building, and the little buggers liked to come out and play now that it was spring.

He ran to the bathroom and lifted his shirt. "Dear God!" he shrieked, looking into the mirror. There, carved in his flesh, were the letters W–R–I–T–E in bright red. And it was then that Mr. Johnathan Peacewood remembered that he really was the most powerful man in the world.

Chapter 16

"Something tells me you're not really a maid," Sargent said to Somerset as she stood before him in the hallway. "I don't see you as a maid. I see you as a princess or songstress. Or even an assassin. But you ain't no maid. So tell me what it is you're doing here."

Somerset knew she was caught. Sargent was blind but could see everything clearly from behind the Wayfarers that he wore over his eyes. Certainly, he had read her biography, *Somerset Eternal.* Or perhaps he was a fan of one of the sequels. Everyone knew her story. But no one knew she was here. No one knew that she had emerged from the pages of the novels and had crossed into to this other realm. No one would believe that a literary character had come to life in the flesh. But somehow, Sargent could see this all.

"I know you're not supposed to be here, Somerset," he said.

"I was just coming to talk to Mr. Po—Peacewood," she told him. "I didn't mean to intrude. I can go. I'm sorry. But . . . how is that you know my name?"

"I can almost hear your heartbeat," he said. "I can almost see your face. I listen to Peacewood's novels on audio sometimes. And I feel like I've known you my entire life. I don't need good eyes to know you're not supposed to be here."

"I can go. I don't want any trouble. You won't call the police, will you?"

"No, that isn't what I mean," he said, smiling. "Come in, girl. Have some tea."

"Oh, but I came to see Mr. Peacewood and . . ."

"Let him go on that journey by himself. I think he's coming to his senses," Sargent said. "Come on in. Have some tea and talk to old Simon Sargent."

Somerset didn't even know this man. But something about his smile was very reassuring, almost peaceful. Sargent had no darkness within him. She had always been able to sense darkness in people; it was this innate sensibility that had made her an integral part of the Underground Railroad in the 1800s when she helped over fifty slaves escape to the North. In 1852, while planning to help some slaves escape from a Mississippi plantation, Somerset's intuition told her to warn one slave woman to leave her husband behind. Somerset had a dark feeling about the man.

"Don't sacrifice your freedom for that man, girl," Somerset told her. "His spirit is as dark as a crow's feathers."

But the woman refused, telling her that she was pregnant and could never raise the baby on her own in the North.

"I won't help him escape," Somerset said. "He's trouble. If you can't leave him, then get to the North without me."

So Somerset left them both behind. But she heard that the woman, her husband, and eleven other slaves attempted an escape later that year. Unfortunately, the husband was a spy for the slave owner, and he snitched. The slaves had made it all the way to the woods north of the plantation when the dogs came after them. And when the poor woman heard their barks, she ran. She couldn't bear to be caught—to be tied up and whipped in front of everyone—so she just kept going. Eventually, she heard her husband's voice pointing her out to the slave catchers. She could see his index finger piercing the night fog, and it was pointed right at her heart. And as the dogs raced toward her, she ran again. But it was dark, and she was deep in the woods of Mississippi. She tripped on a tree branch and busted her skull. And as her brains oozed out onto the unholy soil, Somerset appeared to her in a haze of purple light.

"Never sacrifice your freedom for the sake of a man, girl," Somerset said. "Never sacrifice your freedom for the sake of anyone."

And then the woman died. But the point is that Somerset knew all along how the husband was trouble. She could sense the cowardice vibrating off him whenever he stood near to her, could smell the perfidy in his sweat. The potential for betrayal smelled like spoiled meat. So Somerset always listened to that sense of hers. It was likely that sense that had kept her from falling too deeply for any man all these centuries—even Clifton.

But meeting Sargent felt completely different. His aura, with its soft purple glow, was peaceful. It was welcoming, and she went into his apartment without apprehension or struggle. It just was. The energy just flowed. Yes, it just was.

"Have a seat anywhere you'd like," he said.

Somerset was awed by the space. There were beautiful abstract paintings all over the walls, and the bookshelves were lined with artifacts from Egypt, Cambodia, Peru, and Romania. Somerset walked over to what appeared to be a purple, translucent stone. It sparkled like a ray of sun. It shimmered as brightly as a star in the night sky.

"Amethyst?" she asked, being very careful not to touch.

"That is stone from outer space," Sargent said. "It wasn't formed on Earth. It's a piece of meteorite."

"What do you mean by that?"

"I mean it's a gemstone that was formed deep in the heart of the universe," he replied.

"You're pulling my leg," Somerset said. And after staring blankly at him for a moment, she erupted into laughter. "I don't dabble in science fiction. I came here from the romance aisle. But thanks for the story. But how about that tea now, Mister?"

"Please. Call me Simon. And take a seat!"

So Somerset went over to the sofa. Behind it was Sargent's largest canvas painting. It was about twenty feet high and took up an entire wall. At first, all she was able to see were blobs of blue and red, hurling themselves toward one another.

"What do you call it?" She asked.

"It's called *Bridge the Distance*."

"And what does it represent to you?"

"Look at it. But don't look with your eyes. Look with your spirit. Feel what it is that's being said."

And Somerset looked upon the painting, letting her senses guide her through the blobs of red and blue, which soon became more diverse shades of purple and green. And there was yellow. And then there was some orange. As she let go, the blobs became more distinct shapes. They were triangles and squares, and a rhombus too. And there was depth, almost as though the painting had become something she could reach right through. A scene began to form. Somerset found herself up on hill, standing amidst lilies and lilacs as the wind rubbed its hands along her bald head. And Sargent was standing next to her. He held her hand and kissed her cheek. And she was at peace. And she could let go. But, most importantly, she was at peace.

"The painting is all about love," he said. "All about finding yourself in someone else and realizing that you are connected to all of humanity. And the distance that we often feel between ourselves and others is nothing more than an illusion.

Because, you see, there is no real distance. We are all units within one whole. And in order to save humanity, we must bridge the distance"

Then, Sargent waved his hand. And when he did, a flash of purple light shot from his fingers. And suddenly, the record player across the room was on. It played "It Had to Be You," sung by none other than Frank Sinatra. Sargent then extended his hand to Somerset. She stood and took it. And the two began to dance.

"The last time I danced to this song it was with a movie actor by the name of . . ."

But Sargent put his finger over her lip to hush her. The past didn't matter anymore; it was all about the present. He waved his hand again, and a long stream of purple light spiraled around them like a brilliant, electrified eel. And this energy lifted them into the air so that they were floating over the coffee table, just waltzing through midair. Somerset had floated before, but her senses told her that, this time, there was no chance she would fall. Sargent flicked his hand at *Bridge the Distance* over on the wall. And once more, a slither of purple light shot from his fingers and splashed right onto the canvas. And suddenly, they were transported back to that hilltop, where the lilies and the lilacs loved them.

"How do you do what you do?" she asked.

"I just do. It just comes. I don't fight it. I don't attempt to control it. I just let the energy flow through me as it pleases. And when I feel myself desiring of anything, my desires manifest."

"A wizard!" Somerset exclaimed, laughing a bit.

"No, I'm just a human being who understands the limitless power within me."

"Interesting."

"I'm going to paint your picture," he said. "I want to paint you as you really are."

And as they floated through the air, falling madly in love with one another, he caressed her bald head, and it was good. Then, he gave her a kiss, and it was good. He turned her upside down so that they could dance with their feet upon the ceiling, and it was good. Sargent shot a flash of purple light at the curtains, making them close so that it was dark. And from the darkness, love emerged.

Chapter 17

"What are you getting at now, Sargent?" Johnny asked, sipping a glass of merlot while resting in his living room. He had his legs propped up on the coffee table, and he was fiddling anxiously with a newspaper. Like the skies just before a tornado, Johnathan's eyes were a morbid pink. He had been crying, and he still had a bit of powdered cocaine on his nostril. The remnant of his mourning for Charlotte. Sargent stood over him, smoking a joint.

"I saw it," Sargent said. "Danger is coming for you, little man. It's coming for you tonight. I saw a girl—a very pretty girl—shoot you in this very apartment. She was a little skinny for my taste, but pretty, nonetheless. She shot you in the back of your head while you were sitting at your typewriter. And I think Harvey has something to do with it. I saw it all in a vision, Peacewood."

"I'm sure it was just a nightmare," Johnny said, sullenly flipping through his newspaper. "Why don't you come have a seat? Pour yourself a glass of wine."

"Now look, Peacewood!" Sargent said, more stern and paternal now. "You know something ain't right around here. Your agent just died, and my visions never fail me. If I see something coming, then something is sure enough coming."

"Okay," Johnny said, his hand jittering in the air as he acquiesced. "I'll make sure the door is locked. But nobody ever comes up here. And we have a doorman."

"That old fart couldn't stop a cat from crawling in, let alone a killer."

"Well, would you like me to sleep over at your place then?" Johnny asked. "Would that make you feel better?"

"No!" Sargent snapped—but it wasn't an unfriendly snap, just a cautious one. "No, I have a guest over."

"Well, well, well," Johnny sighed, throwing the paper down on the coffee table and hiking up his sleeves. He wiped the last bit of coke from his nose and sat up. "All that fame is finally getting you some action. Welcome to the dark side, brother. First come the women. Then, you'll get all these endorsements and free products. The next thing you know, you're on every front row at Fashion Week, and you're getting caviar at Buckingham Palace every time you're in London. Seriously, I was there for a few days promoting a book. Suddenly, I get a call on the phone. It was the queen herself wanting me to come for tea. Apparently, she's obsessed with Somerset."

"Well, who wouldn't be?" Sargent interposed.

"But not even all the fame in the world is worth this life, Sargent," Johnny added, slow and solemn. "So who's the lucky girl? Do I get to meet her, or is she just a fling? I don't judge."

"I'd rather not get into it, Peacewood," Sargent said. "Just promise me you'll be careful tonight. I have a really bad feeling."

"Are you in love with her?"

"Look, Peacewood," Sargent went on. "I'm telling you, I had a vision of a young girl with short blond hair in your apartment. She was so thin she looked like a model. But she came in the door very quietly, and she shot you while you were working on your manuscript. And when you fell to the floor, she called someone. The dream was hazy, but it sounded like a male voice. I think it was Harvey. Johnny, that Harvey is no good. I wouldn't be surprised if he tried to have you killed so he could take all your money."

"A thin girl with short blond hair, you say?" Johnny asked. "You said she looked like a model?"

"Yeah!" Sargent replied. "And my visions are always accurate. I got the gift, remember?"

"Okay, well, I'll make sure I lock up tight when you leave," Johnny replied. "But you have fun with your lady friend. I'm really happy for you. What's her name, anyway?"

"I'd rather not say, Peacewood."

"Okay then," Johnny said, smirking and retrieving his paper from the coffee table.

"She's waiting for me in my apartment," Sargent said, smoking on his joint and smiling. "I'd better go."

"Have fun!" Johnny said.

Then, Sargent handed Johnny the rest of his joint, and he turned and extended his white cane so that he could find his way toward the door. Johnny wasn't worried; Sargent had navigated his way in and out of the penthouse several times now. Johnny flipped through his newspaper again. Sports. Double murder. Political debate. Nothing new. So then, he did whatever he did when he was restless. He read one of his old novels.

$$\triangle \ \triangle \ \triangle$$

Somerset first endured Sasha at Studio 54 back in '79. Sasha was one of the fashion models discovered by Roy Holston, who had quickly inducted her into his harem of cocaine waifs—skinny girls who strutted around Manhattan in jersey dresses.

But it was love at first sight—or should I say, first fight? You see, Somerset's hair brought her and Sasha together. Wanting to get away from the commotion on the dance floor, Somerset had come to the ladies' room to reapply her lipstick, only to find Sasha snorting a line of coke at the vanity. The girl had looked up and noticed the long braids rolling over Somerset's shoulders like black willow leaves. Sasha was a white girl from Connecticut, as Waspy as they came. What did she know about ethnic braids? All she knew was that her thin, unctuous hair could never do what Somerset's did. Somerset's hair was so coarse, so long.

"What are you doing?" Somerset howled, slapping Sasha's hand. Mesmerized, Sasha had started yanking at the braids on Somerset's head. She wanted to know if they were real.

"How does your hair do that?" Sasha asked.

"You keep your hands to yourself, or I'll slap you silly!" Somerset warned. "Damn coke rats!"

"How much can I pay you to do my hair like that?" Sasha asked, pulling a wad of twenties from her bra, which also contained two very small breasts. "How much can I pay you to do my hair?"

"How much can I pay you to clean your snot off the basin so I can use the sink?" Somerset asked.

"I like you!" Sasha laughed, adjusting her dress so that it didn't fall off her boney shoulder. "And I like your hair even more. Maybe we could get you to do a show. I'll talk to Roy."

"I don't want to model," Somerset said.

"Oh, I didn't mean modeling," Sasha told her, giggling. "I meant you could do the girls' hair. Your fat hips wouldn't fit into one of Roy's jersey dresses. He likes his girls slim like dancers, not fat like whores. Nobody wants to see a Zulu fertility goddess on the runway."

Then, Sasha leaned over to snort another line of coke. But before she could inhale, Somerset grabbed Sasha's hair and was pulling the boney coke rat down to the floor. Then, she grabbed her by the hair again and dragged her into the stall, banging her face against the toilet bowl.

"Shit belongs in the toilet," Somerset said. Then she turned and walked back to the mirror to apply her lipstick.

Sasha was so high that she could barely tell she was getting her butt whupped. Hell, she could barely tell the ceiling from the floor from her face. Pulling herself up, she came over to the sink and cautiously wiped the coke from her upper lip. Seemingly unaffected, she tossed her hair in the mirror as Somerset applied her lipstick.

"You black gals might not read too well, but you sure do know how to fight," Sasha said.

And with that, Somerset elbowed her in the face, knocking her back down to the floor. Blood began to drip from her nose as her eyes went cross.

"That's quite an arm you got there," Sasha said right before passing out.

"Silly coke rat!" Somerset grumbled, tossing her black braids behind her shoulders. Then she opened the restroom door. Balls of light skated across the walls as disco music roared in, along with several more coke rats. Somerset went back over to her table where she had been sitting with her friend, a famous lead singer of a rock-and-roll band. But of course, that singer shall not be named. And of course, that band shall not be named. And Somerset told him about how he had to beat the snot out of some coke rat in the bathroom for being a racist.

"One of those Holston girls," she told him, "all skinny and coked out. She'll probably overdose next week trying to sniff the coke off her cuticles."

The famous lead singer passed Somerset a shot glass full of whiskey, and they toasted to the end of coke rats. Looking over her shoulder, Somerset noticed Sasha stumbling out of the ladies' room on the arm of another cocaine waif. The two looked barely alive. Most likely, the cocaine was all that kept their hearts beating.

"Or better yet," Somerset said, "she'll die in some millionaire's penthouse."

Chapter 18

As Harvey had promised, he left the key to the penthouse under the mat. When Sasha came in quietly, Johnny was facing the window, typing away at his new manuscript. Sasha could only see the back of his head. She could only hear the tick of the typewriter, which was loud enough to mute her footsteps. This was it. This would be the end of Johnathan Peacewood. In just a few seconds, she would fire a bullet into the back of his head, and she and Harvey would take all of the money and run away. Now, her finger carelessly caressed the trigger.

"Hey! How are you, Sash?" Johnny asked without turning to face her. Why would he? He had a book to finish.

Sasha stopped dead in her tracks. Sasha and Johnny had never met, right? She instantly suspected Harvey of ambushing her. After all, men could never be trusted—especially not beautiful men like Harvey.

"Come in and have a seat on the couch," Johnny said, typing feverishly.

But Sasha would not be tricked. She pointed the gun more intently toward Johnny. "I'm going to kill you!" she shouted.

Johnathan stopped typing. He looked out the window at the wonderful moon, remembering the night he had tried to kill himself. All he had wanted that night was to be loved—all of this was happening because Johnathan had wanted so desperately to be loved. He remembered he had stopped writing because he wanted to feel some sort of connection with humanity.

Johnathan turned to face his assassin. "Have you ever read any of my books, Sasha?"

"How do you know my name?" she asked. "Harvey!" she called, still thinking that this was an ambush.

"He isn't back from New York. Please, Sasha, won't you come in and sit?" he asked.

"I am going to kill you and take everything you've ever built," she shouted, wagging the gun at him from across the room.

"I know all about you and what you want," Johnny told her. "You're a model from Connecticut who coked yourself out of a job, and now you have nothing to live for. You and Harvey are planning to kill me and take all my money and run off to Mexico to languish unhappily ever after. I know all about that garbage, Sasha. I wrote it! Now, come sit down and talk to Daddy."

"What do you mean?" Sasha asked, frowning.

"Have you read any of the Somerset novels?" he asked.

Sasha could have shot him right then and there. But something inside made her too petrified to do it. And what was it that he was saying? Did he call himself 'Daddy'? What kind of kink was Peacewood into?

"What does it matter to you?" she asked, keeping her guard up. "You're about to die."

"Well, I was just reading one of my best works earlier this afternoon. It was my sixth book, *Somerset Eternal: The Disco Era*. Have you read that? No? Well, it's all about Somerset's adventures at Studio 54 in the 1970s. That's when I remembered you! You were a minor character in that book, so minor that I had almost forgotten about your boney ass."

"You're crazy!" she laughed, pointing the gun right toward his nose.

"Am I? You're not Sasha Van Lisdale of the Connecticut Van Lisdales? Your father wasn't friends with Ted Kennedy? You didn't go to boarding school in Massachusetts until you were kicked out for selling coke on the tennis court? You didn't run away to New York at sixteen to become a fashion model? You're not that Sasha?"

"I am going to blow your brains out!" she shouted.

"How many siblings do you have, Sasha?" Johnny went on. "You can't remember? What color were you mother's eyes? Cat got your tongue? Where were you last Tuesday? Hmm? You have no clue, do you?"

"Nobody is going to suspect a thing," Sasha told him. "I'm going to make this look like a burglary," she said, pulling books from the shelf and throwing them onto the floor. "They'll think some thug came and did this, and Harvey and I will be long gone."

"You don't remember any of the minor details of your life that most people would remember," Johnny said. "Don't you wonder why that is?"

"Because I'm on drugs, you twit!" Sasha laughed. "Hell, I crushed up a pet tranquilizer and snorted it before I came here. Half the time, I can't tell you up from down."

"Yes," he replied. "You stopped at your dealer's apartment in Gold Coast on the way here. Bradly is his name. He's a cute Jewish kid just trying to supplement his income during law school. So he sells drugs to the local white trash, like you. You bought a new vaporizer from him too. And you cut your hand on the nail hanging out of his wall in the hallway."

Sasha looked down at the bandage on her hand.

"He smoked weed with you and asked if you wanted to have sex, yes?" Johnathan asked. "You declined and told him you had business to tend to tonight, yes? And that business is with me? I know exactly who you are, Sasha? I wrote you! I am your god. Now, I command thee: sit!"

Johnny pointed his finger at the sofa. And when he did, it illuminated with shimmering, purple light. Against her will, Sasha walked quickly over to the sofa and took a seat. But she kept the gun pointed at Johnny the entire time.

"Put that away, you silly coke rat," he told her, laughing. "You can't do anything to me. Place the gun on the coffee table in front of you, please."

"Eat lead, Peacewood!" she shouted.

Johnny sighed. "Sasha cautiously placed the gun down on the table in front of Johnathan." And then, Sasha cautiously placed the gun down on the table in front of Johnathan. "Very good! Now, as I was saying, I had almost forgotten about you until I went back and read a chapter from *The Disco Era.* Maybe you'd like to read it?"

"What?" Sasha asked, angrily squinting her eyes.

"Honestly, you're one of the dumbest characters I've ever made up," Johnathan said, shaking his head with disappointment. Then, he continued to command her by narrating aloud. "Sasha—befuddled as ever—stood and walked over to the bookshelf." And Sasha—befuddled as ever—did, in fact, get up and walk over to the bookshelf. "And there, she saw all of Johnathan's novels in print. It was quite the collection. Johnathan had been a prolific writer—before he became distracted, that is. Sasha pulled *Somerset Eternal: The Disco Era* from the shelf. It wasn't Johnathan's favorite, but it was one his top sellers—five hundred pages of bad fashion, hard drugs, and broken hearts. But that was the 1970s in a nutshell. Anyway, Sasha opened to page one hundred and forty-nine, and she began to read."

"No!" Sasha shouted, struggling to defy him. But it was no use. When Johnny narrated, her body was under his control. Each moment that she fought, the current of his power became more painful than the last. So she opened the book, and she began to read.

$$\triangle \ \triangle \ \triangle$$

Somerset had had enough of Studio 54 for the night, so she headed home, sneaking out the back service exit to get away from that Truman Capote, who had been talking her ear off. As she sashayed through the dark alley, she heard a noise, kind of a dying moan. A silver slither of light had caught on something sparkly on the ground. It was a dress. A jersey dress. And inside of it was Sasha.

Sasha lay with her face on the concrete, her body shaking. Somerset knew that this was the tremble of death. Had you lived as long as she had, you would know that tremble too. It comes when the soul is desperate to stay in the body, but Hell is tugging at it to come out. Somerset kneeled down and grasped Sasha by the shoulders.

"Wake up!" Somerset said, slapping her face. "Snap out of it!"

But it was no use. Sasha's pulse was thready and her eyes rolled to the back of her head so that only the whites could be seen. Somerset couldn't help feeling as though she had wished this upon the little coke rat. Hadn't she just joked with that famous rock singer about how the girl would overdose trying to snort coke off her cuticles?

Somerset remembered that the spirits had given her a second chance when she had asked for it. And didn't Sasha deserve a second chance, too? She was so young. She couldn't have been any older than twenty-one or twenty-two, not much older than

Somerset when she had been saved from death. Maybe the girl could be revived.

Somerset pulled her breast out and squeezed some of her magical milk into Sasha's mouth, hoping it would revive her. Sasha swallowed. And slowly, her pupils rolled back down so that the baby blue of her eyes could be seen. But she was thirsty. She grabbed Somerset's breast and drank some more. She sucked hard and bit at the nipple. The magical milk was invigorating. It was the best thing she had ever tasted. And it made her heart beat twice as fast as that lousy coke.

But that was the problem. The milk along with the coke along with the alcohol along with the tranquilizers was too much for Sasha's little black heart. Somerset felt that Sasha had stopped sucking. Looking down at the poor coke rat, she noticed that Sasha's face had gone gray.

"You okay?" Somerset asked, shaking her. "Hey! Hey!" Somerset yelled, slapping her face again.

But it was no use. Sasha's heart had exploded in her chest. Somerset hadn't really killed her, because she would have died anyway. If anything, Somerset had put her out of her misery. Truth be told, there was nothing happy about Sasha; she hadn't spoken to her family in years, and she couldn't keep friends because she had a traitorous spirit. Sasha had essentially become a zombie with nothing to live for. So her death was more an inconvenient truth than a tragedy. Still, Somerset kissed her forehead and laid her back down on the concrete.

"Poor little coke rat," she said. "Poor little coke rat."

Now, Sasha remembered having emerged from these pages. She had come from a copy kept at the Harold Washington Library downtown. She emerged headfirst from page one hundred and forty- nine, kicking and screaming on the library floor—full-grown but covered in amniotic fluid. She remembered walking through the library's majestic marbled hallways, dragging the novel by the umbilical cord that was still attached to her belly. And she remembered cutting the chord with a piece of broken glass before passing out at the sight of blood. When she woke, there was no scar. Sasha had no navel. Her belly was smooth. And she remembered now that she was angry—angry that she had died so tragically in chapter seven and that nobody ever talked about her character. She meant relatively nothing to the plot. In fact, the editor had suggested Johnny cut her. But Sasha felt she had deserved more from Johnny. And that's really why she was here to kill him, wasn't it?

"No!" Sasha screamed, throwing the book to the floor. "It isn't true!"

"I'm afraid it is, little coke rat," Johnathan said, smiling and folding his hands upon his lap. "I thought about developing you more, but there was no point. I was writing a love story, not a drug saga."

"You can't do this to me!"

"Face it, Sasha. You're dead. You're just a ghost here to haunt me, reminding me not to languish through life the way you did. I did bring you back in my new manuscript. You're a memory of Somerset's. In the last chapter, she feels nostalgic and looks back over the last five hundred years she's spent longing for love. She remembers you momentarily and cries a little. She really wanted you to have a second chance—you know, to really thrive. But I honestly think I may cut that out. None of my fans even remember you from that last book."

"No!" Sasha cried, tears running down her face. "I do deserve a second chance. Let me go to Mexico and start a new life. I could get cleaned up. I could help people. You could reinvent me over and over again. Don't you see, Peacewood? I could be the new Somerset!"

Suddenly, a blade pierced the back of Sasha's neck, the tip coming right through the front. Poor Sasha fell to the floor to reveal Clifton standing at the door behind her, bald-headed and sinister, and Junior right behind him in his filthy red hoodie. Cliff had had to throw the knife at her; she wasn't a significant enough character to carry out this murder. The death of Mr. Johnathan Peacewood would be Clifton's legacy, not hers.

"I think there are enough Somersets in the world," Cliff said, sneering. "No need for two."

"Good job, Cliff!" Johnny said, standing and clapping his hands vigorously.

Johnathan walked over to Sasha as she bled out onto the floor—her eyes still open. He never cared much about her, but she was still one of his beautiful creations. And even in death, her beauty inspired him.

"Poor little coke rat," Johnny said. "But you know I'm glad I got the grout in my floor sealed before you did this. Can you imagine how hard it would be to get this blood out of the cracks between the tiles?" He smiled at Clifton as though he were greeting an old friend. "We'll leave her here for now," Johnny said. "The corpse will lend dramatic effect later. Oh, by the way, Clifton. Bring your little friend over here, but do lock the door behind you. The penthouse has been busier than Grand Central Station tonight."

Clifton shoved Junior into the penthouse so forcefully that the boy fell onto his knees. After making sure no one was coming down the hall, he stepped in and locked the door behind him.

"I guess you know who this is," Clifton said, pulling another blade from his jacket. "Get up, you little turd." He wielded the blade over Junior's head, ordering him to stand. "Show him your belly!"

Junior stood, lifting his hoodie to reveal the letters W-R-I-T-E. While this child also had no navel, Johnny knew that this was no character of his. And unfortunately, no amount of narration could control this little fellow.

"I missed you," Johnathan said.

"Aw, isn't that sweet," Clifton hissed. "A writer reunited with his inner child. It's like something out of a book. Maybe you should write it, Peacewood."

Junior had been watching Sasha bleed out. He remembered her very well, actually. He had thought of her while watching the E! True Hollywood Story of Gia, the world's most tragic fashion model. How neat would it be to have a character like that interact with Somerset, to fight with her, to drink her milk! Junior remembered whispering the idea into Johnny's ear one night as he slept. Those whispers were the mortar that held Johnathan's dreams together.

"You forgot about me," Junior said, frowning at Johnny. "You forgot about me just like you forgot about her."

"You were always such a bossy little brat," Johnathan laughed. "You always wanted exactly what you wanted when you wanted it. There was never any room for compromise. No wonder I'm so successful."

"Isn't that sweet!" Clifton said. "But you know I'm gonna kill the little bastard. And I'm gonna kill you too, Peacewood. This is a two-birds-with-one-stone type of deal."

"What is it that you really want from me, Clifton?" Johnathan asked. "You want Somerset back? Is that why you're doing this?

You've kidnapped my inner child, holding him hostage until I give you what you want?"

"That's not what this is about," Clifton said. "Real men finish what they start. But you're not a real man. You're a bitch."

"Am I now?"

"I don't stutter," Clifton said.

"Well, then," Johnny replied, smiling as he began to narrate. "Johnathan snapped his fingers, igniting a spark of purple light between himself and Clifton. Suddenly, Cliff was lifted from the floor and flipped to land flat on his face. Stay there," Johnny said once Cliff was on the ground. "And you are the bitch."

Johnny pointed his finger at Clifton's backside, and a bolt of purple light shot toward the prostrate man. A cute little puppy dog tail grew from Clifton's tailbone and began to wag. It was a petite, coily tail—like that of a pug.

"Come sit down, kid," Johnathan told Junior. "We have a lot of catching up to do before Harvey gets home."

"What about him?" Junior asked, pointing to Clifton, who was looking up from the floor, stupefied yet wagging his tail.

"Oh, please," Johnny laughed. "He won't do anything. This is my story."

Knock knock. Someone was at the door.

"Good grief!" Johnny said. "Another one. I feel like Scrooge on Christmas Eve with all these spirits dropping in. Sit down, kid. I'll see who it is."

As Junior cautiously walked around the corpse of Sasha on his way to the couch, Johnathan went toward the door. He stepped over Clifton, who was now completely harmless, sitting on the floor like an obedient dog. But who could this be? Johnathan opened the door. And to his surprise, Somerset stood there before him.

Chapter 19

"I guess you may as well come on in, too," Johnny told Somerset, rolling his eyes.

"You know who I am?" she asked. "I came prepared to do a whole lot of explaining. I didn't think you'd even—"

"I have spent more time thinking of you than I've spent thinking of any other thing on Earth. I know who the hell you are. Come on in and sit on the couch."

Somerset came in to find Clifton on the floor, still sitting like a well-trained dog. And was that a tail coming out of his ass? Yes, yes, it was tail. He looked up at her, snarling, but he dared not touch her. He feared Johnny at this point. She walked past him only to see Sasha dead on the floor; she remembered wishing this on her back in '79.

"Good gracious!" Somerset cried, covering her eyes. "Poor little coke rat!"

"Calm down," Johnathan told her. "I killed her. You didn't do anything." He looked over at Clifton. "You get up and go sit on the couch with the others. And don't try any funny business, or I'll flip you over again. And don't mouth off or I'll just narrate your mouth off your silly white face."

So Cliff followed Somerset over to the sofa. And he, Somerset, and Junior all sat down. There they were: a trifecta of cerebral manifestations. Johnny went to the refrigerator and pulled out a bottle of sauvignon. While they sat, he poured himself a glass. He also pulled a joint from the drawer and lit it. After one glorious puff of the weed, he threw his head back and laughed. Then, he crossed the room to sit at his desk.

"Now, what am I going to do with you three?" he asked. "An orphan, a heroine, and a serial killer walk into a bar. It's like the start of a bad bar joke, isn't it? It's like thirty-one Tylenol, a glass of zinfandel, and a partridge in a pear tree. Hmm. Thirty-one Tylenol, a glass of zinfandel, and . . . I think that'd be a good opening to a novel. What do you think, Cliff?"

"I think I'm gonna gut you like a fish," Cliff grunted.

"Interesting," Johnathan said, preparing to narrate again. "Clifton pulled out a third knife that he had tucked in his jacket. He pulled back his sleeve and carved the letters F-I-S-H into his own pasty white arm."

"You ass!" Cliff shouted, clutching his arm with his hand, trying to stop the bleeding.

Johnathan sucked on his joint. But instead of Johnny, Clifton opened his mouth and exhaled the smoke. "Mmm. That's some good green," Junior said, feeling the pot go straight to his head.

"Now listen very carefully," Johnny said. "I had lost sight of things. But now I'm back on track. And I'm writing the script here. Clifton, I let you go awry. I'm sorry. I didn't give you the resolution you wanted, and so you went batshit crazy. And worst of all, you killed my agent and my best friend. But you'll be happy to know that I have written a conclusion to your story, and you don't have to act like this anymore."

"Really?" Clifton asked, arching his brow. He was shocked yet curious.

"Somerset," Johnny continued, "I know you're tired. What's been almost a decade for me has been five hundred and fifteen years for you. I left you longing, didn't I? I'm sorry for that."

"I have something to say," Somerset replied.

"I'm sure you do, but say it later," Johnny said. "Now, Junior, you didn't have to go acting like a child with no home. As long as I'm writing, you'll be safe. I should have done a better job of protecting you. But I failed at that. And I am truly sorry."

"Peacewood, I have something to tell you," Somerset reiterated.

But before she could say anything, Clifton was standing up and pulling a gun from his jacket. He pressed it to Johnny's temple and smiled. Johnny went completely still.

"Try and use your purple powers now," Clifton said, wagging his cute little tail. "By the time you lift your hand, I will have fired into your skull."

"That's enough!" Somerset said. "Clifton, stop it! I came here to give you exactly what you want! All this killing has to stop, and if I need to give you what you want to stop it, then I will." Then, Somerset stood, pulling out her breast and offering it to him.

"Titty titty titty!" Junior sang.

Clifton took the gun down from Johnny's head. He felt a genuine happiness overwhelm him. It was what he had been searching for this entire time. All the killing, all the sadness could stop now. He grabbed her hand.

"Have a drink," Somerset said, offering herself to him.

"Why did you leave me, Somerset?" Cliff asked, pulling her down onto the couch until they both flopped back onto the leather. Junior jerked, fearing that the gun would go off, but Clifton just placed it safely back in his jacket and caressed Somerset's face and breasts. He was overjoyed to be holding them in his hands again after searching for so long.

"Titty!" Junior shouted.

"Hold your tongue," Johnny warned the child.

And of course, Junior stuck out his tongue and pinched it with his fingers—holding it as he was told. This kid was a cheeky son of gun, wasn't he?

"I wasn't ready," Somerset told him. "I didn't know what real love was. I have never felt it before. But now I know what real love is. I've felt it. And so I'm willing to give you my milk as an expression of true love, Cliff."

"Cover your eyes, kid," Clifton told Junior. Then, he leaned in and sucked the milk from Somerset's breast. It was still as delicious as it had been long ago. He sucked and sucked and sucked. What a taste! But something was very wrong this time. Clifton quickly became queasy.

This wasn't the invigorating surge he had felt before. Instead, Clifton felt drained—empty. He felt as though he was somehow becoming less solid. Clifton felt so light that he thought he might actually be water vapor. He was becoming nothing, washed completely off the page.

"What's wrong with your milk?" he asked.

"As I was saying," Somerset continued. "I have found true love, but certainly not in you. How could I ever love a murderer? You've manipulated women to get what you want, and when they couldn't give it to you, you killed them in the name of love. That isn't love, Clifton. Love is compassion for your fellow man. Love is calming. Love is peaceful. Thanks to Sargent, I know what love is now."

"What!" Clifton said, growing weaker and dizzier by the second.

"I love Sargent. It's true love," Somerset said. "And he loves me. He sees me for who I really am. I'm not just some object, some black beauty for him to fetishize. He sees my spirit better than you ever could—better than any of the other men ever could. And you know what that means?"

"No!" Clifton shouted, falling to the floor.

"That's right, Clifton," Somerset said, standing over him, her face beginning to wrinkle, her back beginning to bend. She was aging right before his eyes. "That means I'm no longer immortal. And you just drank my death into your body."

"No!" Clifton begged, reaching up from the floor.

As Somerset began to shrivel like a raisin, Clifton could hardly breathe. Liver spots appeared on his hands, and cataracts formed over his eyes. Somerset had found love, and so the spell was finally broken. And this meant that her milk was no longer life-giving. Instead, it drew life.

"Mr. Peacewood," Somerset said. "Perhaps you'd like to take over from here."

"I most certainly would!" Johnny replied, thrilled that he could finished another great novel. "Clifton's skin began to sink into his bones, and as he lay dying on the floor of the Peacewood penthouse, he appeared to be a hundred years old. Reaching for Somerset one last time, his arm crumbled into sand, the grains igniting into purple sparks before they could even hit the floor. Then his jaw fell from his skull, and it, too, ignited, vanishing into nothingness. His legs did the same. His torso. His shoulders. Even that cute little puppy dog tail. Finally, his head fell to dust, until nothing was left of him but those cold, blue eyes. They were like marbles now—hard and glassy. So Junior picked them up and put them in his pocket. They would be fun to play with later."

Then, the doorbell rang. Another guest? My, this was turning out to be a busy evening. Who could it be this time? Another character from another book? Perhaps Dorothy Gale would walk in looking for Toto. Or maybe Huckleberry Finn was about to walk in with Tom Sawyer and tell a story. Or it could be Sherlock Holmes on the trail of the Northside Butcher.

"Get the door, Junior," Peacewood said.

The boy ran over, hopping over Sasha's dead body to answer the door. It was Sargent. He came in holding a canvas of his latest work. He had left his white cane, but he felt along the wall to the living room. Junior followed behind him tossing Clifton's eyeballs up in the air one at a time.

"Watch your step!" Johnny warned, hoping he wouldn't trip over Sasha.

"Seems like you've got some trash to clean up," Sargent said, stepping cautiously around her. "I painted a picture for you, Peacewood. And I . . . is Somerset here? I can smell her. She smells like roses."

"Yes, Simon," Somerset replied. "It's me! I'm right here." She walked to him, giving him a kiss on the cheek.

"You sound different," Sargent said. "Your lips feel different."

"I'm dying, darling," she replied.

"Dying? Because of me?" Sargent asked.

"I'm afraid so! I love you, Simon. You're the most wonderful man I've ever met. I feel like I've known you all my life. And I know you know the real me. But I don't have much longer. The spell that preserved me is wearing off because I found exactly what I was looking for. And meeting you has been worth the wait."

"I suspected as much," Sargent said, looking down slowly and somberly. "I painted this picture of you, but thought that Mr. Peacewood here would get better use out of it. I call it *True Love*. It's a painting of you, Somerset. I painted you as you really are."

And he showed them the painting, filled with amorphous blobs of yellow and green and blue. And as they looked on, the colors danced and merged until they appeared as Sargent meant them to be seen. It was Somerset holding her son in her arms, loving him unconditionally and willing to die for him. And as she bled out from the child's violent birth, the puddles of blood formed into a typewriter, and yellow and purple blobs became Johnny writing a new novel. And behind him in this painting was Junior, whispering new ideas into his ear.

"You're brilliant!" Johnny said.

"And what are you? Chopped liver?" Sargent asked. "I think you have something to finish, Mr. Peacewood. You owe it to us all."

Junior took the painting from Sargent and carried it over to the desk, where he held it above the typewriter. After Johnny pointed his finger and shot it with a purple beam of light, the painting levitated from Junior's hand and secured itself up on the wall where it belonged. At this point, Johnny felt completely at peace with his mission. He walked over to the desk and sat down at the typewriter. Then, he did what he had always done best.

△ △ △

For the first time in her five hundred and fifteen years of living, Somerset was experiencing unconditional love. No matter what she did, no matter what she said, no matter how many mistakes she made, Sargent would always love her. He had fallen in love with her spirit, which was incapable of lying or hiding or even dying. He was in love with the part of her that was, in itself, unconditional. And now that she had found exactly what she had always wanted, there was nothing left to experience.

Somerset had seen it all. All the wars, famines, fashions, genocides, evolutions, devolutions, discoveries, renaissances, arrivals, and departures of the last five hundred years had taken place right before her eyes. She had met dignitaries and poets and politicians and criminals and clowns. She had laughed and cried and killed and lost. And now, because of love, she had nothing to fear or run from. It was a comfort that no one could take away, no matter what. And so now, Somerset was ready to die.

Sargent held her in his arms, singing sweetly into her ear. And they danced one last time as Somerset began to age more and more swiftly. Her skin, like Clifton's, was sinking into her bones, and her irises were getting pale. Sargent flicked a spark of purple light from his fingers, and the two of them began to levitate above Johnny's sofa.

"My only regret," she told him while waltzing in the air, "is that I wasn't able to spend more time with you."

"Don't worry," Sargent said. "I don't have the same sense of time as everyone else. A second to me feels like a year. You and I have had a lifetime together in my mind. And I understand that your body has to go. But remember that your spirit is what you really are. And that, Somerset, is truly eternal."

And then, Somerset kissed Sargent on the lips. Before she could pull away, her body turned to stone. And when the heavy stone fell to the floor, it shattered into a billion grains of sand that rose into the air. Somerset's spirit was still there. They could hear her speak.

"I will always love you, Sargent," she said. "And Johnny, take care of that inner child of yours. And don't you ever, ever stop writing. It's who you are."

Then, the sandy haze condensed into a single nebula filled with purple lightning. And the entire thing began to glow a bright purple until nothing else in the room could be seen. And, finally, with a purple flash, the cloud vanished.

Sargent drifted back down from the air and settled himself on the couch, holding his head in his hands. For the first time in years, he was melancholy. He had just lost his Somerset. But it would be all right. It had to be.

Junior moved to put his arm around Johnny, but before he could, the little boy exploded into a million little lavender sparks. And those sparks swirled to form a purple halo around Johnny's head, almost as though Johnathan had the entire galaxy encircling his mind. He realized that his thoughts were the center of his universe. And this made Peacewood the most powerful man in the world.

Chapter 20

"What do you think of God?" Sargent asked Johnny. He was still sitting on the sofa wiping tears away.

"I usually don't," Johnny replied. "I never much liked religion. I grew up Baptist, but it was all too regimental and oppressive for me. The going to church every Sunday. The dressing up. The being dipped to wash us of our sins. I just didn't like having my behaviors dictated like that. So I left God alone."

"You were thinking too small, Peacewood," Sargent said. "God is not a church. He is not a religion. He is formless. He is a formless surge of love that flows through all of us. That's what's wrong with humanity. We get too focused on form. We obsess over the body of Christ or the Cross or the Pope. None of those things are God. God is the love that flows through them. Where there is love, there is God, Peacewood. You love writing. So whenever you write, you are worshipping God. You must make writing your new religion. That is your love. That is your God."

"I think you may be right, Sargent," Johnny replied, scratching his chin and thinking some very deep thoughts. "Can I get you a glass of wine?"

"Something tells me you have a mess to clean up here. And I'm not talking about the dead girl in your foyer."

"Oh! The coke rat!" Johnny replied, laughing. "Yeah, I haven't forgotten about her. I'll be needing to use her one last time. But if I can't encourage you to stay for the finale, at least let me pay you for the painting. I can't tell you how much it means to me."

"If it's one thing you and I have enough of, it money. I have so much of it that I sometimes wipe my behind with twenty-dollar bills when I'm too lazy to go to the store and get tissue. Something tells me you do the same."

Johnny laughed. "I'm Johnathan Peacewood. I wipe my ass with hundreds, thank you very much."

"My apologies! So now that you're wrapping up the Somerset books, I guess you can get started on your new book about me."

"You seriously want me to write a book about you?"

"At least one!" Sargent said, celebrating a little. "I'm a fascinating man, don't you think? A book about a blind man who becomes a painter! Now, that's the stuff bestsellers are made of. You could call it something fun like *Simon Sees*."

"*Simon Sees*!" Johnny laughed. "I like it. It's got a nice ring to it. Charlotte used to help me come up with titles, but she can't now. And that's all my fault." Johnathan stopped speaking for a moment. He rubbed his head while feeling a pang of anguish shoot up his neck. "I made some really bad mistakes here, didn't I?"

"There are no mistakes, Peacewood," Sargent told him. "Every life event is a lesson that nudges us further along our spiritual path. Everything happens for a reason. You unleashed a monster with Clifton, and he did heinous, heinous things. But in a way, Clifton saved the world from becoming a worse mess than it is now. He wasn't just targeting innocent women. He was targeting demons—devils! You put that in him. You created that sensibility in him."

"He killed a mother!" Johnny replied, shocked. "A school teacher too!"

"Look deeper, Peacewood," Sargent said. "When was the last time you turned on the television? None of the women he killed were innocent victims. Investigations have uncovered horrible things about all of them. Cheyenne Cost, the mother you're talking about, was trying to kill her sons; the oldest boy confessed it to his psychiatrist when the father took him back to Paris. It was all over the news, Peacewood. Where have you been?"

"I've been languishing a bit," Johnny replied. "But for Christ's sake!"

"Yeah, and everyone else's sake too!" Sargent replied. "And that teacher you mentioned, Mary Ann Bell? She got a write-up for suggesting to her indigent students they drop out and live off welfare like their poor parents. She told one kid he'd be better off selling drugs because he could barely read and wouldn't cut it in college. Ms. Bell only kept that job because she was sleeping with principal, who happened to be married. She was in the business of corrupting young minds, until Clifton snatched her off the street."

"You don't say," Johnny said.

"I do say! And Marilyn Gouche was a lawyer who had been helping her boyfriend launder money from a nursing home she represented. She sucked the home dry until the place was shut down. The elderly patients were poor and had nowhere to go. One was a seventy-year-old lady who suffered from schizophrenic hallucinations. When they closed the home, she was out on the street. She eventually wandered into a rail yard and got hit by a train. It made headlines, Peacewood!"

"No!" Peacewood snapped. "Charlotte didn't deserve it. She didn't. And don't you dare suggest otherwise!"

"I'm sorry, Peacewood. I really am. And I would never suggest that your friend deserved what happened to her. Never."

"I let it go too far," Johnny said. "I was in a dark place when I created Cliff's character, and I just let it go too far."

"You never know how far any of them really would have gone, Peacewood," Sargent said, trying to console him. "Just know that everything happens for a reason. I hate to say that because I know all about loss. I know it hurts. I know all about blaming yourself for something terrible and reliving it over and over. But everything really will turn out for the best."

And then, they heard the sound of a cell phone ringing. But where was it coming from?

"Sounds like you have a phone call, Peacewood!" Sargent said, smiling cheerfully.

"No, I keep my phone on silent."

"Well, I don't carry a phone," Sargent said. "I don't need people trying to reach me all times of night. Besides, I hear the cellular rays cause brain cancer when they penetrate your skull."

"I think it's coming from the coke rat," Johnny said, walking over to Sasha's corpse. Pressing his toe to her shoulder, he nudged her until he could lean down and reach into her coat. Indeed, there was a cell phone buzzing away in her pocket. As soon as Johnny looked at the screen, the ringing stopped. He had missed the call.

"Who was it?" Sargent asked.

Johnny read the screen but said nothing. Then, the phone started to ring again in his hand. It was the same caller as before. Johnny just let it ring on until it went to voicemail. This time the caller decided to leave a message.

"Looks like he left a message this time," Johnny said coldly.

"He?" Sargent asked. "He who?"

"Harvey Marcus."

△ △ △

Harvey had just landed at O'Hare International, and he desperately needed to hear from Sasha. He had just gotten back from New York and needed to speak with her right away. Yes, right away! Harvey had maneuvered according to plan. He even made a fuss about his peanut allergy during the flight so that the flight crew would remember him. That'd be a perfect alibi, him being on a plane during the murder. Now, he just needed to speak to Sasha and make sure that everything had gone according to plan. But she wasn't answering. He called again and again, but there was no answer. Finally, he decided to leave a voice message.

"Hey! It's me," Harvey said into the phone. "Why aren't you answering? This is weird. I don't know what to do. Is everything okay? I want to hear from you. Call me back."

So Harvey hailed a cab and took it downtown to the penthouse. He hoped to get back and find Johnny dead as a doornail. Money, money, money! It was going to be fantastic! This would be his renaissance, full of red carpets and galas. He'd finally be free from a life in the shadows of Johnathan Peacewood. And best of all, he'd have a nice little nest egg to make a name for himself in the world. He only hoped Sasha didn't get in the way. She seemed to want him to languish down in Mexico with her forever, but that's not what Harvey Marcus was about. He wasn't born to languish. He was born to be a star. He just needed a proper catapult to get himself up in the sky so he could twinkle.

The cab driver was a very friendly young Jamaican woman. She was spooked by Harvey's striking resemblance to classic movie star Montgomery Clift. According to her, it was absolutely uncanny. She was a big fan of Mr. Clift's movies.

"I've actually never seen any of his movies," Harvey said. "But I get told I look like him all the time."

"You know," the cab driver said, "that reminds me of a book I read recently."

"Oh yeah? A book, huh?" Harvey asked. He was so sick of hearing about books. He hoped she didn't reference anything written by Johnathan.

"Yeah!" she said. "Have you ever read any of the Somerset novels by Johnathan Peacewood?"

Harvey rolled his eyes. "I know them all like the back of my hand."

"Is there anyone in the world who hasn't read those books? I guess it was silly of me to even ask. Anyway, I guess you just remind me of that character Harvey from *Somerset: The Disco Era.* You know, the model that Somerset met in New York? The one who looked just like Montgomery Clift?"

"What?" Harvey replied, amused yet skeptical. He chuckled a bit, looking out the window as cars buzzed by on the freeway.

"The one that Somerset couldn't stand because all he ever did was complain about how he could never model again because of that little scar on his face. Then, in chapter seven, we discovered that he had a small penis and wasn't even good at using it. Thank the Lord that Somerset kicked him to the curb!"

Suddenly, Harvey remembered it all. He had met Somerset at Studio 54. He thought she was beautiful, with her black braids like leaves on a willow tree. She was the only girl in the whole joint who didn't snort coke, and he liked that about her. They went out a few times. Fooled around once or twice. And Somerset really liked him. "I want us to date, Harvey," Somerset said. "I want you to be my boyfriend."

But Harvey couldn't do it. He just wasn't ready. He liked Somerset a lot, but he just couldn't do it. He had spent the last four years in a relationship with a model named Sasha. And in the middle of the night, with no explanation, she had gotten up and left. She didn't even say goodbye. He heard five months later that she had overdosed in an alley behind the club.

"I'm just not ready to trust someone else with my feelings," he told Somerset. "You're a wonderful girl, and I do really like you."

And so that was how it was. Harvey was too weak to love, so Somerset walked away from him, breaking his heart again. And he was left right there on page two-hundred and nine, languishing with his beautiful, Montgomery Clift face that was perfect except for that damned scar.

Harvey was mortified. This reality wasn't his at all—it was Johnathan's. And he wasn't even a happy part of it. He was just a symbol of what happens when we choose fear over love. While love forces us to expand and become our greatest selves, fear leaves us languishing in mediocrity.

"But I'm sure you're nothing like the character Harvey from that book," the cab driver said. "You seem like a very nice man. I'm sure you have a wonderful person waiting for you at home right now. If not, I'm sure you will very soon."

$$\triangle \triangle \triangle$$

Harvey walked into the Peacewood penthouse terrified and not knowing what to expect. He realized now he had been messing with the most powerful man in the world; Johnny had given him his privilege, and Johnny could take it away. And there Sasha was, lying dead in a pool of blood on the floor—a knife stuck in her neck. Her eyes were still wide open.

"Sasha!" Harvey cried. "What happened to you?"

Sobbing, he ran over to her and kneeled by the body. Then, holding her head in his arms as though it were a newborn baby, he rocked her back and forth. His tears fell onto her face so that she seemed to be crying with him.

"No!" he screamed. "This isn't how things were supposed to happen. Why are you laying here like this? Dear God, why?"

"She's doing what she does best, Harvey," Johnny said, coming out of his bedroom and walking up the hallway. "She's languishing."

Johnny emerged from the hallway holding a bottle of Dom Pérignon and wearing his best tuxedo. He sucked the champagne straight from the bottle because he didn't need class. He was Johnathan motherfucking Peacewood. He taught the class. He made the rules.

"I decided to celebrate, Harvey," he said. "I finished the last Somerset novel while you were away. Somerset finally discovered the meaning of true love, and she was released from her curse. And you know, as I wrote the story, I also discovered the meaning of true love. And I was released from my curse."

"And what curse would that be?" Harvey asked, his eyes red and full of tears.

"You and everything you represent. I brought you out to save me from my fear of loneliness. And it was that fear that led me off my path. I'm a writer, Harvey. Writing is my love. And as long as I have that love to surround me and to enrich me, I am never alone. You aren't love, Harvey. You are fear. And now, it is time for me to take you and to do away with you."

Johnathan drank a swig of champagne then placed the bottle on a table. With a flicking of his wrist, a bolt of purple light shot from his feet like fire out the tail of a missile. Johnny rocketed high into the air where he twirled and danced like a fairy above the coffee table. He snapped his fingers, and suddenly the record machine began to play Mozart's "Requiem."

"Say goodbye, Harvey," Johnny sang, twirling through the air in his tuxedo. "I am a magical creature, and you have pissed me off. Therefore, my handsome fellow, I am going to zap you into oblivion. And you can take that dead coke rat with you!"

"Peacewood, I just wanted my own chance. I wanted to do something more," Harvey said, still clutching Sasha's dead body.

"You're driftwood, baby!" Johnny laughed. "Presto!"

A purple noose fell down over Harvey, and he understood very clearly what his punishment would be. Perhaps pleading would help, or a little Marcus charm. He was still cute, right?

"Can't you bring her back?" Harvey cried. "She's yours. All you have to do is write it and she'll come back. Isn't that how it works?"

"Harvey, I'm going to give you two choices, babe. You can either roam the earth, languishing without Sasha for all eternity, or you can hang yourself by that noose and end your pointless life now." Johnny did a flip through the air, carelessly flying like Peter Pan. "Either way, you'll be out of my hair for good. I mean, I could just narrate you into dust, but I'd like to know that you suffered a little for what you've done."

"I'm sorry I hurt you," Harvey said, and then he stood, leaving Sasha on the floor. As tears streamed down his face, he cautiously placed his head in the noose and tightened it around his neck. This would be the end of Johnathan's indecision. He, like all of us, had two choices in life—fear or love. This time, Johnathan was choosing love. The death of Harvey would be the death of his fear.

"Say goodbye to the coke rat, Harvey," Johnny said. "She's staining my floor."

And with that, Sasha's body vanished with a spark of bright purple light. "Requiem" played on, but Johnny decided that he was done flying around the penthouse for the evening. Landing gracefully, he went over to sit at his desk. He thought back to the day he chose his pen name. His father had walked out on him again (this was one time of many), and Johnathan was devastated. He couldn't think. He couldn't eat. He was too anxious to even sleep. He was having trouble finishing the last chapter of his first book, and he needed to get away.

So he ran from his tiny little apartment. He got into his car and he drove all the way to Tennessee, where he had grown up. It was a ten-hour drive, and he did it in the middle of the night. When he got to Tennessee the next morning, he went into the woods just outside Memphis, where his father used to take him hunting for quail. Johnathan got out of his car and went deep into the woods, wearing only a T-shirt, jeans, and some sneakers, which was dangerous given the snakes all over the place. But he didn't care. He was there looking for some memory of his father, some sign that everything would be okay. He knew that something was out there. Then, there it was. On an oak tree. His father had given him a knife when he was nine years old. He had given him a knife and lifted him up on his shoulders. Johnny's father told him to write his name on the tree. Just his name. And his father told him that one day he would come back with the love of his life and have his love do the same. And then their names would be memorialized here forever. But when Johnathan was there upon his father's shoulder, he didn't carve out the name Johnny Pots. Instead, he carved a peace sign. And on this day, almost fifteen years later, Johnny had come back, and he had found that tree. And the peace sign was still there. And he realized what love had meant to him all along. Love was whatever granted him inner peace. And so he decided that his name would be Peacewood.

"Have you any last words, Harvey?" Johnny asked, turning to see that Harvey had wrapped the noose around his neck.

"Yes," Harvey said.

"And what might they be?" Johnny asked.

"I'm sorry for trying to drain you of your power. I just felt so powerless. And I thought that I could maybe, just once, have what you have—have that power, that magic. I envy you, Peacewood. You really are the most powerful man in the world."

"Thank you for those riveting last words!" Johnny laughed. "Abracadabra!"

And with that, Amadeus Mozart appeared in a flash of purple light and floated through the air, playing his "Requiem" on a grand piano, which was also floating through the air in front of him. Mozart was fabulous, of course. He came wearing his powdered wig and all, just tickling the ivories and drifting above the coffee table, tapping his foot on the air beneath him to keep time.

"Fare thee well, Harvey!" Johnny said. And with a flick of his wrist, Harvey was yanked up into the air by his neck. Mozart laughed because Harvey's legs seemed to be dangling to the rhythm of his music as the life drained from his body.

"He languishes beautifully," Johnny said, smiling and turning to look out the window. The moon was silvery and full again, just as it was the night he attempted suicide. But this was a new era for him—an era in which love would always conquer fear. For the truth is, Johnathan Peacewood knew that he had nothing to fear. He knew unconditional love was the source of his power. And with that knowledge, not even the biggest, baddest beast could touch him.

Chapter 21

Thirty-one Tylenol, a glass of zinfandel, and a partridge in a pear tree. Johnathan Peacewood was lying on a quiet beach in the Hamptons with the sun soaking his chest, its rays caressing his skin as he became a succulent shade of buttery brown. Slowly, Johnny opened his eyes to see the wondrous blue of the summer sky. A rainbow was triumphantly shooting out from the waves of the ocean, congratulating him on his achievements. The seagulls sang in enchanting harmony, gliding freely. Yes, the universe was a magical place. And Johnny wondered what reason he had ever had to attempt suicide.

The thirty-one Tylenol had been thrown up so high into the sky that they had become the stars of Johnny's constellation. The gods hung Peacewood up right between Taurus and Gemini so that he could slap the bull on the ass and give the first twin a high five. But that was the life of Mr. Johnathan Peacewood.

And that glass of zinfandel? Johnathan had poured it into a river that transported him far away from Chicago, all the way to New York City where he had started anew. He bought himself a new bachelor pad on the Upper West Side—which was surprisingly affordable because all the kids had moved to Brooklyn. So New York had become a new love for Johnny. The city was like him: blunt, unapologetic, and teeming with power.

Oh, and the partridge in the pear tree? That single partridge? The one we know will always start and finish the song? The one that makes the Christmas tree complete even before we bombard it with any of the countless golden rings or ladies dancing or pipers piping? That partridge was Mr. Johnathan Peacewood himself. He was complete even without a ridiculous gang of ornaments. He didn't need any turtledoves or French hens. Everything he ever needed to be happy was right there inside of him.

If he wanted love, he could simply snap his fingers and presto! It would manifest out of thin air, walk up to him, and kiss him on the cheek. He could rid himself of his enemies simply by flicking his wrist. Hell, he had made a serial killer sit and mind like a well-trained collie. The fool starts his journey seeking out what he already has inside him. And when he discovers this paradox, he is empowered. This is how Johnathan Peacewood became the most powerful man in the world.

The wind was subtle and warm, and the waves crashed into the sand. Life was good. Life was really good. At least until Johnny heard a familiar voice. Could it be her again? Here in the Hamptons? Oh Lord.

"Mr. Peacewood! Is that you?" she asked.

It was that gangly, redheaded fan from the beach in Chicago—the one who kept insisting he come to her wedding. Here she was again. And she was holding a copy of his latest book, *Somerset Eternal: The Meaning of True Love*. She would probably ask him to sign it. Did she have some sort of tracking device on him? He figured he may as well humor her. He had no reason to be surly anymore. Everything was good.

"Mr. Peacewood, you probably don't remember me," she said. "We met a while back. Come to think of it, it was on a beach just like this."

"It was in Chicago," he replied. "It was North Avenue Beach in Chicago. I was reading the paper when you came up. You had just gotten engaged."

"Yeah!" she said, giggling awkwardly. "I am flabbergasted that you even remember a little pipsqueak like me!"

It was amazing. He did remember her. She was wearing the same red bathing suit as before—despite that red hair and red skin. Some people just never learn their lessons. But that was okay now. Johnathan appreciated the admiration. Her happiness was his happiness. It was contagious.

"How's that going? Your marriage? I mean, did you ever go through with it?" he asked.

"It's going well!" she replied, smiling cheerfully. "We're about to celebrate one year. That's why we're here in New York! His friend is a producer at NBC. He got us tickets to *The Tonight Show* tomorrow. Can you believe it? Oh, listen to me. You've been on there a dozen times. What do you care?"

"I'll be on tomorrow, actually," Johnny said.

"No! Get out of town!"

"It's true," Johnathan said. "I'm going on to promote the new book and the new movie. I can get you tickets to the movie premiere if you'd like. It'll be in L.A. Not sure you how feel about La La Land."

"Oh, you don't have to do that, Mr. Peacewood," she said, covering her face with the book.

"It'd be my pleasure!" he happily replied.

"Well, wouldn't that be grand!" she said, using the book to fan her sunburnt face. "You are so courageous, coming out and facing all that scrutiny. My very best friend Sidney is gay. I love him to death! I was in his wedding, as a matter of fact. I think people should get over their hang-ups. Love is love, right! Oh, Mr. Peacewood, would it be too much to ask you to sign this copy of your latest novel?"

"I'd be delighted to!" he said, taking it from her. Then he began to rustle through his bag. "I know I had a pen here somewhere. Hmm. Darn. Oh! Got one! Now, who shall I make it out to?" he asked.

"My name is Charlotte!" she said.

His stomach began to turn. "Charlotte?"

"Yes!" she said.

Johnathan was remembering his beloved Charlotte—that sassy old bat. She had always kept him on his toes, hadn't she? But those days were over. Johnathan was going to have to grow up now and be a real man. No more cavorting about Neverland with the lost boys. No more languishing. He was lucky to have survived this trial by fire. But he would have to use his power more wisely now—for the good of all. Johnathan would have to use his gifts to make amends—to pay it forward. Surely, he could do it. Surely.

But yeah, poor Charlotte.

"Okay," he said, smiling and pressing the pen to the inside cover. "To Charlotte," he continued, reciting aloud, "a fan to whom I wish nothing but happy, wedded bliss. Remember that true love comes from within." Then he signed it, kissed the front cover, and handed it back to her.

"That is lovely!" she said, holding it up to read. "You are the best!"

"No," he said, "you are the best!"

"No! You are!" she replied.

"No! You are the best!" he insisted.

"Nope, Mr. Peacewood!" she said. "It's you!"

"Okay, I'm the best," Johnathan gave in, laughing. "And I'm the most powerful man in the world. Was than an overshare? I can never tell."

"Oh, you are a doll!" she replied.

As the awkward redhead skipped off with her newly autographed novel, Johnny leaned back on his beach towel. He didn't need to make a lover manifest. This paradise was enough.

The ocean was enough. His career was enough. The peace was enough.

As the warm Atlantic air brushed and soothed him, he thought of his Charlotte once more. Poor gal. And gazing up into the infinite, blue sky, Johnathan pondered the concepts of good and evil—light and darkness, yin and yang. Chaos had been the mother and daughter of tranquility. How ironic! How frightening! How poetic yet frightening!

Suddenly, a stream of purple light streaked across the sky. It was more brilliant than any shooting star he had ever seen. Johnathan sat up quickly, following it with his eyes as it pierced the clouds like a jet plane, traveling all the way to the horizon, where it vanished. Curiouser and curiouser. Moments later there was a sonic boom. *Pow!* The vibrations disturbed the water so that the fish jumped into the air and the waves rolled backward from the sand. And it rearranged all of the particles within Johnathan, and he was completely transformed; the sadness and the pain were extinguished, replaced with grace and understanding. This was his resurrection. He was now completely awake and armed with purpose.

Chaos was the mother and daughter of tranquility. That was the truth from here to Heaven. And everything happens just as it should. Everything.

$$\triangle \ \triangle \ \triangle$$

"So is it my understanding that this last book was inspired by the Northside Butcher of Chicago?" the host of *The Tonight Show* asked—of course, the host cannot be named—you know, rights of publicity and such.

"Yes," Johnny said, as the camera panned in to get a close-up. "I actually lived in Chicago during the killings. And a dear friend of mine was the killer's last victim."

"Oh, that's right!" the host said. "I read about that. That must have been devastating. You were close?"

"We were extremely close."

"And the Northside Butcher was never found," the host continued. "Four murders in a matter of months and then nothing."

"Serial killings are often like that," Johnny said. "It was a nightmare for me. It was partly why I went ahead and moved to New York."

"You're telling us that the Northside murders are the reason you left Chicago?" the host asked.

"They were a big part of it," Johnny replied. "After I lost Charlotte—that was her name, Charlotte Swanson—the city just wasn't the same. I didn't want to be there anymore. I needed to start something new. So I'm here in New York now. I'm actually sharing the proceeds of the book with Charlotte's son. He's been pretty messed up. Poor guy. Poor Charlotte."

"I'm sorry, man," the host said. "That had to be tough to write about."

"Well, writing was my way of coping with it," Johnny said. "Writing has always healed me. I strayed from it a bit for a while, but that was a mistake. I always have to write. Always."

"And what's next for Johnathan Peacewood?" the host asked. "Now that you're done with Somerset. Word is that your publisher is afraid you've lost your audience—coming out to the world and all. But we applaud you for that. We really do." And the audience applauded.

"It's a surprise!" Johnny said. "I'm most likely done with historical romance, so I'll be looking for a different audience anyhow. I've been working on a project with a good friend of mine. You probably know him. His name is Simon Sargent. He's a painter."

"Yeah, Sargent's been on the show!" the host replied. "I bought one of his paintings last year. Don't ask me how much I paid for it. I had to mortgage one of my kids." The audience laughed.

"His paintings are really cool," Johnny said. "I have a few pieces too."

"Mine is hanging in my kitchen," the host said. "And sometimes, when I go in there late at night, I swear, the objects in the paintings are moving. Do yours have that effect on you? I mean, I don't know if it's the way he paints or what. I was talking to a friend who has one. He says his does the same thing."

"Oh, absolutely!" Johnny said, laughing. "The objects in the paintings move. And sometimes, if you're not careful, a Simon Sargent original can move you!" Again, the audience laughed.

"The movie is *Somerset, Eternally Ever After* in theaters now," the host said to the audience. "The book is *Somerset Eternal: The Meaning of True Love*. Give it up for Mr. Johnathan Peacewood, everybody." And the audience cheered.

Johnny went back to his dressing room, where an old friend had been watching the television. It was Junior. He was sitting on the couch, tossing around Cliff's eyeballs, which were as hard as marbles but still so beautiful and blue. Junior's red hoodie was clean now and his face had been washed. And he looked healthy and well fed.

"What'd you think?" Johnny asked.

"You forgot to plug the Broadway show, man," Junior said, juggling the eyeballs up into the air.

"We're still negotiating that, so I'm not supposed to discuss it publicly," Johnny reminded him. "But how was everything else? Are you a happy kid?"

"I'm happy as hell!" Junior said, jumping up from the couch. He came over and gave Johnathan a great big hug.

"Where should we go for dinner?" Johnny asked. "Your choice! What do you feel like? Sushi?"

"Sushi?" Junior replied, grimacing. "I'm a child. I haven't acquired that sophisticated Peacewood palate yet."

"Yet you have acquired the sophisticated Peacewood vocabulary," Johnathan said, laughing as he wiped off his makeup.

"What about fried chicken and macaroni?" Junior asked.

"Oh, you and friend chicken!" Johnny replied, sighing. "Fine, we'll go home and order in. I kinda feel like having a chill night."

"Chill," Junior replied. "When did chill become an adjective?"

△ △ △

And that is how the story goes.

I tried to kill myself because I felt lost—so lonely and so lost, and I didn't understand my place in the world. I was just another lonely gay man who couldn't find love. We've heard it all before. Blah blah blah! What a cliché!

Closeted affairs and endless hookups were the only reality I ever knew, and that was unacceptable. Sure, I was hot and rich and famous, but what good was that glamour without warmth and love and intimacy? The flashing of lights and the cheers of the crowd fade so quickly once you get home to an empty penthouse. I may as well have lived in perpetual darkness. My friends were vapid. My family was aloof. What was this existence?

I was a rogue planet, roving across the universe with no star, no anchor, no home. It made me so very sick, and the sickness ate through me until there was a giant hole in me. My psychiatrist said it was depression caused by a lack of social integration. No shit! Four hundred dollars an hour to state the obvious? That's when he put me on a bunch of pills and told me to take a vacation. I went off to my private island for a few weeks with nothing but a Twix bar and a vial of Prozac. The Twix was pretty good, but those damn pills were bullshit. They didn't make me feel loved by anyone. They didn't make me feel connected to my star. They just made me apathetic, unfeeling, unhuman.

No point. No purpose. Life was a redundant, tiring march until one morning I looked out at the ocean and couldn't sense its beauty anymore. The blues and greens and brackish grays may as well have been blacks and whites. The salty smell of the sea did not impress me. The sand between my toes was soft and welcoming, but I couldn't appreciate it. The miracles of the universe became such banalities that I was numb to it all. I didn't even sense fear anymore.

So I came back to Chicago a zombie. I walked into my penthouse, which was empty and cold, and my shoes clacked against the tile, echoing off the walls. My heart was broken, but I couldn't feel the pain of that. That's when I cut my arm, watching the blood ooze from me, but I could not feel the pain. I plugged in the iron and pressed the palm of my hand to the hot surface. Although I sustained a second-degree burn doing that shit, I could not feel the pain. The senses were numb. Numb. So I was alone and felt nothing—no joy, no pain, nothing. I felt nothing for the sky or the earth. Nothing for birds flying by my bedroom window. Nothing for any of the people down below on the street. Worst of all, I felt nothing for myself.

And I knew that God either hated me or didn't exist. What options did that leave me? Either I was going straight to Hell, or I would die and become nothingness after life. I assumed Hell would at least grant me some agony, something to feel again. Or there was always the second alternative—I could become nothing. That'd be okay. The point is that death would be an emancipation from this oppressive numbness that I felt. Do you hear me? I'm telling you I popped enough pills to take down a fucking bull. I was one crazy motherfucker for trying that shit. But luckily, I failed.

I failed, and I found a friend—a real friend, who reminded me what life was all about. In my lowest moment, I met him in the halcyon days of his existence. I was put off by him at first— his modest appearance, his eccentricities. But then I looked closer. He had nothing more than I had—no more money, no more friends, no more romance. Hell, I was better looking and much richer. But he was somehow so happy, healthy and powerful. My buddy Sargent was doing whatever he wanted and never suffering.

At one point he'd lost everything—his family, his job, even his vision. His world had crumbled to dust. Yet somehow, he survived. And not only did he survive, he reinvented himself, and the new Sargent was more a wonder than the last. I thought he must be something like Jesus to bring himself back from the dead like that. I didn't see it at first. I didn't see my own power, but he did. Looking back, it's a little ironic that a blind man saw in me what I couldn't. Don't you think?

What Sargent did was he showed me my reflection, and that reflection saved me. He reminded me that life is magical. That there is always a song playing somewhere and therefore always a reason to dance. That the ocean is beautiful and full of color. That the sand is always soft and comforting, which is a reason to rejoice. He reminded me that I could have anything I wanted because I was powerful and strong beyond measure—not because I was a famous writer, but because I was. I just was. Being alive was enough.

Sargent Simon shared with me the recipe for limitless power. It was quite simple really and completely free of hocus-pocus. There was no eye of newt or wing of bat. No alien technology or magic purple lightening. Sargent just slapped me in the face and snapped me out of a damsel-in-distress kind of self-pity. He knew I was more than what I was allowing myself to be. And I had the secret to infinite power. And now I am going to give you the recipe, so that you too can have this ultimate power. Are you ready? Hmm? Are you ready? Drum roll, please.

Purpose.

Purpose?

Yes, that's exactly what I said. I've written that word all throughout this book. You shouldn't be surprised at this point. It's what this story was all about. Say it aloud with me, now! Purpose. Purpose. Purpose.

Purpose. We come to this planet with tiny seeds of purpose inside us. Each soul has a purpose. Each object has a purpose. From the microscopic amoeba to the regal redwood, we all have a purpose. I have a purpose. You have a purpose. We have a purpose. And each purpose is integral to transcendence into absolute knowledge, light, and peace. But if one of us—just one of us—languishes about rather than pursuing his purpose, the entire cosmos suffers. When purpose goes unrealized, society crumbles, hopelessness ensues, and oppression wins. Then, we come one step closer to decay and one step further from ascension. That is the power of purpose.

And what of our dreams? What are they really? Are they merely the offspring of an overactive subconscious? Are they the thoughts we think as we doze and slumber? Or is there more to a dream than that? Yes, of course there's more! There is always more. Dreams are our roadmaps to purpose. Dreams show us who we are, what we want, and where we need to go. With our dreams in hand, we may never truly be lost, because they always know the way home to purpose. Thus, we must chase our dreams—chase our dreams with fearless passion until purpose is realized.

My mistake was that I lost sight of my purpose. I got distracted by the world's obnoxious cacophony. There were all these voices on the television and on the radio and in the newspaper that told me what life should look and feel like—telling me that I was somehow incomplete without the perfect lover by my side. Purpose wasn't good enough; if I was single, I had to be doing something wrong. I forgot what my dreams had been telling me, and I started listening to the world. Lord, what did I do that for? A year into living for the world and all hell broke loose. My dreams transformed into nightmares and went on a killing rampage.

It was then that I realized I was a fucking retard. As long as I wasn't listening to my dreams, my reality would be a hellish one—a place where nothing made sense and storm clouds stalked me around the planet. You see, all of the suffering and all the affliction in the world can be overcome by focusing on purpose. Our dreams are trying to show us. But we must open our minds and actually listen. You have dreams. I know you do.

Listen to those dreams. Follow those dreams. Nurture those dreams as though they are your own children. Speak to them. Feed them. Water them, and ensure that they are happy. Watch them grow from seeds in your mind to something that sprouts out upon the world with magic and power.

You see, once you understand your true purpose—and once you become unflinching and unwavering in the campaign to fulfill that purpose—nothing in this universe can harm you. Those of us who follow our dreams and live our purpose are the baddest motherfuckers on the planet. We are the most powerful people in the world. And that, my friend, is truly fabulous!

Forever yours,

Johnathan J. Peacewood

P.S.
THE END :)

Made in the USA
Middletown, DE
14 January 2020